"This doe...
M...

"It is to your advantage... ...all in this venture.
Why in the world would you offer help?" asked Jane.

Rydell took a single step toward her and reached out.
"Been askin' myself that question all morning."

"And what is your answer to that question?" Jane's voice
had steadied, but it dropped to a whisper.

"Damn—darned if I know," he admitted. And before he
knew what he was doing, he closed his fingers around
her upper arm. She didn't move, just looked at him.
Unable to help himself, he pulled her toward him. And
his mouth found hers.

Her lips were warm. He'd never known such
excruciating sweetness. Instinctively he broke free. He
didn't think he could stop if he didn't call a halt now.

"You're right, this doesn't make sense," he breathed
against her temple. "No sense at all."

* * *

The Courtship
Harlequin Historical #613—June 2002

Praise for Lynna Banning's previous titles

The Law and Miss Hardisson
"...fresh and charming...a sweet and funny
yet poignant story."
—*Romantic Times*

Plum Creek Bride
"...pathos and humor blend in a plot
that glows with perception and dignity."
—*Affaire de Coeur*

Wildwood
"5 ★s."
—*Heartland Critiques*

Western Rose
"...warm, wonderful and witty—
a winning combination from a bright new talent."
—Award-winning author Theresa Michaels

**DON'T MISS THESE OTHER
TITLES AVAILABLE NOW:**

#611 MY LADY'S PLEASURE
Julia Justiss

#612 THE DARK KNIGHT
Tori Phillips

#614 THE PERFECT WIFE
Mary Burton

The Courtship

Lynna Banning

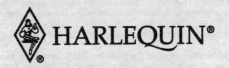

HARLEQUIN®

TORONTO • NEW YORK • LONDON
AMSTERDAM • PARIS • SYDNEY • HAMBURG
STOCKHOLM • ATHENS • TOKYO • MILAN • MADRID
PRAGUE • WARSAW • BUDAPEST • AUCKLAND

ISBN 0-373-29213-9

THE COURTSHIP

Visit us at www.eHarlequin.com

Printed in U.S.A.

Please address questions and book requests to:
Harlequin Reader Service
U.S.: 3010 Walden Ave., P.O. Box 1325, Buffalo, NY 14269
Canadian: P.O. Box 609, Fort Erie, Ont. L2A 5X3

Dedication

For my mother, Mary Elizabeth Banning Yarnes

Acknowledgments

With grateful appreciation to Jean Louise Banning,
Suzanne Barrett, David Woolston and my agent,
Pattie Steele-Perkins

Chapter One

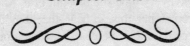

Dixon Falls, Oregon
1874

"Jane Charlotte, don't you dare step one foot out that door without straightenin' your hat! Why, it looks just like a puffball that's been knocked plumb off center."

With a sigh, Jane poked one finger against the stiff straw creation she'd clapped on top of her dark hair and felt it shift an inch to the right.

"Now, pull your waist down and tuck it in nice, honey. Y'all can't go traipsing into town looking like you've got no maid to tend you."

Jane faced her mother, who was reclining on the worn green damask settee, an open copy of Tennyson clutched in her thin fingers. "We have no maid, re-member, Mama? We left Odelia at Montclair with Aunt Carrie, and Juno ran off with that sharecropper in Dillon County after the War. We're on our own out here."

Her mother's unblemished ivory forehead wrinkled. "Truth to tell, Ah don't *like* to remember, but never you mind. Tuck in your waist, now, honey. And tell your father where you're goin' in such a fizz."

Jane's throat closed at the mention of her father. Papa was dead and buried in the orchard, and her chest ached every time she thought of it. Mama didn't want to remember this, either—that they'd laid him to rest three days ago. Some days, Mama fancied herself back in Marion County, sitting on the porch in the shade of the tupelo tree, sipping lemonade.

"I won't be gone long, Mama." She bent to kiss the smooth, cool cheek and patted her mother's hand. "You find a nice poem by Mr. Tennyson to read out loud after our supper, you hear?"

"You speak to your father before you leave, Jane Charlotte. Ah don't know what he'll say to your goin' out unchaperoned...."

Jane bit her bottom lip. *Papa's dead,* she wanted to scream. *Don't you understand? He's gone!* But such an outburst would serve no purpose; Mama would forget it within half a minute, and Jane's throat would hurt for hours from screaming. Her mother refused to accept unpleasantness; she simply pretended it didn't exist. Maybe she should thank the Lord her mother preferred the past; it kept her from being frightened of the present, and Jane was frightened enough for both of them.

She straightened her spine, smoothed down the folds of the dark blue sateen skirt she had made over from a ball gown of her mother's, and moved to the front door. The paint around the lock plate was flaking off, revealing the bare wood beneath. It needed fixing.

Everything needed fixing—the house. Their lives. Even herself. It had been ten years since she'd first delved into her mother's clothes trunk; how much longer could a few outdated ball gowns last? And the house—it had gone to wrack and ruin since her mother's health began to fail.

"'Bye, Mama. I'll be home in time to make your tea."

"Jane Charlotte, tell your father..." The small, clear voice faded as Jane descended the porch steps.

Tell your father. She gritted her teeth. She'd like to tell him a thing or two, like to shout the truth at him: *Papa, you dragged us away from everything we knew, everything we loved, and you didn't take care of us, Mama and me, nor our property, and...and now you up and die and we're practically starving!*

Hush up, now! No well-bred Southern lady rails at a dead parent no matter what they'd done, leastways not in public. And certainly not among Yankees! She marched down the path to the front gate, groaning aloud at the sight of the weed-infested border of sun-withered Sweet William and the overgrown roses massed along the fence. Well, great heavens, she couldn't keep up the cooking and the cleaning and the pruning and lovingly dribble wash water on the roots like Mama did before she took sick.

Oh, Papa, whatever am I to do? A sick, hard knot formed in her midsection. She didn't feel like herself anymore. At that, she gave a choked laugh. *Be truthful, Jane.* For months and months, even before Papa died, she had felt like a fledgling sparrow who'd fallen out of its nest. No matter how hard she tried, she couldn't fly back in.

Well, fly you must, ready or no. She swung the gate shut, wincing at the *screak* of the rusty hinge—one more thing to attend to—and twitched her skirt free of the fencepost. It took all her willpower to steady her breathing. She felt for all the world like David girding himself to meet Goliath.

Only this was worse. She snapped open her mother's best black silk parasol. At the bottom of their dusty, sun-baked hill lay the town, and there waited The Enemy. Goliath was a Yankee.

She straightened her hat and ordered her feet to carry her forward. *I am sorry, Papa, but you left me no choice.*

"She's comin', Dell! Miz Jane. Walkin' up the street lookin' jes' like a queen."

Rydell Wilder's entire world spun to a stop. "You sure about that, Lefty?"

"Dad blame-it, my eyesight's good as it ever was. Ever since you started this here bank 'stead of ridin' shotgun for me, you never b'lieve one thing I say. I tell you it's *her*."

Rydell stood up and stared into the old man's face. Lefty Springer was the only person in the entire world he'd ever confided in. He'd trust the man with his life if it came down to it; after all, Lefty had trusted him with thousands of dollars in payroll shipments from the time he turned sixteen.

Barton Springer—Lefty, to those few who knew

how he'd lost his right arm at Shiloh—never spoke a word unless he had to. The old man had been the first customer at the bank Rydell had established in town when he was a week shy of twenty-three, and he was the only patron allowed to use the private side entrance to his office. Rydell waited for the details.

Lefty looked at him expectantly, and Rydell chuckled. He didn't believe for one minute that Miss Jane Charlotte Davis was heading for his bank. Not unless hell was freezing over. But the old man's sharp blue eyes sparkled, and then his gaze narrowed.

"Got over it, didja?"

"Sure thing, Lefty." He grinned at the lie. "Another ten years or so and I won't care about breathing, either."

"Thought so. Dell, I came to warn ya—she looks like she's made up her mind to somethin'."

Rydell shook his head as a queer pain stabbed into his heart. "Jane Davis hasn't been allowed any kind of life to make up her mind *about*. Her folks pretty much saw to that. Offhand I'd say she's just visited the mercantile and is headed toward home."

"She's comin' this way, I tell ya." The old man twirled one branch of his drooping gray mustache with his left forefinger. "Thought ya might like to be prepared, is all."

Rydell grasped the older man's shoulder. "Thanks, Lefty. Buy you a beer later."

When he was alone, Rydell tipped his chair back, propped his boots on the desk, and closed his eyes.

Jane.

All these years he'd carried her name and the memory of the shy, frightened girl who'd treated him with kindness when he'd chased a group of bullies out of the schoolyard. She was new in town, from the South he gathered from her speech. Maybe fourteen or fifteen, and she looked...different. Her clothes were too fussy for a small town like Dixon Falls, her manners too formal. The other students surrounded her as she walked home, tossing rocks and chanting. *"Queen Jane, Queen Jane, she's got no brain. She's stuck-up, too, and awful plain."*

The taunt made him mad. They'd bedeviled him, too, but he could fight. Jane could not, so when it came down to it, he'd done it for her. When it was over, she put her small, soft hand on his and whispered two simple words. Thank you.

He'd been fifteen. She didn't come back to the school; he heard later that her folks taught her at home. Rydell had finished his schooling, rode shotgun for Lefty Springer, and watched from a distance as wide as two oceans while Jane grew up in the big yellow house on Dixon Road.

He'd tried hard to forget her.

Wilder's Bank sat at the far end of the town of Dixon Falls, an imposing two-story white-painted building, the only structure along the main street that looked strong enough to withstand the winter snows and the hot, dry July wind without the roof sagging and the paint peeling off. Jane hesitated a moment, then stepped onto the board sidewalk.

A silver-dollar-sized spot of sunlight seared her chin. Peering upward, she noted the hole in the faded black parasol and groaned aloud. She could patch it with a scrap of silk from Mama's trunk. Or she could live with it. What she'd *like* to do was toss the blasted contraption into the horse trough in front of the Excelsior Hotel, but she knew there wasn't enough money to purchase another. That sad fact was what brought her into town in the first place.

She would manage with the damaged parasol. She needed something much more important than that, Jane thought with a shudder. And it was waiting inside the bank—her last hope for survival. For the hundredth time in the last three days, she wondered how she could live through the humiliation.

Inside the bank it was mercifully cool and quiet. The gray-painted window shutters were closed against the midday heat. It was, she noted, the only building in town that *had* shutters. In the dim light she drew in a slow, careful breath and walked resolutely to the counter. The air smelled of lemon oil and tobacco smoke.

The young man behind the iron grill blinked. "Yes, ma'am?"

"I would like to speak with Mr. Wilder, please."

"Yes, ma'am. I'll just step in and see if he's busy."

Jane willed her gloved fingers to rest in a ladylike manner atop her reticule while the clerk disappeared through a doorway. What if he's occupied? What if he wants to see all our family private papers, Papa's will and the deed to the house? *What if he says no?*

"Just step this way, ma'am. Mr. Wilder's always happy to see a pretty lady."

I'll just bet he is. Rydell Wilder had a Past, her mother had whispered over the years. Papa had been less subtle. "No background, no breeding, and a damned Yankee besides."

Clamping her lips tightly shut, she followed the young man in icy silence, listening to her black leather shoes tap-tap on the polished wood floor. When the clerk thrust open a heavy oak door, Jane's heart jumped.

She couldn't. She just couldn't.

But you will. You must. She sucked in a breath so deep her corset pinched and forced her feet through the doorway.

The man behind the desk rose. "Jane," he said, then caught himself. "Miss Davis."

"Mr. Wilder."

"I was sorry to hear about your father."

Jane steeled herself, stepped toward him and extended her white-gloved hand. Too late she saw the dark smudge on the palm, where she'd laid her hand on the dusty front gate.

He didn't seem to notice. "It's been some time since I've seen you," he said, his voice low and oddly tense. "How are you? And your mother?"

"Why, we're just fine, Mr. Wilder. Thank you for inquiring."

He hesitated, an alert, almost wary look in his steady gray eyes. Well and no wonder, she thought. Papa never did like him, and made no bones about saying so.

"Please sit down." He drew up a slat-back oak chair and gestured. Jane noticed the cuffs of his white shirt were rolled back, revealing tanned wrists and forearms sprinkled with dark hair. The sight made her uneasy. The dark jacket that matched his trousers lay on the chair behind the desk.

She wished he would put it on. Rydell Wilder was tall and lean and good-looking, even if he was a Yankee. His mouth, especially. Unsmiling as it was, the lips were well-formed. She remembered from school days that he rarely smiled. His mouth had seemed thin, pressed into a hard line. Well, he had been struggling then, she reminded herself.

As she was now, she admitted with an inward sigh. How time altered things.

He settled himself into the chair behind the desk. "What can I do for you, Miss Davis?"

"I—" Her throat closed.

"Yes?"

"You know...about my father's death." It was as far as she could get at the moment. She worked to keep her breathing steady.

"I do know. And I am sorry, as I said."

Honey, not vinegar, she reminded herself. To catch a fly, a Southern woman uses charm and lightheartedness. She tried to smile at him.

"Mr. Wilder, my father—through no fault of his own, mind you—left us with some...er...obligations."

"Debts, you mean." The bank owner's voice was gentle but firm.

"Why, yes, I suppose you could call them that."

Do not prevaricate, Jane. It is beneath you. Papa owed everyone in town, from the liveryman to the mercantile owner. She'd found the notes in the box of private papers in the chiffonier. Even Mama didn't know about them. She'd rather die than admit their existence to a Yankee. But...

"Oh, all right, debts."

"How much?"

"Over two hundred dollars."

His dark eyebrows rose. "Are there assets?"

Jane's stomach clenched. "Just the house. Papa built it when he came out West after the War to work for Uncle Junius on the newspaper. Since Uncle passed on a year ago, well, the house..." She swallowed hard. "It's in need of some few repairs, but it's all we have now."

Rydell leaned forward, folding his hands on the desk. "And?"

And. Jane stared at his hands. The long, tanned fingers sent a jolt of awareness into her belly. His hands had held guns, had handled gold. His hands, she had heard her mother whisper, had touched women. Many women.

She wrenched her gaze away, studied the wall behind his dark head. "Well, Mr. Wilder, I have come to a decision. A very difficult decision, you see, because..." Her voice faltered.

"I can imagine," he said quietly. "This must be hell—uh, hard for you."

With all her heart she wished he hadn't said that. The very last thing she wanted was understanding. It stripped her pride away, left her exposed. Vulnerable.

But, in for a penny, in for a pound.

"I have decided to establish a business in Dixon

Falls. A dressmaking shop. I am quite a capable seamstress, you see...." She made another attempt at a smile, but tears stung under her lids. All these years she had dreamed of going back to Montclair, imagined how it would be when they lived again with Aunt Carrie. Odelia would help with Mama, and they would plan picnics and a ball in the summertime. To think that now she had to beg like a common...a common laborer.

Oh, God, can this really be happening? I am sitting here in Rydell Wilder's bank at noon on the hottest day yet this July, asking—begging!—for money?

"How old are you, Jane?"

His voice was low and quiet, but the question sliced through her muddled thoughts. She stiffened. "How old...? Not 'How much do you need?' or 'How do you intend to proceed?' but 'How old am I'? Why on God's green earth would you want to know that?"

"I know how much you'll need," he said. His mouth quirked toward a smile. "And how you intend to proceed; you'll roll up those lacy sleeves and go to work. What I need to know is what my risk is."

"*Your* risk? What about *my* risk? I am prepared to offer our home as collateral."

"I don't want your home. As you said, it's in disrepair, and besides..."

Every nerve in her body jangled into excruciating attention. "I am twenty-six years old," she blurted. "If you don't want the house, what *do* you want?"

He did smile then, a slow, sensuous curving of the lips, and a light flickered deep in the cool gray eyes.

He paused, assessing her with an odd mixture of amusement and pain. "I want to make you a deal."

"What kind of deal?" Her voice sounded tight.

Rydell waited a full minute before answering her. She would never know how many years he had thought about such a moment, a time when Jane would again turn to him for help. His chest felt like a horse had ridden over it.

He'd wanted Jane for so long he couldn't remember a time when seeing her didn't make him ache. He knew about the debts her father had incurred, about the state of their house. At least a dozen times he'd planned to go to her, in spite of her father's disapproval, and offer a proposal of marriage.

"I'll lend you three hundred dollars, enough to pay off your father's...obligations, rent you a store, and get you started in business."

Jane sat bolt upright. "You will? Just like that?" She narrowed her eyes. "With no collateral?"

Rydell smiled. "A deal, as I said."

That she wanted to be independent surprised him. He had to admit he admired her for wanting to try setting up her own business, but the truth was he wouldn't give a moldy flapjack for her chances of success. She was a lady with a capital *L,* refined manners, soft voice, gentility.

He'd always admired that, too. Oh, Lordy, she was so close to being his he couldn't think straight. He was facing the biggest gamble of his life.

"If you succeed in your business venture," Rydell said carefully, "you simply repay the loan."

Jane stared at him. "And if I can't?"

Rydell took a deep breath and tried to keep his voice steady. "Well, here's the deal. I'm going to hold you yourself as collateral."

"Me?" Jane echoed. "What happens if I fail?"

He sent her a quick look, his eyes unreadable. "If you fail, you marry me."

Chapter Two

For one unsettling moment, Jane thought she was going to faint. "I beg your pardon? I think I must have misheard—"

Rydell held her gaze. "You heard it right. If you go broke sewing dresses, then you'll marry me."

She fought a wild desire to pinch herself. *"Marry you?"* Her voice was definitely not her own. She tried again. "Marry you? Why on earth would I do that?"

He regarded her with a steadiness that made her heart skip erratically. "Maybe because you're up a creek."

Fury brought her to her feet. "Now just one minute, Mr. Wilder. I am not 'up a creek' as you so crudely put it. I admit my father's passing has caused a small problem, but problems are not new to me. I will persevere, and I will triumph."

Rydell nodded. "Oh, you'll persevere, all right. But you're not equipped for life the way it shakes out in the West—your folks made sure of that. They treated you like a hothouse violet. For a woman like you—a lady—you've pretty much got three choices, as I see it. One, work yourself into an early grave keeping up that house for your ma. Two, take a job in a saloon—or maybe worse. Or..." he lowered his voice "...three, get married. I'm offering you a respectable way to survive."

Jane bit the inside of her cheek so hard she tasted blood and sank onto her chair. "My parents did not overprotect me," she snapped. "They cared for me, taught me about the finer things of life, about history and art and music. Mama encouraged my piano studies until she..." Her voice trailed off.

"You're twenty-six, Miss Davis. Your father discouraged every unattached male within a hundred miles from comin' anywhere near you. I'd say you're well on your way to being an old maid."

Jane expelled a pent-up breath. "And just what gives you that idea? Yankee gossip, most likely."

Rydell leaned closer. "Is that what you dreamed about while you were growing up? Caring for your mother for the rest of your days?"

"You do not know one thing about my mother!"

Rydell chuckled. "Once nice thing about living in a town as small as Dixon Falls—when you don't know what you're doing, somebody else is sure to."

A corset stay dug into her midriff and Jane jerked upright. "Well, I never!"

"Look, Miss Davis. We already have a schoolteacher here in town, and you don't look strong enough to shoe horses. So what the hell else are you gonna do?"

"I..." Her mind whirled. "How would you know about my piano?"

"I listened some, over the years," he said quietly.

The look on his face made her pause. "Just how do you know that my father discouraged potential suitors?"

"I know because I was one of them. Your father said I wasn't fit to shine your boots. He thought a rootless kid with no family background wasn't worth spit."

Papa said that? Well, she supposed he knew more than she did about such things. "Besides," Jane murmured. "You're a Yankee."

"Still am," Rydell said mildly. "But the war's over, Miss Davis."

"For you, maybe. Not for us. My daddy and mama lost their entire plantation when the Union army came marchin' through. Papa never forgave the North for that. The only reason we came west was because Father was ruined, and Uncle Junius needed help on that awful newspaper of his."

"The way I see it, your father never really settled in Dixon Falls. Oh, he ate and slept out here all right, but he stayed in the past. He kept your mother imprisoned there, too."

"He did no such thing! Why, Mama went out lots of places!"

He went on as if she had not spoken. "And—forgive me for saying this, Jane—he kept you there, as well. Locked up in that house up on the hill, arranging bouquets and practicing the piano—preparing yourself for a life you'd never have."

Jane flinched. The words stung because they were true. The only times she was allowed to attend a town social, even visit the mercantile for soap or a spool of thread, Papa always accompanied her. She had been allowed no friends. Sometimes she'd felt so lonely she thought she'd die.

Looking back on it, she wondered why she'd put up with things the way they were. Rebellion, of course, would have been unthinkable. A state could secede from the Union, and fight a long and bloody war over it. But a daughter didn't secede from her family. That was beyond the pale.

Then, before she knew it, it was too late.

Deliberately, she changed the subject. "I would prefer that you hold my home as collateral for the loan, Mr. Wilder. Not my...person."

His face changed. "It isn't the house I want, Jane."

"And *you* are most certainly not what *I* want!" She managed to keep her voice steady, but her hands shook like dry leaves in a wind. For an instant she thought of jamming them under her skirt, but discarded the idea immediately. A lady never sat on her hands, not even when frightened half to death. Or mad enough to commit murder.

"Yeah, well, I figured as much. Nevertheless, those are my terms."

Honey, she reminded herself. *Not vinegar.* She unclenched her hands and drew in a slow, careful breath. A whalebone stay jabbed anew. The best way to forget all her troubles was to wear a tight corset; it was hard to concentrate.

As soon as she could trust her legs to support her, she rose. "Very well, Mr. Wilder. You have the advantage of me at this moment, since I do need the money. But, sir, while I may be forced to accept the terms of your wager, do not for one moment harbor any hope of winning. I am an excellent seamstress, and I intend to succeed at dressmaking if it's the last thing I do in this life."

His lips twitched. "I understand."

"And," Jane continued, unable to stop the words roiling in her brain, "I promise you that if I ever *do* marry, it will be of my own free will and never, *never* because I have lost a wager. I am not in the habit of gambling."

"Certainly not."

"Neither am I in the habit of failing. I shall *not* fail!"

"Of course." His voice was annoyingly calm. He slid open the top desk drawer and counted out three crisp one-hundred-dollar bills from his private cash supply. Folding them in half, he handed the money to her.

"There's an empty storage room next to the mercantile. I own it. You can rent it for three dollars a month, as is." He extended his hand toward her. "Agreed?"

Jane slipped the currency into her reticule. "It is indeed agreed, Mr. Wilder. Thank you." She laid her hand in his and gave it a businesslike shake. Even through her glove, heat from his palm surged from her fingertips to her elbow, and she snatched her hand free.

"As we have nothing further to discuss, I will bid you good afternoon."

Which was most certainly *not* what she wanted to say. Sometimes she wished she wasn't a Davis at all, with ladylike manners to remember and a reputation to uphold. Just once she'd like to say what was really on her mind—that Rydell Wilder was a lowdown snake in the grass, an upstart with no sense of propriety and a grievous lack of breeding. Why, he'd even said "hell" in the presence of a lady. The world had come to a sorry place when the likes of him owned the only bank in town!

She resisted an overwhelming urge to slam his office door as hard as she could. Instead, she closed it quietly, relinquishing her grip on the polished brass knob when the latch clicked. The last thing she saw before the door swung shut was Rydell Wilder's steady gray eyes looking at her from behind his big walnut desk.

Oh! She could gobble down a whole keg of nails, he made her so mad!

The minute she was gone, Rydell folded his fingers into a fist. Jane Charlotte Davis hadn't a clue how hard real life could be, but by thunder she was going to find out. Was he crazy to lend her the money that could take her out of his life once and for all? Could she possibly make a go of setting up her own business?

Not one chance in a thousand. He rose and paced to the window opening onto the street. A flash of blue caught his eye, sending a familiar ache into his chest.

Oh, hell. Even if she could sew ruffles around a

circus tent, she had no experience in trade, no understanding of life in a dusty Oregon lumber mill town.
All he had to do was watch and wait—he figured in
about ninety days he'd be a married man.

God help him, he wanted her to fail!

Maybe he wasn't so crazy. He'd worked and
sweated for ten years to offer Jane something more
than the rough life of a freight line owner's wife. He'd
eaten beans and biscuits for months on end, saved the
pay he'd earned riding shotgun for Lefty, and in-
vested it. When Lefty grew too frail to drive the
wagon, Rydell had bought him out, and after a few
years saw his chance to establish a bank. It was a
smart move. Owning a bank made him a lot of money
and brought him the respect of the entire town. Now
he ate steak every night, shared an occasional drink
with Lefty, and was sought after by all the single
women, respectable or not.

The only hunger he hadn't eased over the years was
his longing for the shy girl with eyes like a summer
sky and thick chestnut hair that hung to her waist.
She looked different now, more filled out and sure of
herself. He was older, too—work-hardened and female savvy. Even so, the thought of even touching
her hand made his heart stutter.

*Leave it alone, Dell. Don't think about her any-
more.*

Ten long years he'd waited for a chance, and now
it was here. He wondered if she remembered him,
from before he'd become a man.

He wondered if she knew how a man could feel
about a woman.

* * *

"Walk you home, Miz Jane? Barton Springer's the name, case you don't remember. Drove a wagon for Wells Fargo and knew your daddy."

Jane tipped her parasol so the shade covered the man's weathered face. "Mr. Springer, of course I remember you. You were a great help to my father and Uncle Junius at the newspaper office."

He grinned and fell in step beside her. "Sure sorry to hear about your pa, Miz Jane. 'Specially so soon after Mr. Junius. What you gonna do, now he's gone?"

"The first thing I will do, Mr. Springer, is stop by the mercantile. I am going into business."

His bushy gray eyebrows twitched upward. "You, ma'am? All by yourself?"

"All by myself. I'm going to rent the store next to the mercantile. Then I intend to purchase some bolts of fabric—muslin, I think, or perhaps sateen—and some thread. Oh, and maybe a lantern so I can work in the evenings."

"You gonna need some help totin' them things, Miz Jane. I'm puttin' myself at your service."

Jane surveyed the bent figure trudging beside her. He looked healthy enough, but his right shirt-sleeve was pinned up, indicating a missing arm. She couldn't bear to embarrass him by declining his offer.

"That is most thoughtful of you, Mr. Springer. First, however, I wish to inspect my place of business. Mr. Wilder said it was right next to the mercantile, but I don't recall seeing anything that looked like a store."

The old man gave her a sideways look. "No won-

der in that, I guess. 'T'aint much of a store, more like
a...well, you'll see fer yourself, it's just yonder.''

"I don't care what it is, Mr. Springer, it's a start.
For me, it's a whole new life!" For a fleeting moment
she wondered at herself, talking so freely about her
plans. She'd been taught never to speak of things
other than the weather and recipes for rheumatism
medicine and who's having a baby, and here she was
chattering on about her ideas. Maybe it was because
Mr. Springer's blue eyes snapped with intelligence.
Or was it because he was a sweet, frail man whom
she sensed was a bit lonely for company? Perhaps he
was a kindred spirit. His interest in her venture
seemed so genuine she didn't even mind too much
that he was a Yankee.

"You don't mind me sayin' so, Miz Jane, you been
frownin' somethin' fierce ever since you come outta
the bank. I never seen anyone look more serious."

Jane stopped midstride and stared at him. "'Serious,' Mr. Springer, does not begin to describe my
state of mind. I am committed. Determined. *Resolute!*" She stopped herself from adding "desperate"
only because he was pointing at something behind
her.

"There 'tis. Your store."

Jane whirled to see. "Where? I don't see a— Oh,
you mean that little add-on next to the...? Oh. Oh,
my." Her heart sank.

A tilting clapboard structure no wider than the back
end of a wagon leaned against the mercantile building. She stepped closer. The single window, slightly
wider than the plain plank door, was so grimy she

could not see through the glass. No matter. At the moment, she couldn't face looking inside. A weathered wooden sign swung on a chain in the wind. *Mercer's Feed & Seed. Cash Only.*

"Used to be Rafe Mercer's feed storage room. Looks kinda worse for wear, don't it?"

Jane's mouth was as dry as field cotton. "It looks like the darky quarters back home in Marion County. Only not as clean."

"Miz Jane, I jes' gotta say this. This ain't no kinda place for a lady. Why don't you take your momma and go back where you come from?"

She bit down hard on her lower lip. "I cannot, Mr. Springer. My mother is…unwell at the moment, and…"

And she had no money for train fare, other than what Mr. Wilder had lent her. Besides, even if her mother could travel, she couldn't leave Dixon Falls with Papa's debts still unpaid, and now, on top of that, there was the bank loan to pay back.

The old man's eyes narrowed in unspoken understanding. "I bet you'd hightail it outta here if'n you could find a way."

"I'll find a way," Jane said quietly. "And the first step is to take down that awful sign and scrub that window." She nodded her head politely. "Good day to you, Mr. Springer. I'd best visit the mercantile and purchase an extra bar of lye soap."

"You tell Mr. Mercer I'll tote yer supplies on over to your store for ya. Meanwhile, I think I'll mosey on down to the Silver Cup and have some words with an old friend."

* * *

"Dell, you outta be horsewhipped fer what you're puttin' that gal through. This ain't no way to court a lady like Miz Jane."

Rydell downed the last of his whiskey and looked at Lefty across the oak table. "The courting part comes later. First, she's got to give up that fool notion about supporting herself and her mother by making dresses."

"You gonna let her work herself to the bone so's you kin pick up the pieces? Dell, her hands ain't never done nothin' but play the pi-anna and embroider tea towels."

Rydell looked straight at his friend. "I want a wife who's a partner, not a decoration."

"Then choose some other gal. Lord knows you'd have yer pick."

Rydell ignored him. "Jane's got more inside her than she knows," he said. He smoothed one finger around the rim of his glass. "I've waited for ten years. I'm willing to wait some more."

Lefty plunked his beer glass down so hard the liquid sloshed over the side. "You waited ten years cuz her daddy ran you off. Now that he's gone, why'nt you jes' grab her? I seen you do that with plenty of other women, so don't say you don't know how. Jes' do it!"

"Lefty, you ever think about a man and a woman? What it means for them to be together?"

"Hell, yes, all the time. Nuthin' complicated 'bout that. Hug 'em, kiss 'em, and rope 'em quick."

Rydell grinned. "You're a smart man, Lefty. How come you're so dumb when it comes to women?"

"I'm a good forty years older'n you, boy, so I know what I'm yakkin' about. Women is women."

"There's more to it than that. Jane is...Jane. She's not ready."

The older man groaned. "You're a smart man, too, Dell. How come *you're* so dumb when it comes to Miz Jane?"

Rydell rose and clapped his friend on the shoulder. "She's a spinster. Overeducated. Underexperienced. But I like her. Always have. She deserves the chance to learn who she is."

Tossing a coin on the table, he strolled toward the saloon doorway. "Besides," he said over his shoulder, "she won't suffer long. As green as she is in the ways of the world, inside of a week she'll drop into my hand like a ripe peach."

"I don't think so," Lefty muttered. "I think you're the one who's gonna learn the lesson."

But his words, punctuated by the *swish-whap* of the swinging doors, echoed in an empty barroom.

Chapter Three

"Here's your tea, Mama." Jane lowered the silver tray onto the table next to the upholstered settee. "I fixed it just the way you like it."

"Why, thank you, dear. Such a nice custom, don't you think? Whenever Ah am in a tizzy, Ah just have my tea and soon it's all better."

Jane gazed past her mother's pale blue eyes to focus on the rose-flowered wallpaper on the wall behind her. How Mama clung to the past, especially when things upset her. Her entire day was made up of rituals from when she had been a belle—hot cocoa served to her in bed, roses arranged in crystal vases, tea every afternoon. Then the War came, and their lives were shattered. Until the day he died, her father referred to that dreadful fighting as The War of Northern Aggression.

"I went to town today, Mama. To the bank and the mercantile." She forced a gaiety she didn't feel into her tone.

"I trust you were properly chaperoned?"

Jane hesitated, her hand on the handle of the silver

teapot. "No, Mama," she said softly. She lifted the delicate painted china cup and tipped the pot forward. Her hand shook as she poured.

"Your father spends entirely too much time fussin' over those peach trees of his. We've already got a cellar full of jams and jellies, and Ah can't bear the thought of another crop comin' on. We must ask Jonas to bring his darkies to help."

Darkies! Jane met her mother's dreamy gaze. Jonas had been her father's overseer at Montclair. Numb, she tried to think what to say.

"Mama? We haven't laid eyes on Jonas, or his darkies, for over a decade. Are you feeling a bit tired?" She set the teacup down and took hold of her mother's soft, cool hand. The skin was so transparent a tracery of blue veins showed through.

A dull pain pressed near her heart. Her mother was growing frail. Washing the kitchen floor and changing the bed linen, as they had done together each Saturday morning since they'd come west, would soon be out of the question. From now on, Jane would have to manage by herself.

"Mama, I spoke to Mr. Wilder at the bank this afternoon. I—I'm going to start a business."

"Wilder? I don't recall the name, dear. Who are his people?"

Jane let an inaudible sigh escape through her lips. As far as she knew, Rydell Wilder *had* no "people." Anyway, she didn't want to think about him.

She moved toward the kitchen. "Finish your tea, Mama, while I fix our supper."

She concocted a sandwich of sorts using sliced tomatoes and cheese melted on the biscuits left over from breakfast. Jane wasn't the least bit hungry, and her mother ate both portions.

After washing up the dishes, she opened all the windows and the front door to catch the cooling evening breeze, then pulled the cherrywood sewing cabinet into the front parlor. Tomorrow she'd have to find someone to load it into a wagon and haul it down to her store. But first, she had to scrub the place six ways to Sunday with a bucket of hot soapy water and a broom.

Her mother settled on the settee, propping her feet on a crewelwork-covered hassock to relieve the swelling in her ankles. The kerosene table lamp sent a pool of light over the book open in her lap.

"Jane Charlotte, just listen to what Mr. Tennyson writes. *"The old order changeth, yielding place to new....* Whatever does he mean?"

A sob bubbled up from Jane's throat, and she clamped her jaws tight shut. She thought of Papa, lying cold and still in a grave behind the orchard, of Montclair before the Union army came, the way the sun lit the tupelo tree as they drove the buggy down the drive for the last time. The old order.

"It means that things change," she murmured. "That we must look forward, not back."

Right then and there she decided she detested Mr. Tennyson. Things weren't supposed to change, especially if they were beautiful things—peaceful summer days and evenings so quiet you could hear the darkies singing from their quarters beyond the stables, a father who was strong and brave, a mother like a small exquisite bird entertaining dinner guests dressed in shirred emerald satin and petticoats so wide she had to move sideways through doors. Why, *why* did such lovely things have to be destroyed?

Worst of all, why did she now find herself beholden to that aggravating know-it-all Mr. Rydell Wilder? Merciful heavens, he looked at her as if he owned her already!

She frowned as something stirred her memory. There was a boy once, who looked something like Mr. Wilder around the eyes. He'd walked her home from school that first day, and she noticed first that he was tall, with a shock of unruly dark hair tumbling over his forehead, second that he was barefoot. He had shoes, he'd told her…. He just didn't wear them except in winter.

He had a gentle voice, she recalled. He explained about being new in a town and said he would watch out for her. She remembered that his shirt was clean and pressed, but the sleeves were so short his wrists stuck out. When he saw her staring at them, he unbuttoned the cuffs and rolled them up. His knuckles were scraped raw from a fight he'd been in. She wanted to cry at the sight of those bony wrists.

Odd that she'd think of that now. It was so long ago, but for some reason remembering it made her feel warm inside.

"Jane Charlotte, Ah want to read some of this lovely poetry to your father. He is partial to poetry, you recall. Wordsworth and Shelley are his favorites."

"Mama? Mama, I've tried to explain about

Papa...." Oh, what was the use? Mama had always refused to acknowledge things that were unpleasant.

Jane stood up, aware that her chest felt tight. The skin over her cheeks burned. She opened her mouth, then snapped it shut. Perhaps it would be wiser to—

"Miss Davis?" A low voice spoke through the front door screen. Jane froze as the tall form of a man loomed on the porch. With the lamplight from inside, she could not see him clearly in the dark. Mercy me, at least she'd latched the screen! Otherwise he could walk right in.

"Who's there?" she blurted.

Her mother looked up from her volume of poetry. "Jane Charlotte, where *are* your manners? Is that any way to greet a caller?"

A lazy laugh rumbled from the front porch. "Thank you, Mrs. Davis. It's Rydell Wilder. May I come in?"

Jane stood as if transfixed. Come in? Few people— and decidedly fewer men—ever crossed their threshold.

"Jane Charlotte." Her mother's light, clear voice carried over the thudding of her heart. "Don't keep your guest standin' on the porch."

With reluctance, Jane moved forward and unhooked the latch.

Rydell stepped through the doorway. "I'm obliged, Mrs. Davis. If you hadn't interceded, I might have frozen to death." He sent Jane a quick look, amusement dancing in his eyes.

"It's a warm summer night," Jane snapped. "People don't freeze to death in July."

Her mother stirred on the settee. "Wilder," she murmured. "Wilder...have we been introduced?"

"Some years back, ma'am. When your husband was associated with the newspaper office."

"Oh, yes. How nice to see you again, Mr. Wilder." Jane stepped forward. "What do you want?"

"Jane Charlotte!" Her mother had not raised her voice, but Jane jerked guiltily just the same.

"Ah expect you wish to see my husband, Mr. Wilder? We were just about to have our afternoon tea, won't you join us? Jane, go set the kettle on and call your father."

Rydell's gaze held hers for a long, long moment, and then he dipped his head in a barely perceptible nod. "Thank you, Mrs. Davis, but my errand concerns your daughter." He turned to face Jane.

"You left something in my office this afternoon." He pressed a white envelope into her hand. "The key," he said in a low voice. "You'll need it to unlock the store." He closed her fingers around the stiff paper.

An army of white-hot needles marched along her skin where his hand touched hers.

"Jane Charlotte, do let us have some tea! And call your father."

Jane fought the urge to scream.

"Please don't trouble yourself," Rydell said. He looked straight into Jane's eyes. "There's no need to bother Colonel Davis. I'm sure he has pressing business elsewhere this evening."

He released Jane's hand, bowed to her mother, and

turned toward the door. Jane noticed his leather boots were polished to a shine.

"Lefty Springer'll be there tomorrow, if you need help," he said.

"I need no help, thank you." Her hand still tingled, and the sensation made her slightly dizzy. It felt as if that part of her body didn't belong to her any longer, but belonged instead to him. *Goodness, what if he touched my shoulder? My chin? Would those parts of me feel the same? As if they belonged to a different person?*

Rydell grinned at her. "Like I said, Lefty'll be there. You can fire him if you want, but I warn you, he's almost as stubborn as his employer."

It took her a moment to grasp his meaning. By the time she'd thought up a retort, he had disappeared through the doorway. The screen banged shut behind him.

Her mother sighed. "My, what a nice young man."

"He's a Yankee, Mama!"

"Is he? Well, fancy that. A Yankee in Marion County."

"Mama, we're not in..." Oh, what was the use? Maybe it was better this way. At least Mama was not suffering the awful grief widows usually endured.

Jane's mind buzzed. Her hands itched to be busy. Part of it was the need to escape rather than watch her mother retreat into her pretend world. The rest...well, she couldn't bear to think of that just yet. Her skin felt stretched tight along the length of her spine and across her shoulders. The sensation was so

intense she half expected her body to split in half.
She needed to *do* something!

Her pulse hammering, she climbed the stairs up to
the attic for her pattern box and the worn copy of
Godey's Ladies' Book.

All at once she could hardly wait to begin.

Jane twisted the key in the rusty lock and pushed
the plank door wide. A puff of hot, musty air washed
over her, smelling of chicken mash—earthy and
slightly sweet. For a moment she felt she might lose
her breakfast.

She leaned over the mop bucket she'd brought from
home, clamped her hand across her stomach, and
closed her eyes. She could not do this. The only thing
she'd scrubbed in her life was her mother's already-
spotless kitchen floor, and this was a far cry from that.
This, she acknowledged, gazing at the cobweb-
swathed walls and ceiling and the grains of something
moldy heaped into the corners, was one step above a
henhouse. Or maybe a step or two below.

Merciful heavens, she had borrowed good money
to set up a dressmaking shop in a pigsty! The smell
was overpowering.

Another wave of nausea swept over her. She
clenched her jaws tight and convulsively swallowed
down the bitter saliva pouring into her mouth.

When she could raise her head, she fumbled in the
pocket of her blue work skirt for a handkerchief,
folded it in half cross-wise, and tied it over her nose
and mouth. The scent of lavender masked the odor of

the stifling room just enough; if she left the door open
and worked fast, maybe she could manage it.

She took the bucket outside, filled it at the pump
near the horse trough in front of the hotel across the
street, then lugged it into the mercantile. Mr. Mercer
had offered to heat water for her on the potbellied
stove next to the candy counter. While she waited,
she rolled up the sleeves of her high-necked white
waist and began sweeping down the walls.

Debris, dirt particles, even what looked like de-
cayed bird droppings rained down on her. She rolled
the sleeves back down to protect her arms. As she
worked, a thick yellow dust rose and hung in the air
like smoke. It made her cough, and her eyes began to
smart, but she gritted her teeth and worked steadily
until Mr. Mercer poked his head in the doorway.

"Here's yer water, Miz Davis. 'Bout to boil, it was,
so watch yerself, it's awful hot." He plunked the
brimming bucket onto the floor.

Jane leaned on her broom to catch her breath.
"Thank you kindly, sir."

The storekeeper shook his balding head. "Saddest
thing I ever did see," he murmured.

Jane took his comment to heart. "I find I am quite
surprising myself. It is hard work, but it just wants a
bit of pluck and dash and it will all come straight."

"Oh, I didn't mean that, ma'am. I mean the
thought of a lady turnin' my feed store into a dress-
makin' shop. Too ladyfied for the likes of Dixon
Falls."

Jane stared at the wiry man in denim overalls
standing before her. "Ladyfied? Why, you have

ladies here in Dixon Falls, do you not? Ladies who
wear dresses?''

"We got women. Not ladies. Not like you 'n yer
ma, that is.''

Jane gave him her warmest smile, then realized he
couldn't possibly see it under her handkerchief mask.
"Oh, we are all pretty much the same under the skin,
don't you think?''

"I dunno, ma'am," he mumbled as he turned
away. "I jes' dunno.''

"Well *I* do," Jane announced to the dust swirling
in his wake. "Women are women. We all wear corsets and underdrawers and shimmies and petticoats.
And dresses," she added. "Handsome dresses that I
intend to conjure from pattern pieces and my own
imagination.''

With that, she unwrapped the square of lye soap,
drew out the kitchen paring knife she'd brought in
her pocket, and began to shave slivers of soap into
the bucket of hot water. She swirled her broom to and
fro, and when the suds bubbled to the top, she
plunged the straw in up to the stitching and sloshed
the soapy implement back and forth along the length
of the wall.

Droplets of dingy water and soapsuds splatted onto
her clothes, and her hair, neatly pinned up this morning, began to loosen and now straggled about her
face. She felt sodden, and her fingernails were so dirt-
encrusted she could not bear to look at them. She
could just hear Mama's reproachful voice. "Jane
Charlotte, what *have* you been doin' with your
hands!'' Even if her mother had a voice that was al-

ways soft and regulated, she brooked no mistreatment
of hair or skin; such a transgression was worse than
disobedience and elicited as sharp a criticism as if she
had volunteered to spy for the Yankees.

Oh, well, it couldn't be helped. She'd paid off all
of Papa's debts first thing this morning; by this evening, she would have the place for her business. She
positively must be a success. She had to repay Mr.
Wilder's bank loan or suffer a fate worse than death—
marriage to That Man. That Yankee.

She worked through two more buckets of hot water
before the walls and floors were cleaned to her satisfaction. She would *not* open a business in dingy
quarters! Her back and shoulders felt as if she'd been
yoked like an ox to a Conestoga wagon. Every muscle
in her neck screamed. Even her derriere was sore.

By the time she got around to washing the front
window, she was so tired her legs would no longer
support her weight. She sank down onto her knees,
dipped a clean rag into her still-warm water bucket,
and addressed the lower half of the expanse of glass.

And that was how Rydell found her. He tapped on
the open door and lifted his foot to step over the
threshold when her voice stopped him in his tracks.

"You get one speck of dirt on my clean floor and
I'll dump this mop bucket over your head."

Her back was toward him, but he realized she could
see his reflection in the glass. He eased back onto the
boardwalk step. "I brought your supplies from
home," he called.

She scooted around on her bottom to face him.

"What *are* you talking about? I haven't sent for anything yet."

Rydell caught his breath. She was filthy from head to toe, her hair bedraggled, her once-white waist half pulled out of her water-splotched blue skirt. A ridiculously feminine-looking embroidered handkerchief, folded into a triangle, covered the bottom half of her face. She looked like an angel-bandit. A dirt-streaked and very weary angel-bandit.

He resisted the impulse to scoop her bodily from the floor and carry her off to his private suite at the hotel. And a bathtub.

Her eyes flashed fire. "Have you come to gloat over my difficulties?"

"Believe me, Miss Davis, I would not gloat over a lady in your current...situation."

"Then what are you doing here?"

Rydell pushed down the chuckle that threatened. "Lefty Springer got bucked off a horse this morning. I came in his place."

Jane glared at him. "To do what? Laugh at me? I must be a pretty sight, all wet and dirty and so tired I could..." She stopped abruptly as her voice wobbled.

He tore his gaze from her face and studied the floor instead. She was tuckered out, close to breaking. He had predicted as much, but now that it was before him, he wanted to spare her pride. He concentrated on the toe of his boot.

"I came to help, Jane. Lefty gave his word, and I back him up. Always have. His leg's hurt, so I came instead. Your sewing machine and some boxes of patterns and such are in the wagon out front.''

Jane looked up at him in silence. The blue eyes under the dark eyebrows grew shiny. ''I do thank you, Mr. Wilder.'' Her voice sounded choked up. ''And I apologize. I am so tired I hardly know what I am saying.''

''Rafe Mercer'll help me unload. You ready for your things?''

Jane tossed her cleaning rag into the bucket and got to her feet. ''How did you know what to bring?''

''I asked your mother. She was very helpful.''

''Mama? Why, she hardly knows where she is, let alone where I am or what I am doing.''

Rydell nodded. ''I think she understands more than you think. What's important to her is you. I convinced her I was helping you.''

She shook her head. ''That does not exactly make sense, Mr. Wilder. It is to your advantage that I fail in this venture. Why in the world would you offer help?''

Rydell took a single step toward her, reached out and pulled down the handkerchief mask. ''Been askin' myself that question all morning.''

''And what is your answer to that very question?'' Her voice had steadied, but it dropped to a whisper, whether from emotion or exhaustion he couldn't begin to guess.

''Damn—darned if I know,'' he admitted. The scent of lavender floating in the air made his insides ache. Oh, God, he wanted to...

Before he knew what he was doing, he closed his fingers around her upper arm.

She didn't move, just looked at him. He saw fear, and then something else in her eyes. Unable to help himself, he pulled her toward him, lifted his other hand to her shoulder, and bent his head. When his mouth found hers, he lost all track of time.

Her lips were warm and tasted of salt. He'd never known such excruciating sweetness. Instinctively he probed for more, then broke free. He didn't think he could stop if he didn't call a halt now.

"You're right, this doesn't exactly make sense," he breathed against her temple. "No sense at all."

Chapter Four

"No," Jane said in a faraway voice. "It most certainly does not make sense." She wanted her words to come out crisp and proper-sounding. Instead, she sounded as if she just woke up this morning and wasn't sure where she was. His mouth on hers had felt simply heavenly, as if the sun and all the stars tumbled down and kindled a glow inside her.

Merciful Lord, she must not feel *that* way about it! After all, Mr. Wilder had taken a great liberty. She should be outraged instead. She snapped open her eyelids.

"If I had the strength to lift my arm, I would demonstrate how a lady responds to such an ungentlemanly assault."

He said nothing, and with every passing second she became more aware of his arms about her. "Kindly unhand me, Mr. Wilder. I will then proceed as if your grievous action never took place. Back home in Marion County, such behavior would likely cost you your life."

Rydell lifted his arms away from her. "You're not

in Marion County, Jane. Out here, nobody's gonna challenge a man to a duel just because he lost his head and kissed a lady without her permission."

Jane sniffed.

"Next time," he said with a grin, "I'll ask permission."

She took an instinctive step backward. "You will do no such thing! This is a wild, unprincipled country, and I'll have you know—"

"It is that," he acknowledged. "But it's getting more civilized every day. Got a school, now. A hotel and two churches. Even a Ladies Helpful Society."

She would have stalked out the door, but the mop bucket and broom sat in her path; she felt so whirly-headed she didn't think she could walk straight enough to get past them.

"I apologize, Miss Davis. Got carried away by the smell of your handkerchief, I guess."

She looked him in the eye. "See that it never, never happens again."

To her surprise, he turned his back on her. "I'll bring in your sewing machine." He removed his jacket and began rolling up the sleeves of the starched white shirt he wore underneath. His bare forearms looked so...so...unlike Papa's. Papa's hands and his short, plump arms had always been milk-white.

A funny tingle went up the back of her neck. This man's skin was sun-bronzed, and sinews rippled underneath. Indecent. No proper gentleman in the South ever bared his arms in the presence of a lady.

He grabbed up the mop bucket and moved through the open doorway onto the board sidewalk.

"Never," she repeated into the silence. Her breathing steadied.

In the next moment he reappeared, balancing her sewing cabinet on one shoulder.

Her head pounded. Her legs trembled. Oh, she wished he would just go away! Go do whatever bankers did at the end of the day.

This is ludicrous, Jane Charlotte. You'd think she had never scrubbed a floor in her life! Here she was shaking with exhaustion, her muscles refusing to obey her commands. And it was all his fault.

"Never," she repeated under her breath.

"Where do you want this?"

Jane jerked. "What? Oh. There, by the window."

He bent his knees and tipped his broad shoulder forward. The cabinet legs clunked onto the scrubbed plank floor, and he shoved it gently against the wall and stepped away. She pounced on it with a clean rag, flicking off the veil of dust on top and refusing to look at him.

"Here's your pattern box," he announced after his next trip out to the wagon.

She desperately wanted him to stop. She would *not* be beholden to him.

"And the iron and your button jar. Didn't know it took so many things just to sew a dress."

"Didn't your mother sew?" she snapped. She regretted the words the instant they passed her lips. From what she remembered about Rydell Wilder, he'd lived on his own, without mother or father, ever since he'd come to Dixon Falls as a boy.

"No," he said, his voice quiet.

Oh, bother. She'd been rude and she was sorry. But she didn't want his help. His very presence in the tiny store made her thoughts tumble like the bits of colored glass in Aunt Carrie's brass kaleidoscope. He had touched her. Kissed her. And now he acted as if nothing unusual had occurred.

But it had. She couldn't get it out of her mind. His mouth had pressed hers, and a sweet, silken warmth kindled in her belly. Back in Marion County, she would be hopelessly compromised by such an event. Out here in this wilderness they called Oregon, one pair of lips touching another didn't carry the same significance. What an uncivilized place!

It would certainly matter to Papa. Papa would have Mr. Wilder horsewhipped or betrothed within the hour. But Papa was gone.

And so the significance of being kissed by Mr. Wilder, or lack of significance, is up to you, Jane Charlotte.

Oh, she couldn't think a bit straight. She was so tired she knew if she took a single step she would totter just like Granny Beaudry. Her grandmother had been near eighty when they left Marion County; at the moment, Jane felt nearly as old and just as frail. She'd worked too long without stopping to rest. Had eaten nothing since her meager breakfast of toast and tea.

Had felt decidedly wobbly ever since Rydell Wilder had kissed her. All she wanted to do now was get him out of the store, away from her.

"I will arrange the chairs and the dressmaker's

mannequin later," she announced. "Thank you, Mr. Wilder, and good afternoon."

He straightened. "Whatever you say, Miss Davis. Lefty'll come by tomorrow, see if you need anything. He's pretty handy, even if he has only one good arm. Sensitive about it, though."

"It will be a relief to have him instead of... I mean—"

Rydell chuckled. "Got your brain tied up some, I'd say."

Jane sucked in a quick breath. "Whatever do you mean?"

"All of a sudden, your tongue doesn't quite know which way to flap." He grinned at her. "That's not like you."

"Just what gives you a harum-scarum idea like that?"

"Instinct, I guess. Woman savvy. Either you don't like me..." His grin widened. "Or my kissing you meant something."

Two thoughts collided in her brain at the same instant. One, she hated him. Two, she liked the kiss. "I believe," she said with all the ice she could muster in her tone, "the former statement will suffice to explain why I want you to depart before I—"

"Talk plain English, Jane. This is the frontier, not a parlor."

"Out," she snapped. She snatched up the broom and whacked it across his knees. "Out!" Fury gave her the strength for two more blows before he backed out the doorway, still grinning. She heard his lazy laughter as he climbed into the wagon and rattled off down the street.

Jane leaned against the broom handle to steady her shaking body. Even if she *was* a lady, the next time that man kissed her, or touched her, or even looked at her sideways, she would kill him! She had no time for such nonsense; she had work to do. Dresses to sew. A loan to pay back.

She propped the broom in the corner, swiped her dust rag over the sewing cabinet one last time, and surveyed the rudimentary beginnings of her new life. Rough, uncultured town and Mr. Rydell Wilder be damned. She would succeed or she would die trying.

"You mean you jes' grabbed her and bussed her, right there in front of the store window? Lord love ya, Dell, you're gonna scare the bejeesus outta the lady."

Rydell watched his friend hobble to the potbellied stove in the corner and splash more hot coffee into his mug. "She didn't act scared, Lefty. She acted more like she'd been poleaxed. Truth is, I don't know exactly what came over me."

"You're the one that's poleaxed. What were you thinkin' of, fer God's sake?"

Rydell shifted on the hard wooden chair, the only available seat in the tidy one-room cabin Lefty Springer called home. The older man occupied the neatly made-up cot on the opposite wall.

"I wasn't thinking."

"Well, I guess not, son! Like I said, all you have to do is stand still and wait. Don't push her—ladies like Miz Jane may look soft, but they can be stubborn as a mule and twice as skittish.''

Rydell sipped the black sludge his friend called coffee and nodded in silence.

''Somethin's eatin' at you, Dell. I seen it right off.''

Again Rydell nodded. He'd fought his way to acceptance, and then respectability, in this small, close-minded town, overcome his background, his lack of education and polished manners. It had been a long, hard pull. He'd worn patched britches that were too short for his long legs, learned to spell and do sums with the younger children and been ridiculed by the older ones, watched through the hotel dining room window to learn proper table manners.

What bothered him was not that he hadn't succeeded. He had. He'd lived in the tiny shack down by the river and eaten beans and biscuits for ten long years, worked hard, and saved every last penny. Now he owned the bank, dressed in suits that fit, ate whatever he wanted. The townspeople had begun to overlook his hard-scrabble beginnings, began to patronize his bank, even hint that their daughters were unmarried.

The only thing his life lacked now was Jane, and that was the problem.

''Well?'' Lefty clicked his thumbnail against the tin cup balanced on his left knee.

Rydell met the older man's sharp blue eyes. No use hedging to Lefty. He'd always seen right to the core of a man.

Rydell exhaled. ''To be honest, I see something in myself I'm not sure I like.''

Lefty's bushy gray eyebrows waggled. "Yeah? What?"

"I guess I'm afraid that something I've worked hard for in this town might slip away."

"Why would it?" Lefty snapped. "Hell, kid, half the town borrows money from your bank to pay the other half fer somethin' or other, and pays you back interest for the privilege. I told you at the start, it was a good idea. You ain't got a thing to worry about 'cept where you're gonna build a house for Miz Jane."

Rydell worried his forefinger around the rim of his coffee mug. "What if there's more to it? See, inside I still feel like maybe I don't belong here among all these decent, respectable folks."

"'Cuz of your pa, is that it? Why he never gave you his name?"

"Partly."

"Well, spit it out, son. I've been cooped up here a day and a half with a swole-up knee and I'm gettin' hungry for a hotel dinner."

Rydell smiled in spite of himself. Lefty always had a hard time when he couldn't move around much. Seemed to remind him of that Army hospital when he lost his arm.

"I never knew who my pa was. Whether he was a good man, or a card sharp. An honorable man or a thief. "

"So," the older man said, heaving his weight off the cot. "You're not so sure who *you* are, izzat it?"

"Partly."

"Partly! Lordy, Dell, you'd a been a good lawyer.

You gonna string this out 'til the dining room closes? Tell me the other part and let's eat!''

Rydell stood up and set his cup in Lefty's spotless dry sink. "The other part is this: The man who marries Jane Davis will automatically be respected."

"Shore will. So?"

"Even if that man turns out to have a horse thief as kin, having Jane as a wife would protect him."

"Yup. What's the problem?"

"The problem is that it doesn't work both ways. Such a man couldn't protect Jane in the same way. Coming from a family like hers, being associated with him would ruin her."

Lefty clapped his good arm on Rydell's shoulder. "Son, I've known you since you was sixteen and so skinny-ribbed and knob-kneed you looked more like a baby moose than a man. And I've watched you fall for Miz Jane like a felled tree and moon for her these ten years while you turned yourself inside out to grow up and get yerself established."

"That obvious, huh?" Rydell grinned at the older man.

"Plain as a duck's bill to me, though I doubt anyone else cottoned on to it. You always were good at keepin' secrets."

Rydell flicked a glance at Lefty's face. How much did the old man know?

"You're growed up now, Dell. You're a fine-lookin' feller with half the gals in Douglas County sweet on ya. What the hell else do you want? You want to marry Miz Jane, you go ahead and marry her. If she'll have you."

A fifty-pound lead weight rolled off Rydell's chest. "Should have been a lawyer yourself, Lefty. You talk just like you know all the answers."

"Ain't the answers that's important, it's the questions. An' the question here is, what the devil's got into you? No matter about yer pa, you've got everything to gain by marryin' Miz Jane. Now come on, so's I can get some supper before my stomach caves in."

Rydell shortened his stride so Lefty could keep pace with him with his injured knee. With every step he took between the old man's cabin and the Excelsior Hotel he turned the matter over and over in his mind.

He wanted Jane. Had always wanted her, ever since that day in the schoolyard. He used to walk out to their place on the hill after it got dark and listen to her play the piano. The rippling notes floated like pearls on the warm air, and he stood for hours outside the trim white picket fence and gazed at a world he knew nothing about. A world that excluded him. He wanted her anyway.

He stepped off the walkway and started toward the hotel, then stopped dead in the middle of the street.

"Whatza matter?" Lefty complained.

"Nothing. Everything."

His dream was within reach, now. He wasn't going to give up. Nothing on the face of the earth was going to stop him.

Jane dragged herself up the hill to her house as the red-orange sun slipped behind the mountain tops. Just as she reached for the front gate latch, a tall, well-built Negro man stepped out onto her porch.

"Miz Jane?"

She stared at him. She'd seen him about town, but she didn't know his name.

"It's Mose, ma'am. Mose Freeman. The blacksmith."

"Oh, yes. What are you doing here?"

"Was jus' walkin' home past your house and I smelled somethin' funny, like hot iron. I know that smell, see, and I knock and I come on in cuz sure as God made sweet corn, I smell fire."

"Fire! Is Mama—?"

"Well, ma'am, your momma, Miz Davis, she boil all the water outta the teakettle, an' it settin' on the stove glowing red. So I dunk it into a dishpan of water. No harm done, Miz Jane."

"Oh, thank you, Mose. Mr. Freeman. Thank you so very much!"

The soft brown skin of his face crinkled into a smile. "You better go on in, cuz your momma sayin' how she wants her tea."

"Yes, of course," Jane managed over the tight feeling in her throat. "I am indeed grateful."

With a wave, the man was off down the road, and Jane opened the front door.

"Jane Charlotte, is that you?"

"Yes, Mama." She smelled something sharp and smoky in the air. The scorched teakettle.

Her mother's silvery voice echoed from the parlor. "Abner came to make tea, but Ah don't believe it's ready just yet."

"It wasn't Abner, Mama." She moved into the room. "You haven't laid eyes on Abner since we left home. Or Odelia or Aunt Carrie, either. That was Mose Freeman, the blacksmith."

"The blacksmi... What *have* you been doin'? Your hair looks all windblown, and your skirt! My stars, that hem is simply filthy!"

Jane gazed at her mother's slight frame curled up under a crocheted afghan on the settee. "I told you about my shop, Mama, remember? My dressmaking shop?"

Her mother looked up, a blankness in her pale blue eyes. "Why, no, dear. Tell me all about it while we have our tea. Abner? Ab—?"

"Mama." Jane felt her heart squeeze tight. *Oh, Mama, please. Please don't leave me like this.*

She turned away and forced a lightness into her voice. "I'll fetch the tea, Mama. And then I'll make us a nice supper."

And then I will go to bed and cry until I can't feel anything anymore.

"Jane, do call your father. He's been out all morning and must surely be tired."

Try to remember. Oh, please, Mama, just try a little bit.

The teakettle was ruined. Jane boiled water in the gray enamel saucepan and made hot milk and bread for their supper. It was a pitiful offering, but she was so tired she couldn't think of anything else. Besides, they were running out of staples.

They ate in silence. Jane listened to the moths batting against the lighted dining room window, the *ting* of her mother's silver spoon against the edge of the china soup bowl. The air was warm and smelled of rain. She closed her eyes and tried to concentrate. *I cannot bear this alone. I cannot.*

She had to take care of Mama.

She had to open her shop, had to stitch up at least one garment to sell—otherwise they would run out of flour and tea and molasses before the week was up. And she had to bake bread, do the washing and then the ironing, scrub the—

"Jane Charlotte, honey, you look plumb worn out."

Jane clenched her fist in her lap. "I'm fine, Mama."

Her mother reached across the table and smoothed her soft fingers over Jane's hand. "We will be all right, Jane. Things are difficult just now, but they will work out. The Beaudry women have always been strong."

"I'm only half-Beaudry, Mama," Jane said wearily.

The fingers tightened on her hand. "Half," her mother said, her pale blue eyes looking into Jane's, "will be sufficient."

Chapter Five

"**A**nything else this morning, Miz Davis?"

Jane drew in a deep breath. She had inspected every bolt of yard goods Mr. Mercer had in stock—crisp yellow percaline, rose and pale green checked gingham, airy white dimity. Nothing seemed just right. She wanted something unusual, something eye-catching to display in her shop window. Something that would stop the ladies of Dixon Falls in their tracks.

"Miz Davis?" the mercantile owner reminded.

She scanned the shelves of fabric once more. "There, on the top. What is that red?"

Rafe Mercer pushed a ladder into place and clambered up four rungs. Reaching out his long arms, he grasped the bolt and dragged it off the pile, balancing it on his shoulder. "Muslin, ma'am. Ordered it by mistake."

He descended the ladder and plunked the fabric down on the polished wood counter before her. "Ten cents a yard."

Jane's head began to buzz the way it always did

when she began to envision a new design for a dress
or a hat trimming. Yes, she could see it now. And in
red, just the thing. The eyes of every woman in town
would be glued to her store window display!

"And the blue, next to it?"

With a sigh, the thin, graying man propelled his
skinny legs up the ladder again. "Cambric," he called
down to her. "Bought extra this year for the big
Fourth of July doings at the schoolhouse on Sunday,
but the ladies decorating committee didn't use it all.
Sell it to you for…eight cents a yard."

"Seven cents," Jane countered. "And I will offer
you one dollar for the bolt of red muslin." Oh, how
Papa would bellow if he knew she was bargaining!
But her money was borrowed; she certainly could not
afford to squander it.

Mr. Mercer's thin face blanched. "Ma'am, that's
near thirty yards of muslin."

"Ordered in error, I believe you mentioned." She
swiped her gloved forefinger across the rolled fabric
and held it up. "Unless I am mistaken, Mr. Mercer,
this has been on your shelf for a good while, long
enough to collect dust. Seven cents."

"Oh, all right, Miz Davis. A dollar for the bolt.
That'll be, lessee, two dollars and five cents alto-
gether. You need any thread?"

In her mind's eye she was already laying out the
yardage and marking the gathers. And two bright colors, red and blue, just perfect for the Fourth of July.
Every female in Dixon Falls would want one.

"Miz Davis?"

Jane jerked to attention. "What? Oh, yes, thread,

if you please. Two spools of Brook's cotton.'' She counted out the coins while the mercantile owner wrapped up her parcels.

''I'll send the Harrelson boy over with your purchases, ma'am. The flour and tea and such I'll deliver to your house on my way home this— Ah, good morning, ladies.'' He turned his attention to the two new customers sweeping through the doorway. ''Mrs. Tanner, Miss Price.''

Jane shut her reticule and fairly floated over the planked floor, her brain whirling with ideas. She'd done it, made the first purchase for her new business! The feeling was so heady, and so unexpected, she suppressed an urge to laugh out loud.

Jane Charlotte, just you stop and think what Papa would say.

For a moment her elation dimmed. Of course Papa would disapprove. How could he not, coming from a long line of gentleman plantation owners? Working with your hands for a living was ''common.'' *Face it, Jane. You yourself are now an employed woman.* A shopkeeper.

And Mama…she dared not think about Mama. She would *not* think of them, she resolved. She was doing what she had to do, either that or marry, and the only offer she'd had was from Mr. Wilder and it hadn't been the least bit proper. To succeed she had to care for her widowed mother and earn enough money to keep them fed and clothed until they could return to Montclair. It would take every ounce of concentration and fortitude she could muster, but it would all come straight in the end. She knew it would.

The two ladies passed her by. "Good morning," she said automatically. Jane heard one of them give an audible sniff.

She should have addressed them by name, but she realized suddenly she did not know which one was which. Was Mrs. Tanner the dark-haired woman in gray, or was that Miss Price? The latter had golden ringlets and a merry laugh, but looked too young to be married. In fact, both women looked to be not a day over twenty.

For just an instant a dart of envy pricked her. By comparison, at twenty-six, she herself would be considered "old." And probably stiff-necked, as well.

Behind her, she heard the two young women whisper together, and then a soft giggle. They were talking about her. She could feel it in her bones. Pain swallowed up her envy.

She had lived here in Dixon Falls ever since she was fifteen years old. Eleven full years, and she still felt like an outsider. Oh, people were polite enough; no one had ever been unkind to her except for schoolboy bullies years ago. But somehow she felt separate from everyone else, as if she didn't belong.

She closed the door of the mercantile on the happy laughter of the two women, punctuated by Mr. Mercer's deeper tenor voice. "Right this way, ladies. Allow me."

An empty feeling yawned in the pit of Jane's stomach. *I feel so alone.*

In the next moment, she felt her spine stiffen. *Jane Charlotte, you stop that this instant.* Don't you dare go all mooney over your lot in life! Just because Papa is gone and Mama isn't well doesn't mean you are any less than you were before, does it?

Certainly not. She'd had private tutors, had studied history and Latin and Greek grammar, took years and years of piano lessons from Mama. She knew how to serve tea and plan a dinner party—everything a proper young lady should know. She was Ready.

But ready for what? What was it all *for?* She'd lived all these years in suffocating isolation. A bell jar. She'd never been allowed to join the other young people at socials because they "weren't the right sort," Papa said. She was never allowed to walk into town unless Papa accompanied her. No friends ever came to call. She had been so lonely growing up she hadn't *wanted* to grow up!

But she had. She'd gone right ahead and done it, and before she knew what had happened, she had turned into an old maid.

Her steps slowed. Was this some kind of punishment for coming to live in a town full of Yankees?

She unlocked the door to her shop, surveyed the dim interior, and rocked back on the heels of her black buttoned leather shoes. She would need a kerosene lamp, even in the daytime. And a stove of some sort to heat her sadiron. And…

She gazed at the tiny space, small as a shoe box. At least it was clean. The air still smelled faintly of soap. She would bring the long cheval dressing mirror from the upstairs bedroom and Aunt Carrie's bust form. What amazing foresight her mother's older sister had shown when she insisted that the padded dressmaker's form come west with them. Jane had used it ever since to fashion new garments for herself out of her mother's old gowns. She used the illustrations in *Godey's Ladies' Book* for inspiration, and the fabrics had lasted through many remakings. She knew the styles had grown outdated over the years, the skirts too full, the tops too ornate, too stiff and formal for a small dusty town in Oregon. She always looked different. Out of place. And the townspeople still called her Queen Jane.

"But no more," she vowed. It would be sheer joy to work with something crisp and new from the mercantile! With her first earned dollar, she would send for the latest edition of Godey's book. "And," she announced to the silent cherry sewing cabinet, "since I cannot any longer use our dining room table, I will need a cutting board. A nice big one. Propped up on...what?" she muttered to herself. She hadn't the faintest notion. Barrels? Stacked-up old trunks?

"Sawhorses! Yes! Now where can I find—"

"Beggin' yer pardon, Miz Jane..."

Jane whirled to see Lefty Springer standing in her open doorway. "Mr. Springer."

"Lefty, ma'am, remember? Mose down to the blacksmith shop, he's a pretty fair carpenter. Bet he'd cobble you up a pair of sawhorses quicker'n a frog snaps flies."

"Of course! The perfect thing. Oh, I do admire a man who can think." She headed for the door, then stopped dead in the middle of the room. She couldn't go traipsing around town, down to the blacksmith's shop, without an escort; it just wasn't done. Mama would have a fit.

"Mr....Lefty, I am so glad you came visiting this morning. I need your help."

The old man beamed.

And when Mrs. Evangeline Tanner and Miss Letitia Price stepped through the mercantile doorway and onto the board walkway, they gasped and pointed.

"Well, did you ever see the like!"

"Queen Jane and that old one-armed freight wagon driver!"

Jane rested her fingers on Lefty's extended good arm and was skipping—skipping!—across the street in the company of an old man who couldn't stop grinning.

Rydell counted out ten dollar bills and handed them through the cage to the trim, gray-haired woman on the other side. "There you are, Mrs. Manning."

The woman folded the bills into her black crocheted bag and smiled at him. "Thank you, Mr. Wilder. Now, you'll remember to come on out and meet my granddaughter sometime, won't you? She's come all the way from Kansas City to visit for the summer."

He watched the woman's small black shoes move toward the bank entrance and shook his head. Only yesterday it seemed, Mrs. Manning's daughter, Eula, had moved back East to be married; now Eula had a grown-up daughter looking to do the same thing. All of a sudden, he felt old.

And left out in an odd way. He'd sent Josiah, his bank clerk, home to be with his wife. The young man was so nervous at the prospect of their first child he

was useless this morning, but—Rydell had to laugh—
he himself wasn't much better. All morning he'd done
nothing but think about Jane Davis.

A small grimy fist appeared on the counter before
him. "Kin you save this for me, mister?" The fingers
unfolded to reveal a single copper penny.

Rydell leaned forward. A round freckled face
peered up at him, wide blue eyes questioning.

"You want to deposit this in the bank?"

"Yessir. Else my brother'll grab it from me. Will
you save it for me?"

"Sure thing, son." With a chuckle he slid the coin
into a bank envelope. He'd not been much older than
this when he'd started saving pennies, only there
hadn't been a bank then. Rydell saved all his earnings
in a pickle jar secreted under his mattress.

"What's your name, son?"

"Tommy. I helped the Queen Lady down the street
set up a sawhorse 'n she done paid me."

The Queen Lady? Did he mean Jane? He dipped
the pen in the inkwell and scribbled on a piece of
notepaper.

"Okay, Tommy, here's your deposit receipt. When
you want your money, just show it to the clerk."

The boy nodded, and the round face disappeared.

A sawhorse? He'd step down the street and inves-
tigate, but he couldn't leave the cash drawer unattended. He'd wait until noon, when he could lock up
the safe.

Customers drifted in and out for the next hour, and
Rydell's curiosity grew. What the devil did Jane want
with a sawhorse?

The clock on the wall tick-tick-ticked toward twelve. At one minute before noon, Tommy's freckled visage reappeared at the counter.

"Mister, I got 'nother 'posit to make."

Rydell reached for the envelope marked Tommy. "How much this time?"

"One big an' one little. Here's the little one." He plopped another penny onto the smooth wood surface, and Rydell added it to the envelope.

"'N here's the big one." With both hands he lifted a tiny ball of orange fur and set it on the smooth oak surface. "It's lost. I found it in the alley back of the livery stable, but if I take it home, my brother'll steal it for sure."

Rydell eyed the clock. "Okay, Tommy. I'll take care of it." He scooped the purring kitten into his coat pocket, where it curled up and burrowed its nose into a corner seam.

"Thanks, mister."

Rydell sent the under-clerk to lunch, closed up the safe, and locked the front door of the bank. Then he headed up the street to see what Jane was up to.

"That's it. A little to the left. No, too much, Lefty. Yes, right there will do nicely." Jane cocked her head, assessing the position of her new cutting board, a discarded door plank Mose Freeman had carted from Tanner's lumberyard. With a sawhorse propping each end, it made a perfectly level, smooth surface on which to sponge-shrink her yard goods and lay out pattern pieces. Already, a bucket of water and her sadiron were heating on the small oil stove Lefty

Springer had "found" for her. It looked so new she suspected Lefty had actually purchased it from Mercer's Mercantile.

The old man's interest in her new business touched her heart. He'd even volunteered to watch over the shop while she'd walked up the long hill to check on Mama and boil up some eggs for her lunch. She left Mama dozing on the settee, and Jane hoped she would sleep until suppertime, when she would return to fix the evening meal.

All morning she'd worried about another teakettle incident—or worse. What if Mama fell and couldn't get up again? What if she went out to the orchard to look for Papa and couldn't find her way back? A hundred dangers suggested themselves as she organized her little dressmaking establishment. A hundred reasons why she felt torn in two.

She didn't really know any of the women in town, much less the farm wives that lived out in the country and came into town only occasionally. Not only did she have to start her business, she had to befriend her clientele, women who were virtual strangers. She would have to work hard to make them think of her not as Queen Jane, but as a capable dressmaker.

And of course Mama needed her attention, too. Merciful heavens, how could she be in two places at once?

She blotted the perspiration from her face with a damp wadded-up lace-edged handkerchief and tried to think. The hot, still air smelled of dust and acrid smoke. The heat from her little stove made it stifling inside the shop. Lefty perched on an empty nail keg positioned half in, half out of the doorway, whittling on a piece of oak.

"Why'ntcha sit yerself down, Miz Jane? You're gonna melt into a puddle if'n you don't slow down and rest a bit." He motioned to a second upturned keg.

"Oh, I just can't, Lefty. I must get this muslin sponged before suppertime so I can cut out my patterns first thing tomorrow. The Fourth of July is only two days away, and I simply must be ready by then! It offers such a wonderful opportunity for my...well, my first original creation."

With his boot, Lefty pushed his wood shavings out onto the board sidewalk. "Cain't sew if you cain't stand up."

"Oh, but I can," Jane countered. "I sew sitting up. It won't matter a whit if my legs won't hold me up, I can seat myself at the sewing machine. I intend to finish my—"

Through the open doorway stepped a tall figure, and Jane gave a little gasp. Her heart somersaulted at the sight of Rydell Wilder.

"Why, howdy, Dell. Come to oversee yer investment, have ya?"

That man! What right did he have to come barging in without even a by-your-leave? Jane grabbed a length of red muslin and hastily draped it around the padded bust form in the corner. Surely it wasn't proper for a gentleman to see a lady's...well, replica of herself, without a stitch of clothing?

All at once she was doubly grateful for Lefty's presence in the tiny shop. Her brain seemed as sluggish and sticky as molasses, and her stomach felt as if thousands of bird feathers swirled inside it. She was afraid of him.

Afraid he would kiss her again.

Afraid she would like it.

She stared at him, her tongue stuck to the roof of her mouth.

"Miss Davis."

"If you have come to watch me struggle, you can turn right around and…I declare you're watching me just like a hungry tiger stalking its prey."

"I assure you—"

"Waiting until I fail, and then you'll pounce on me." She heard Lefty make an odd choking sound, but he lowered his head so she couldn't see his face.

And then she noticed something strange. Mr. Wilder looked lopsided. The right pocket of his well-fitted suit bulged out of proportion, and then, right before her eyes, it moved.

Mesmerized, she watched the dark fabric pooch out. Unable to contain her curiosity, Jane moved forward, eyeing Rydell Wilder's coat pocket.

Chapter Six

Jane stopped two paces in front of Rydell, narrowed her eyes and pointed at his coat pocket. "What have you got in there?"

With a sheepish grin, Rydell plunged his hand into the opening in the soft worsted and brought forth the orange kitten. Jane's eyes widened.

"Why, the darling little thing! Wherever did you find it?" She took an involuntary step forward, stretching both hands toward the tiny ball of fur.

"A young...bank patron found it in back of the livery stable. He entrusted it to me for safekeeping."

Jane's hand darted toward the animal, then retreated. If she touched the kitten, her skin might brush against his. She laced her fingers together behind her back. But oh, how she longed to smooth her fingertips over that soft-looking fur.

The hand holding the kitten moved nearer. "Jane?" a low voice spoke. "Would you like to have it?"

Yes! All those years when she was growing up she'd longed for a pet, something of her very own to care for. Papa always said an animal would make too much work for Mama.

"Oh, no, I couldn't. It really belongs to your patron, you see, and I just couldn't—" She broke off as Rydell offered the kitten. Taking extreme care not to touch the hand of the man who stood before her, she extended one finger and nuzzled the tiny face. A small pink tongue licked her forefinger, and at that moment her hand brushed his.

A zing of awareness raised the fine hair on her forearm and danced on up past her elbow. Her heart beat so loudly she could hear it. Could he?

He just stood there, looking at her with those knowing gray eyes and that firm, unsmiling mouth. It gave her the shivers.

Lefty grinned at her from the doorway, then dropped his gaze to the oak piece in his lap. *Snick, snick* went the blade of his pocketknife, and then he began to hum a tune to match the rhythm. Little Brown Jug.

A spell seemed to have fallen over her. She could neither move nor talk nor even think rationally. Why, merciful heavens, what a silly bit of nonsense!

She ordered her knees to bend, knelt and set the feline onto the plank floor. On wobbly legs, it headed for her sewing basket, climbed in and curled up next to the calico-covered pincushion. The soft rumbly purring rose into the quiet room, and no one moved.

She couldn't bear this awful tension one more minute! With a toss of her head she rose and planted both hands on her hips. "Gentlemen, I have work to do."

Lefty hefted himself off the nail keg and slipped

his knife into his trouser pocket. "Guess I'll go next door to the mercantile and rustle up some food for puss, there." He glanced pointedly at her sewing basket. "Mebbe find an old box for him to sleep in."

The old man tramped off down the board walkway, and suddenly Jane realized she was alone with Rydell Wilder. She positioned herself so the sewing basket was between them.

"It's a her, not a him," Rydell said.

Without thinking, Jane snapped out a retort. "What makes you so all-fired certain?"

Rydell chuckled. "What makes me certain? It's very simple, Miss Davis. I looked."

Oh! Why had she said that? He made her so skittery inside she couldn't think clearly, had just blurted out something—anything—to wipe that smile off his face.

But it hadn't. Now he was laughing and she could feel the color wash up her neck and flush her face. Even if he did make her as nervous as a partridge chased by a hound, she must learn to think before she spoke!

"Forgive me, Jane. I didn't mean to upset—"

"Oh yes you did! You marched in here fully intending to interrupt my work and disrupt my peace of mind."

She faced Rydell with fire in her eyes. "I see your game, Mr. Wilder. Just you take yourself out of my establishment and...and keep your nose out of my business."

She was off on a tear now, Rydell decided. Plain

as the pearl buttons on her blouse. He'd try to change
the subject.

"About the cat—"

"Just never you mind about that cat. I will take
excellent care of him—her—so there is no need for
you to come sneaking around to check on him. Her."

The guffaw that escaped him added fuel to her fire.

"Oh! If I weren't a lady, I'd...I'd..."

He was gone before she could finish the thought.
Later, as he and Lefty watched from the window of
the Excelsior Hotel dining room, Jane Davis marched
down the street at a pace so determined, her face looking so resolute, Lefty put down his fork and followed
her with his eyes.

"Sure does *look* female, Dell. But she walks like
a damn Reb general. You real sure this is the one you
want?"

"I'm sure. Thought about it for ten years."

The older man shook his head. "Well, you ain't
failed at anything yet. Still, there's always a first
time."

Rydell surveyed his friend across the blue checked
tablecloth. "Not for me, Lefty. Nothing's going to
stop me, not even Jane."

He sliced off a juicy chunk of steak and forked it
into his mouth. It had never tasted so good.

At six o'clock the next morning, Jane tucked her
mother's breakfast tray on the table beside the bed,
donned her hat and gloves, and walked down the hill
into town. The air hung hot and still, as if life in

Dixon Falls had suddenly stopped. For a fleeting moment, she wondered if she was dreaming.

No, there was Mr. Mercer in a white canvas apron, sweeping the boardwalk in front of the mercantile with a worn-down broom. *Swish-scratch, swish-scratch.* She nodded as she passed, and he leaned on the broom handle, watching her unlock the door to her shop.

The only sound in the air, the faint ching of metal against metal, had to be Mose Freeman the blacksmith one block over next to the livery stable. She'd never before realized how early working people had to drag themselves out of bed to...work. From now on, this would have to be her regimen as well.

The scent of coffee floated from the hotel dining room, and for an instant she considered crossing the street and lingering over a cup. Then, with a sigh, she pushed open the shop door.

The kitten, snuggled in her sewing basket, blinked two bright blue eyes and watched Jane fold her gray shawl and lay it, along with her veiled straw hat and her gloves, on one of the two nail kegs that served as chairs. The cat yawned, stood up, and arched her back. Then she skittered into the box of sand Lefty had brought yesterday evening.

Jane turned her attention elsewhere. The red muslin lay stretched out on the makeshift cutting table. Time to begin.

The kitten stepped daintily out of the box, ignored the flour-sack-lined box Lefty had fixed, and dove under Jane's full gathered petticoat.

"Oh, pshaw," she said aloud. She couldn't take a

step without fear of stepping on it, and she had a million things to do.

"Kitty, come out of there!" She lifted her skirts and peered underneath. The cat swung off the floor, clinging to her petticoat ruffle. "This is a business establishment," Jane announced. "Not a circus." She shook the cat free, poured some milk from a jar she'd brought from home into a saucer, and surveyed the length of fabric that awaited her. She had sponged and pressed it last night after fixing Mama's supper; now it awaited pattern pieces and her sewing shears.

While the kitten lapped at the saucer, Jane rummaged in her box of patterns. Yes, this one! She could substitute a lace inset in place of the band of embroidery, and for variation could add a contrasting ruffle of the blue chambray. Unusual…and just right for Fourth of July.

She pinned and snipped and basted all morning while the sun flamed in the clear blue sky. The heat in the shop was suffocating, even with the door propped open to catch whatever breeze there might be. Perspiration soaked the high neck of her dress and made her fingers so sticky it was almost impossible to hold the sewing needle steady.

By noon, the kitten gave up her game of batting a spool of thread about the floor and lay panting in the sewing basket. Jane herself was so wilted she wondered how she could manage to walk back up the hill to fix her mother's lunch.

But she didn't have a choice. She pinned on her hat, drew her gloves over her perspiring fingers, and marched home. An hour later, she returned to the store, poured a jar full of lukewarm water into the cat's dish, and resumed her basting.

Townspeople straggled past the store window. The ladies peered in at her, then moved on. One eyed the draped bust form in the window and gave an audible sniff.

Pulling a nail keg up to the sewing cabinet, Jane seated herself, threaded the bobbin, and positioned the pieces of red muslin under the presser foot. She balanced both feet on the treadle and with a thump and a whir she was off, stitching a waistband, adding a generous band of lace, turning up the hem.

She held up the finished garment for inspection. Exactly right! A boldly flounced apron in this bright red color—there wouldn't be another one like it in the whole county. In the entire state of Oregon! With trembling fingers, she tied her creation around the waist of the bust form in the window. My, it certainly did give the old gray jersey-covered form a lift!

In the next hour she cobbled up an even frillier apron in blue, with a double ruffle at the hem, lined in the red muslin. The garments were so pretty she did a little two-step of delight about the floor. And practical, too. Aprons were…aprons. Every woman wore one. And these—in such bold colors and with the extra-feminine trimmings—why, a woman would practically dance through her chores in one of Jane's creations!

By teatime, the dress dummy sported five gorgeous aprons, artfully pinned to the padded covering so the ruffles showed to advantage and the form was discreetly covered.

By suppertime, she was so tired all she could think about was crawling into bed and sleeping for a week. But she had done it! She had launched her business.

Despite her exhaustion, as she trudged up to the house on the hill she felt like singing. *You and me...little brown jug, don't I love thee.* She hummed all the way home.

Until she reached the front gate and saw smoke pouring out of the kitchen chimney and her mother calmly sitting beneath the maple tree in the front garden.

"Mama? Mama, whatever are you doing out here?"

Her mother's watery blue eyes looked unfocused. "Why, Ah'm waitin' for your father, Jane Charlotte. He ought to be along any minute now, and I expect his brother Junius will stay to tea."

Jane knelt in the dirt beside the frail woman and put her arms around her. "Oh, Mama, don't...don't you worry about Papa. He's...he will be here directly. Why don't you come on into the house now, and I'll make some supper for us? Come on, now."

She helped Mama to stand, then slid an arm about the old woman's still-tiny waist and walked her up the porch steps into the house.

The stove top was red-hot, but no pots or skillets sat on top. Thank the Lord, Jane breathed. Mama had stoked up the fire, then probably forgotten all about it. A chill went through her entire body. Mama should not be left alone.

What should she do now? She had a business to

operate, but how could she bear to leave her mother alone with her mind so confused?

Maybe Mama could come to the shop with her during the day? No. That was out of the question. The shop was already so hot and uncomfortable it made Jane half-sick with headache by afternoon. Besides, how would she feed her mother? Mama would rather die than eat in a public hotel dining room.

Could she sew at home? Certainly. But making up the garments was only the first step. Selling them was even more important. She couldn't sell anything if she couldn't display it in the window and be present for fittings.

"Jane, I think I must lie down for a bit. Ask Abner to make some tea, won't you dear?"

Abner again. And Papa and Uncle Junius. *Dear God, what was she to do?*

She settled her mother on the green settee, plumped up two damask-covered pillows and slid them beneath the small graying head. "Rest now, Mama. Just—"

She pressed her knuckles against her mouth and turned away. *Oh, God, help us!*

A wagon rattled up the hill, slowed at the house and stopped. Probably Mr. Mercer with the flour and molasses.

Footsteps crunched up the path, and a knock sounded at the front door. Jane swallowed hard. She would not cry before any of the townfolk. She would *not.*

"Please, just leave the supplies on the porch," she called.

Another knock. Maybe it wasn't Mr. Mercer.

Maybe it was that Yankee reprobate Rydell Wilder. "Go away." She shouted the words as loud as she could with her voice so shaky. "I'll thank you to leave me alone!"

One more imperious rap and the door flew open. "I ain't never gonna leave you alone, child. You oughtta know better'n that."

"Odelia!" Jane peered at the handsome dark-skinned woman as if seeing a ghost. "Is it really you?"

"Las' time I looked, I was me. You got some different notion?"

Jane flung herself at the woman and wrapped her arms tight around her. "Odelia! Oh, I just can't believe my eyes."

"I's real, all right. But you about squeezin' the breath out of me. Don't 'spect I'll last too long if you keep this up."

Jane released her and brushed the back of her hand over her eyes. "Whatever are you doing here?"

The plump black woman sighed. "Well now, honey, I got some hard news. Miss Carrie, she passed over."

"Oh, no. Not Aunt Carrie."

"The pneumonia took her, Miss Jane. She didn't suffer none. An' after she was buried, I say to myself, "Delia, what you gonna do now?' So I decide to take the money Miss Carrie left me and come out west. Now your aunt's gone, I guess I belong here with you and Miss Leah."

"Odelia, you know you're free now. Papa saw to the papers before we left Montclair."

"Sure, I know that, honey. I didn't come cuz I had to, I came cuz I wanted to. I belong here with you-all. Miss Leah an' you the only family I got."

Jane's heart lifted. "You mean you'll stay? You've really come to stay? Oh, you dear old thing!" She hugged the woman again.

"Old? Hmmmmph. Where's Miss Leah?"

"In the parlor. Asleep, I think. Oh, Mama will just bust when she sees you! But…"

Odelia's dark eyes studied Jane. "But? What 'but' you got to tell ol' 'Delia?"

Jane took one of the woman's soft, work-worn hands in her own. "Mama is…well, she's been real tired since Papa died. She seems…confused at times."

The older woman nodded once. "Part of Miss Leah gone to be with your papa, honey. Might be she ain't never comin' back."

Tears stung under Jane's eyelids.

"Now, now, Miss Jane. You show me where you gonna put a frisky woman like me to sleep so's I can settle in."

"Oh, Odelia," Jane sobbed.

"Then you tell me what vittles you got for yo supper, and—"

"Oh, thank you. Thank you for coming to us."

"My baby girl, you all grown up now. It's gonna be all right, jes' you wait and see. 'Delia knows about these things, yes she do. I got me some fine big plans, and ol' 'Delia ain't never been wrong. Trust me, child. Things gonna be jes' fine."

Chapter Seven

By the next afternoon, Jane had created seven more aprons, no two alike. Each was a unique combination of sensible practicality and feminine whimsey—blue with a wide red ruffle, red with insets of dark blue lace gleaned from an old gown of her mother's, even a reversible one, red on one side, blue on the other, with two heart-shaped pockets in the contrasting color.

Knowing that Odelia was caring for her mother, she worked straight through lunch. The kitten, christened General Lee with a sprinkle of drinking water on its head, chased empty thread spools or snoozed, purring like a train engine, in the sewing basket.

By midafternoon, the dress dummy in the window looked like a Christmas tree festooned with bright colored aprons. She folded a piece of cardboard in half, printed "Aprons, 50 cents each" on it, and propped it beside the display.

A few women stopped to study the window. Through the door Jane had propped open for fresh air, she heard their footsteps stop and then words whispered back and forth.

"Not like any apron *I* ever saw…"

"Who would have thought…"

"Very striking colors…"

"Outlandish!"

But not one passerby entered the shop. She slashed ten cents off the price, but still no one paused more than a few moments before moving on down the street. By three o'clock, she was famished and disheartened.

Not one buyer. Perching on a nail keg, she studied the dozen garments she had created and listened to her stomach rumble. Was there something wrong with her designs? Or—worse—were the women of Dixon Falls avoiding her?

But why? She had done nothing to them. She didn't even know any of them well enough to ask the question that burned in her brain. An uneasy feeling invaded her midsection. She turned her back to the doorway and squeezed her eyes tight shut. What if she didn't sell a single apron?

Footsteps, then a man's voice. "Jane, is something wrong?"

She jerked her shoulders straight. That odious Mr. Wilder, what was he doing here?

"I am quite all right, thank you." As if in contradiction, her stomach gave a gurgling squeal. She tightened her abdominal muscles.

"You've been here all morning. Have you had your lunch?"

"N-no. Not yet. I was just going to sweep the threads up off the floor." Her belly spoke again.

"You need to eat first. Come on."

The thought of food made her mouth water. "I cannot leave the shop unattended. What if a customer came?"

"Have you had any customers?"

"Well, no. Lots of ladies pass by, but..." she became aware of a headache starting at the base of her skull "...none of them come in."

Rydell gazed at the decorated bust form in the window and let out a low whistle. "You make all those?"

"Yes, I did. It took an entire day of sewing and eighteen yards of fabric. I simply must sell some of them, which is the reason I cannot leave the shop."

"Horse feathers! You're hungry. Leave a note on the door."

Jane eyed him with suspicion. "That would suit you just fine, would it not, Mr. Wilder?"

"It might."

"If I absent myself from my post of duty, and thus fail to make any sales, I will 'go broke,' as you say out here in the West."

"You might."

"And then you will reap the benefit by forcing me to accept your proposal when I cannot repay your loan."

"Well, hell, Jane, I don't want you to starve to death before I can marry you!"

"I see. Has it occurred to you that I might prefer the former to the latter?"

To this, he said nothing. He didn't need to. Jane

recalled the terms of his offer with blinding clarity. *"If you fail, you marry me."*

She slid off the nail keg and started toward the broom resting in the corner. "Excuse me, I must sweep out—"

"Oh, no you don't." He stepped in front of her. "The last time you had a broom in your hand I had bruises on both knees. This time it's my turn." He reached behind him, grabbed the broom handle, and made as if to sweep at her shoes.

"Out, Jane." He snatched her hat off the peg on the wall and held it out to her. "Now lock this door. We're going to the hotel dining room."

"Oh, I couldn't do that! It's a public place."

"So is this. If you've got the sand to go into business, you've got the sand to be seen in public. That's where your customers expect to see you, not holed up in your fancy parlor at home."

Jane frowned. He was right, blast his hide.

A light-headed sensation washed over her. Maybe she was hungrier than she'd thought. Or maybe the prospect of sitting across from this tall man who smelled of pipe tobacco and pine soap was what gave her a sudden attack of the vapors.

"Actually," he said as he cupped his hand under her elbow, "there's something I need to talk to you about."

Oh, horrors! And in the Excelsior dining room? Where everyone could see them? Mama would switch her good if she heard tell of it.

Her heart squeezed at the thought. No, she wouldn't switch her. Even if Mama did hear about her eating lunch with Mr. Wilder, she would not recall it later. Odd, how their roles were reversed. Now it was Mama who needed to be looked after and Jane who was in charge. Even Odelia, who had raised her from birth, looked to Jane for directions.

Her shoulders sagged as if a fifty-pound bag of flour had been laid across them. Mr. Tennyson was right—the old order was changing. *She* was changing.

She wasn't at all sure she liked it, but she did have to put something of sustenance in her stomach, or else she could not carry on. Very well, lunch it would be.

She pinned on her hat and arranged the veil.

In public.

With a man.

Forgive me, Papa, but it's a matter of survival.

"Ready?" Rydell offered his arm.

"Wait! I forgot something." She was still a lady, and ladies, whatever befell them, conducted themselves with decorum. She ducked back into the shop and rummaged in the jumble on the cutting board.

"A woman never appears in public without her gloves."

Every step she took across the street and down the board sidewalk to the Excelsior dining room brought Jane closer to despair. She was hungry, sure enough, but the flutters in her midsection had nothing whatever to do with the prospect of the juicy steak sandwich and tall, cool glass of lemonade she envisioned. How, she wondered, when young women were being courted, did they manage to concentrate on anything beyond their own physical beings? With Rydell Wilder's long, warm fingers cupping her elbow, her brain could barely form one coherent thought! No wonder girls made such ninnies of themselves at coming-out parties. The first touch of a man's hand would send them into paroxysms of delight.

Well! she huffed to herself. That's as may be for a mere girl, but she, at twenty-six, was steady as a flagpole and sensible to boot. Far past the ninny stage and not the least inclined to giggles and fluttered eyelashes.

In fact, were it not for an annoying shortness of breath and the strangest tingly feeling where his hand pressed the inside of her elbow, she would pronounce the presence of Mr. Wilder at her side of no consequence whatever. She simply refused to think about it.

At the top of the hotel steps, Rydell lifted his hand from her arm to swing open the glass-fronted dining room door, and sanity returned. Her heart stopped. What if someone saw her entering the hotel with Rydell Wilder? She would be ruined!

The waitress looked up from the pile of blue checked napkins she was folding and her lined face lit up. "Rydell Wilder! Well, it's a good afternoon after all."

"Afternoon, Maggie."

"You're kinda late for lunch and too early for dinner."

Jane's stomach tightened. No lunch? And compromised in the bargain? With an inward groan she turned to leave.

"Wait," Rydell commanded. "Maggie'll fix it up, won't you, Maggie?"

The plump woman goggled at Rydell. "Why sure, Dell. You know I'd do anything for you."

Rydell touched Jane's arm once more, and the fight went out of her. "Over here, by the window," he said in a low voice. "You can keep an eye on your shop while you eat."

Mercifully, the dining room was deserted. No one would ever know she had dined in public. With a man. Besides, she was so hungry she didn't think she could last another minute without food. Even a crust of bread would suffice.

"Could you rustle up a sandwich for the lady?"

Maggie nodded. "Anything for you?"

"Coffee." He pulled out the chair for her and as she seated herself his hand brushed her shoulder. A shimmery current ran across the nape of her neck and down her backbone. Hunger was giving her hallucinations.

"Miss Davis," he began when he had settled himself facing her. She lifted her eyes to his and caught her breath. He was looking at her so oddly, his steady gray eyes so intent she felt a giddy urge to laugh.

"Jane," he amended. Her heart skipped.

A cup of coffee slid in front of him, and a tall glass of something appeared at her elbow. Lemonade! She peered at the waitress. Had she spoken out loud of her thirst? Or was Maggie a conjure-lady, the kind Odelia had told her about, who could read minds?

The woman gazed back at her, a hint of amusement in her soft brown eyes. "All the ladies drink cold tea in the summer, but somehow you just looked like a lemonade. I'll be gettin' your sandwich, now.''

Jane stared after her. She had barely given the woman a glance, but Maggie had observed a good deal about *her*. Was there was something significant in the exchange between them? Something she should notice?

At the sight of her lunch plate, the thought vanished. God be praised, a steak sandwich! She drew off her gloves and laid them in her lap.

''Jane,'' Rydell began again. ''The July Fourth social is tomorrow.''

''Yes, I know. I have never before been allowed to—that is, I have never attended.'' She cut a dainty bite of her sandwich, speared it with her fork, and gobbled it down.

''Well, that's just it. Around these parts, the Fourth is a big whing-ding, with speeches and games and a big dance. And an outdoor supper.''

Jane nodded and sipped her lemonade.

''You might want to...'' He hesitated, swallowed, then tried again. ''Things can get pretty wild.''

Jane blinked. ''Wild? How do you mean, 'wild'?''

''Rowdy. Just high spirits mostly, but...well, I wouldn't want you to be shocked.''

''So that's why Papa wouldn't let me attend.'' She spoke half to herself, but across the table from her Rydell licked his lips and nodded.

''Why, Mr. Wilder, you are warning me to stay away, are you not?''

''Not exactly.'' The tanned, regular features betrayed nothing, but his fingers drummed the table-cloth.

"Then what, exactly?"

"I, uh, well, I thought you might like to, uh, make an appearance, seein' as you've never joined in on the town doings before."

"Yes, I might." She forked another precise square of her sandwich into her mouth. Why did the man look so uncomfortable all of a sudden? As if his shirt collar was too tight or his trousers pinched?

"I'll have to see to Mama first."

Rydell cleared his throat. "Jane, if you do attend, I'd like to offer my protection."

Her hand stilled. "Thank you kindly, but I will not need 'protecting.' Our maid, Odelia, arrived yesterday evening. Odelia usually accompanies the womenfolk wherever we go."

He rocked his chair back and gave her a long look. The silence pressed on her until the hand holding her lemonade glass began to shake.

"What I mean, Jane, is that I'd like to escort you."

"Why, mercy, whatever for?"

His mouth pressed into a line. "To be with you. After all, if we're to be married, a bit of court—"

"Married!" Her knife clattered onto the thick blue china plate. "Married?" she repeated in a lower tone. "Whatever makes you think...oh, yes. Our bargain." With dainty motions, she patted her lips with the gingham napkin and counted to ten.

"I think—" she enunciated each word slowly and carefully "—that marrying will not be necessary. Or advisable. For one thing, Mr. Wilder, I am going to make a success of my dressmaking shop, and I intend to pay you back every penny I owe you.''

Rydell began to smile.

''And for another, when I marry—*if* I choose to do so—it will be a gentleman of the South, not some upstart Yankee out in the middle of the Oregon wilderness.''

Rydell grinned at her. Her stomach floated up and spiraled over, and he just sat there smiling, his teeth looking so white and clean she wondered if he scrubbed them with sand.

''Just the same, Miss Davis. Should you attend the social tomorrow, it would be my pleasure to pro—er, escort you.''

With a quick movement he caught her hand in his. Her palm felt tickly. Without conscious thought, she squeezed her fingers into a fist, and he encased it entirely within his own.

His eyes shone with lazy warmth. ''I think you have a customer.'' He tipped his head toward the window.

Across the street, a tall figure bent to peer into the dress shop window. Jane snatched her hand away and stood up. ''A customer! I must fly!''

Rydell half rose from his chair, but Jane had already darted out the door, spilling her gloves onto the floor. He scooped them up and stuffed them into his coat pocket just as Maggie reappeared.

''More coffee?'' He nodded.

''That one eats like a bird, don't she?'' She removed the plate with the half-eaten sandwich. ''Looks to me like she needs some settling.''

"Yeah. Some."

"I think you got Queen Jane caught in your craw, Dell. Ain't like you to not know what to do with a woman."

Rydell tipped his head back to look at the waitress. "Maggie, you're a smart lady."

"Well, then?" She marched back to the kitchen with the plate.

He rocked his chair back on two legs and watched Jane cross the street, head held high, skirts lifted just enough to clear the ruts but not show an inch of ankle. Maggie was dead right. It wouldn't work to just wait until Jane's business folded and he claimed her as winnings. Given half a chance and a few dollars, she'd hightail it back home to the South and leave him with an empty house. And an even emptier bed.

He clunked the chair down. Well, that's it, then. He'd have to do some mighty skilled courting to get Jane into the nest. Best thing would be to get started right away.

Tomorrow. Fourth of July.

Chapter Eight

Her heart in her throat, Jane approached the woman inspecting her shop window. Maybe she would be her first customer!

"Perhaps you would care to step inside for a closer look?"

The woman slowly straightened, taking her time in turning away from the display to meet Jane's gaze. She was tall, even taller than Mr. Wilder, with a proud carriage and high, pronounced cheekbones. The gathered yellow calico print skirt touched the tops of soft-looking moccasins, and a wide belt of fringed deer-hide cinched in the blue-striped man's shirt the woman wore with the tails hanging free.

Jane suppressed a gasp. An Indian woman!

Eyes black as currants looked back at her with calm intelligence. "I buy."

Jane jumped at the voice that spoke. It was low, but it rang with authority. "Yes, of course. Which apron would you prefer, Miss...um, Mrs...."

"Name Mary Two Hats. I choose."

Jane ushered the woman inside the tiny shop,

where she scanned the room, nodded, and glided toward the apron display. She unpinned three red ones with double ruffles and two blue ones with lace insets, then held up five fingers. "How much?"

Five? She wanted all five aprons? "That will be two dollars and a half."

The woman rummaged in a deerskin pouch looped onto her belt and came up with two silver dollars and two quarters. She held the money out to Jane. "Pretty," she announced in her low, ringing tone.

"Thank you," she managed. She knew she was staring, which was certainly rude, but she couldn't stop herself. An Indian in her dress shop! Mama would faint dead away.

Mary Two Hats grasped Jane's hand and dumped the coins into her palm. "Make more. Next time yellow." With a solemn nod, the woman gathered up her garments, rolled them into a ball, and stepped out the door on silent feet.

Jane stared at the money in her hand. Her first sale. Two whole dollars and a half! Why, that was enough to purchase a whole bolt of sateen or even embroidered eyelet. She could make a fine morning dress for summer and any number of fancy petticoats and shimmies. What did it matter that her first customer was an Indian woman? She had actually sold something she had created out of her own head and sewed with her own hands. She was so proud she could pop!

Odelia took one look at Jane when she came in the front door at suppertime and propped her hands on her rounded hips. "What you lookin' so shined up about, Miss Jane? You take on a fever?"

Jane emptied the contents of her bulging reticule on the dining table. "Look!"

Odelia's dark eyes narrowed. "Where you get dat money? You rob Mr. Wilder's bank?"

"Don't be silly, Odelia. I sold five of my aprons and— How did you know Mr. Wilder owns the bank?"

The older woman tapped her head with one finger. "Ol' 'Delia know everythin', honey. You know dat. 'Sides it ain't no secret. An' 'sides that…well, just never you mind. I made chicken an' dumplings fo' supper, so you just set yourself down 'fore it gets cold."

"I can't. I owe the blacksmith a dollar for fashioning a cutting table for me, but I was so excited when I left the shop I plumb forgot to pay him. I must do it at once."

Odelia laid a commanding hand on Jane's shoulder. "You eat. You cain't keep runnin' on spunk and a li'l bitty dab of hot mush fo' breakfast. I go find Mr. Blacksmith and pay him his due."

She leaned over and selected a silver dollar from the pile of coins. "Miss Leah lyin' down, honey. You have yo'self a li'l rest an ol' 'Delia be back 'fore you can say 'shoefly and molasses pie.' Now, where I find dis here blacksmith?"

Mose Freeman looked up from his anvil to see a sight he never dreamed he'd see in Dixon Falls. A handsome, erect woman with skin the color of milk-thinned chocolate moved toward him with purposeful steps. The setting sun at her back sent flames across the sky. To Mose it looked as if the woman was walking right out of heaven with a vermilion and purple mantle trailing about her shoulders.

My Lord, what an evening! He was having a vision.

"You the blacksmith here 'bouts?"

And, Lordy, Lordy, just listen to that voice! Soft like a dove's, with the lilt of Home.

"I be the blacksmith. Name is Mose Freeman."

"How come you still hammerin' past suppertime? You free?"

"'Course I'm free. Don't I look free? Workin' late, count of tomorrow's Fourth of July."

"What you look like is tuckered, Mister Freeman." She gave him a slow, deliberate once-over. "Never did see a man so handsome an' so woebegone-lookin'."

Mose grinned at her. "Woebegone, you say? Only woebegone thing 'bout me is that it's Saturday evenin,' an' I achin' for to pick my guitar and dance some."

"Hunhh."

"You don't b'lieve I kin dance?" He laid his hammer on the support block, backed up a few steps, and executed a snappy polka step with a heel-click thrown in.

Odelia's expression did not change. "Mighty fine feet you got there, Mr. Free-man."

Mose bobbed his head at the compliment. Immediately she changed the subject.

"I got somethin' for you, from Miss Jane Davis.

She say you earned it, but I don't see how, with all the dancin' you doin'." She produced a silver dollar and sent him a smile that made his knees feel like warm blackberry jelly.

"You thank Miz Jane for me," Mose said as he accepted the coin.

"Thank her yo'self. You goin' to be at the big July gatherin' tomorrow."

It was not a question. "How in blazes you know that, woman?"

Odelia's fine black eyebrows rose and she shrugged. "Dunno how, jes' do."

"About Miz Jane..." Mose hesitated. "She never been to a Dixon Falls to-do. If she's comin', you'd best keep an eye close on her."

Odelia sniffed. "Don' you worry none. 'Delia look out fo' her care-about folk. 'Delia smart as three whips and strong like an oak tree."

"You need to watch out for yourself, too, Miss 'Delia. Things get mighty rambunctious around here on Fourth of July. Now I knows a handsome, woebegone man might watch over you, if you was to—"

Odelia clucked her tongue. "Sound to me like you goin' have you hands full of guitar and your shoes full of hot sparks."

But her luminous dark eyes looked straight into his, and in that instant Mose knew something was in store for him. Something a handsome, woebegone man needed more than food or drink or cash money for a service.

Oh, yes, Lord. What an evening. A beautiful evenin.' A Glory-to-God evening!

"I be there," he said quietly. He looked at Odelia, picked up his hammer and resumed his work.

The Fourth of July dawned hot and still under a sky so blue it looked like it was painted. Jane dressed with the same feeling of anticipation she remembered from Christmases at Montclair, a dancy sensation, as if a flock of swallows swooped about under her corset stays.

At noon, when her mother finished the lunch set before her and had curled up on the settee for her nap, Odelia pressed a towel-swathed wicker basket into her hands and propelled her out the front door. "Miss Leah sleep fo' two-three hours. *We* is goin' to the picnic!"

The walk down the hill to the log schoolhouse, erected by the townspeople in the meadow at the opposite end of town from the bank, gave Jane time to conquer her nerves. She had never been allowed out and about at a Dixon Falls fête. Mama had disapproved of her being seen in public without a chaperon; Papa had disapproved of the type of young men she was likely to meet. Today she had made her own decision.

She wore a gauzy dress of mint-green flounced dimity and a wide-brimmed straw hat trimmed with dark green ribbons. For some reason she could not name, she felt youthful and pretty, like a young girl at a coming-out party. She'd piled her hair on top of her head, and the occasional breath of warm air made the back of her neck prickle. Something was going to happen today. She could feel it, sure as the sun shone above them.

And had she known then what it was to be, she would have picked up her skirts and headed for home right that minute.

Fourth of July in Dixon Falls was celebrated the same way every year. By ten o'clock in the morning, the arrangement of sawhorses and wide pine planks serving as the supper table was draped with six of the largest tablecloths owned by the women of the Picnic Committee. To Jane, they looked like an arrangement of flags—three spotless white muslin, two gingham checks, and a blue striped seersucker.

As the morning wore on, covered dishes appeared, along with potato salads, apple and cherry pies, three-and four-layer cakes, plates of oatmeal cookies and ginger snaps. Kegs of beer for the men, pitchers of lemonade and cold tea for the ladies. Children snatched cookies and were shooed back to their games of Run Sheep Run and hide-and-seek. Jane skirted two girls turning a jump rope and chanting while a pinafore-clad friend hopped over the rope in rhythm. "When I was a schoolgirl, a schoolgirl, a schoolgirl..."

She stifled a sudden longing to join them. She had never played jump rope. Jump rope took three people—two Turners and one Jumper. In her brief attendance at the Dixon Falls school, Jane had never been invited to join in any of the games.

She quickened her pace toward the plank benches that had been dragged out of the schoolhouse and arranged in front so the townspeople could sit and listen to the patriotic speeches delivered from the schoolhouse steps. Jane settled onto the end of an already crowded bench and Odelia squeezed her ample hips down beside her. She closed her parasol and took out a small folded paper fan.

Farm wives clambered out of wagons, set their offerings of food on the supper table and gathered in knots in the meadow, nodding over needlework or mending while they listened. Jane squinted into the sun to examine their garments. Dark blue or brown skirts in twill or denim and plain, unadorned waists, covered with a serviceable neck-to-hem apron with no flounces. Dull, dull, dull.

The mayor spoke first. Despite the shade cast by the surrounding maple trees, by the portly man's second sentence, ladies' fans began to swish to and fro in the heat. At her side, Odelia flapped one corner of her apron to make a breeze.

Then the sheriff spoke. "Let's all enjoy ourselves, folks, but don't want nobody to get shot or throwed off his horse cuz some damn fool fired off a gun. So I'm asking you to stash your firearms in the schoolhouse, gents, and we'll all be safer."

The younger schoolchildren recited The Declaration of Independence and the schoolmistress led the older ones in "Yankee Doodle" and "Hail Columbia." All at once Jane realized how much she had missed singing in a choir as she had in the Methodist church back home.

She leaned toward Odelia. "I wish they would sing Bonny Blue Flag," she whispered.

Odelia rolled her eyes. "You touched in the head, honey? Ain't no Yankee gonna sing dat!"

Jane sighed an acknowledgment. Mercy, but she was homesick. Not for Montclair exactly, but for some place where she fit in. Where she felt she belonged. She gazed around her at the townspeople spilling off the crude benches onto the grass, ladies in wide-brimmed hats dotting the meadow like brilliantly colored mushrooms.

And she didn't know a one of them. Even the two young women she'd met at the mercantile on Thursday, Miss Letitia Price and Mrs. Evangeline Tanner, were strangers. She guessed the one with the blond corkscrew curls and a yellow striped dress was the unmarried one; the young woman studied every male that passed, then leaned over to whisper to her dark-haired companion.

Jane began to take note of the men herself. A sunburned Lefty Springer stood talking to Mr. Wilder and several other men on the shaded side of the schoolhouse. Rydell Wilder, in his wide-brimmed gray hat, seemed taller than any of them. He leaned casually against the log wall, facing her. At such a distance she could not be sure where his eyes were focused—on the man next to Lefty, the one that looked like Mr. Mercer from the mercantile? Or on her? A little dart of awareness pierced her chest. Except for the blacksmith, Mose Freeman, she did not know any men in town.

A choking sensation stopped her breath. She was a stranger in her own town! She had lived in Dixon Falls for eleven years in almost complete isolation, like a princess in a tower. Well, she wasn't a princess! She was flesh and blood, with hopes and fears just like anybody else.

And, she realized at that moment, she was lonely.

She wanted to belong. She wanted to have her existence make a difference to someone. She reached her hand to Odelia's firm, warm arm and gave it a soft squeeze.

"Ah know, child. Ah know."

Tears burned under her eyelids. She loved Odelia. She loved Mama, too. Surely she made a difference to them? Then why did she feel so empty? So lost?

Across the heads of the seated townspeople she caught Rydell Wilder looking at her, his gray eyes steady, penetrating. Almost hungry looking. He straightened and touched two fingers to his hat brim. Then he looked away.

Heat washed over her body in lazy waves. She unfolded her fan and fluttered it before her face.

"Need sumpin' cool to drink?" Odelia whispered.

Jane nodded. She prayed the speeches would end soon. A pitcher of lemonade sat on the shaded corner of the supper table.

Odelia rose. "Come on, honey. You gonna expire wid all this patriot palaver."

Rydell watched Jane move away from the schoolhouse toward the supper table, her handsome, dark-skinned maid at her side. Her voluminous skirt, of some light, frothy-looking material, belled out as she moved, the ends of the wide green ribbon encircling her waist trailing behind her. She looked cool and deliciously soft. Fragile. She stepped around a group of men starting a game of horseshoes.

"Gal like that in a town like this looks kinda out of place, don't she?" Lefty remarked. "Like a swan in a dirty waterhole."

Rydell didn't answer for a moment, just watched her float across the ground like a gauzy-winged moth, her little black slippers barely skimming the earth. The old, familiar tension built inside him. Suddenly he snatched off his hat, slapped it hard against his thigh.

"Dammit, Lefty, she makes a man ache just looking at her."

"An' you ain't the only one." The older man cut his gaze to the horseshoe players. One man, a man Rydell did not recognize, followed Jane with greedy eyes. He licked his lips, then said something to his companions in a low voice. The men laughed and nodded. Only when a tossed horseshoe landed at his feet did the stranger shift his gaze.

"Who's that dark fellow, Lefty? You ever see him around here before?"

Lefty squinted, pursing his lips with the effort. "Nope. Got expensive boots on. Bet that shirt's linen. Lotsa starch, 'n mighty fancy-lookin' embroidery."

"Forget his shirt. Look at his face. Seem familiar?"

"Nope. You think maybe he's on a Wanted poster somewhere? Dell, I swear, ever since you started drivin' for me, you see outlaws everywhere."

Rydell frowned. "Something about him bothers me."

Lefty spit a stream of tobacco juice into the dirt. "Maybe it's the way he keeps lookin' at Miz Jane. Kinda like a wolf that hasn't eaten fer a week or so."

"Maybe."

"On t'other hand, maybe it's that roan gelding he's got picketed yonder." He cast a surreptitious glance at Rydell. "Mighty fine-lookin' horse."

Rydell remained silent.

"You plannin' to ride today, Dell?"

Rydell studied the roan. "Wasn't planning on it, no. Let somebody else take it this year."

Lefty's rust-colored eyebrows waggled upward. "Don't sound like you, Dell. 'Specially since Miz Jane…"

Rydell pinned his friend with a look. "You know as well as I do that'd scare hell out of her. I'm having enough trouble just talking to her, let alone—"

A horseshoe clanged onto the metal stake, and the men cheered. Lefty coughed to get his attention. "What if somebody else claims her?" Once again he looked pointedly toward the horseshoe pit.

Rydell watched the dark-haired stranger lean down and retrieve the iron with slow, self-assured motions. Light as a breath, a prickle grazed the base of his neck.

"Guess I'll go saddle up Mischief."

Chapter Nine

Lefty grinned at Rydell. "Better hot-foot it," he said. "Them speeches are 'bout over, and they're gonna run the race afore the picnic."

Rydell clapped his friend on the shoulder. "Stay close to Jane." He strode off to the sound of faint applause drifting from the direction of the schoolhouse, peeling off his coat as he went in search of his horse.

"Ladies and gents," a voice boomed over the sound of children's laughter and the ring of horseshoes against the metal post. "We've waited a whole year for this, and now it's time."

People began to gather at the near end of the meadow, pressing close and jockeying for position. An excited hum filled the air.

Rydell quickened his pace.

At the table, Odelia handed Jane a glass of lemonade. "Here, honey. Now, I gotta go check on Miss Leah."

Jane nodded, listening to the mayor's now-hoarse voice bellow instructions. "This year the Annual

Ladies Capture Race offers a prize to the winner of one hundred dollars in gold. Whaddya think of that, folks?''

Beside her, Odelia jerked upright, her black eyes snapping. ''What he say, child? A hun'erd dollars?''

''In gold,'' Jane responded. She watched, fascinated, as the mayor climbed up on a beer keg to continue his address.

''Mmmm, hmm, hmmm,'' Odelia breathed. ''In gold. I check on yo' momma after dis heah race.''

Jane stifled a laugh. Odelia had always loved a game of any kind, especially if there was money involved.

''We gotta git up close, Miss Jane. Don' want to…miss nuthin'.''

Carrying her lemonade in one hand, Jane raised her parasol and let Odelia elbow a space for them both at the front of the crowd.

''Now,'' the mayor shouted, ''the rules are the same. No shooting. No whippin' another man's mount or stealing his woman. Ever'thing else is allowed.''

Jane cocked her head. *Stealing his woman?* Surely she must have misheard the man. She stared at the mayor, his pear-shaped body teetering on top of the beer keg.

''Remember, it's once around that big cypress at t'other end of the meadow, then grab your sweetheart for the final leg. Don't hurt her none, though, or she won't give you a kiss at the end!''

A kiss! The man was babbling. Surely no man would…

A horrifying thought exploded in her mind. Out here in the uncivilized West, *anything* could happen. An uneasy feeling crawled up her spine, as if a cold finger pressed on each and every one of her vertebrae. She couldn't get the word "capture" out of her head. Just what—or who—was to be captured?

Five horsemen lined up at the starting line, a lanky schoolboy on his father's strawberry roan; Mose Freeman on a skittish white mare with a black slash across her face; Rafe Mercer on an overfed-looking bay. The fourth rider was a dark-haired man on a sleek, prancing roan gelding, and then Rydell Wilder trotted up on a beautiful black mare. He was coatless, his shirt unbuttoned at the neck, the sleeves rolled up to his elbows.

She heard Odelia's breath hitch. "My, my, ain't them jus' beautiful."

"Odelia," Jane murmured. "You are a caution."

The dark face lit up as if an oil lamp had been kindled within her. "Das' right, honey. Ah got a right keen eye! Jes' look," she breathed, her gaze riveted on the riders. "Dat man an' dat horse look like they glued together."

Jane nodded, suddenly unable to speak. The sight of Rydell's hands on the reins, the play of muscle in his forearms, made her mouth go dry. She averted her eyes and gulped a mouthful of lemonade. Yes, glued together. Rydell moved with his dark horse like he walked, with a lazy, long-legged grace. He looked strong and capable and...

Jane swallowed. Somehow vulnerable. Looking at

the V of bare skin at the base of his neck seemed an almost intimate act.

Jane Charlotte Davis, whatever is the matter with you? You have no cause to gawk at this man. At any man! It is most improper and…and…well, it's just not done.

Besides, he's a Yankee. She downed another gulp of lemonade. *No Yankee has a right to make me feel this way.*

The starting gun popped, and they were off, five clouds of dust heading for the far end of the meadow. When the air cleared, Rydell and the dark-haired stranger were neck and neck, but in the lead was Mose Freeman on the white mare.

Around the cypress tree and back toward the crowd they thundered. As the horses approached, Odelia stepped forward and raised one arm. The white mare slowed, and the crowd scattered. Odelia reached toward Mose, and he leaned down, grasped her elbow, and hauled her up behind him.

What on earth…? Had the woman gone crazy? Thunderstruck, Jane watched her old mammy grab the blacksmith around the waist.

"Git up there, Beauty!" He spurred the horse forward.

The move was so unexpected, yet so well coordinated and without a single word exchanged, Jane's eyes filled with tears. Such unspoken understanding was beautiful to see.

Then someone screamed, and she looked up to see the stranger and Rydell heading straight toward her. The next thing she knew, a long, hard arm went around her waist and her lemonade glass flew out of her hand. She felt herself being lifted off the ground and plopped down onto a horse. Or rather on someone's lap on a horse.

Her hat tumbled off and rolled off the horse's rump as an arm of steel closed around her waist. Out of the corner of her eye, she saw Rydell's black mare dance sideways. It was the other man, the sharp-faced one with straggly ear-length hair, who had her.

"Jane," Rydell yelled. "Hold on tight!"

Another voice rumbled in her ear. "Don't fight it, sweetheart. Just relax and enjoy it."

All at once she understood. The second lap of this uncivilized horse race involved kidnapping a woman and keeping her captive until her abductor crossed the finish line.

The rider spurred his mount, and Jane's head snapped back. Dust blinded her, clogged her throat. Another horse pounded behind them, and then Rydell appeared on her left. He was alone in the saddle.

"Jane, don't fall off. Don't fall!"

Terrified, she grabbed the pommel with her right hand and held on so tight her fingers ached. She wanted to scream, to jab her elbow into the man's ribs. Instead, she concentrated on staying seated as the gelding thundered toward the cypress tree marker. Her free hand grasped for something to hold on to. Sitting across the man's lap as she was, the only thing she found was his forearm, the one gripping the reins. His right arm clamped even tighter about her waist.

He smelled of sweat and something sickly sweet, and his hot breath rasped in and out past her ear.

"Wilder! Get outta the way!"

Rydell swerved his mount out of the stranger's path, but kept pace, riding parallel to the roan until both horses closed on Mose Freeman on his white mare. Odelia clung to the dark man's broad back, her cheek pressed against his plaid shirt.

Mose gave a quick look behind him, said something to Odelia, and slackened his reins. The other two horses split, galloped around the dark couple, and rounded the tree going in opposite directions.

As their paths crossed, Jane caught a glimpse of Rydell's face. Unsmiling, his jaw set, he sent her a look that stopped her breath. "Trust me," his eyes said. "You can do this."

But she didn't know whether she could! Her head pounded. The wind scoured her face. Her teeth rattled whenever she opened her mouth, so she kept her jaw clenched. Far down the field she could see the mayor atop the beer keg, and a clot of people cheering and waving hats and fans.

Halfway to the finish line, she felt the horse ease up, then veer toward the schoolhouse. Rydell followed them, and Mose and Odelia flashed past heading for the finish.

The rider slowed the roan to a walk and nuzzled Jane's neck with a bristly chin. Jane jerked upright.

And then the horse stopped. A rough hand crawled over her breast and forced her chin up. "Don't care about the money," he muttered. "Just wanna kiss this pretty lady."

Jane released her hold on the pommel and with

every ounce of strength she possessed, drove her elbow into the man's midriff.

"Now wait a minute," he began. "You gonna behave or do I have to—"

"Let her go," Rydell's voice ordered.

"Why should I?"

Without answering, Rydell dismounted, advanced toward the roan and grabbed the bridle. "Are you all right, Jane?"

She found she could not speak.

At that moment, Odelia appeared, brandishing the black parasol. "You let mah baby alone! What you think you doin', grabbin' at her like that?" She flailed away at the man's denim-clad legs with the umbrella. He made a grab for the weapon, and Rydell closed his hands around her waist and lifted her out of the man's grasp. She had never been so glad to see anyone in her life.

"Jane, are you all right?"

Dazed, choking back tears of frustration and anger, all Jane could do was nod her head.

"No, mah baby ain't all right! Jes' look at her, tremblin' all over like a pore li'l leaf." Odelia whacked the man's thigh again with the parasol.

Rydell set her on her feet. "Are you all right?" he repeated.

"I am p-perfectly all right, just m-mad as a wet hen!" Her legs buckled as if her bones had turned to applesauce

Rydell gathered her up into his arms, and she turned her face into his chest to shut the tall, unkempt man on the roan out of her vision. As long as she lived, she would never forget the look in his eyes, the reek of his breath.

Rydell spoke over her head. "You ever lay a hand on her again, I'll kill you."

"Sure ya will, you son of a—"

Odelia walloped him again. "You even look at her, Ah wring yo' neck jes' like a Christmas goose! Now, git."

The stranger stepped his horse sideways. "Town's not too friendly, is it?" he said to no one in particular.

Rydell started for the schoolhouse steps, but Odelia stopped him. "Ah go check on your momma now, honey. Best you let Mistah Rydell look after you fo' a li'l bit. Miss Leah not gonna like seein' you all shook up."

Jane kept her eyes shut tight until she felt the enveloping chalk-dust-scented coolness of the school-house interior. "Is—is he gone?"

Rydell glanced out the open window. "He's gone."

The surge of relief made her insides flip-flop. All at once she felt light-headed.

"Did he...?"

"I wouldn't let him k-kiss me. But he touched me most shamefully." She bit her lower lip to keep from weeping. "You may put me down now, Mr. Wilder."

"With all the benches moved outside, there's nothing to sit on. Can you stand?"

She longed to stay right where she was, safe, with his strong arms around her. But mercy me, she couldn't spend the afternoon with her arms about his neck, clinging to him like a frightened kitten. "I can try."

Rydell lowered her feet to the floor, and she stood, swaying, then took a shaky step. He kept his hand at her waist.

"I do not need further support, thank you."

Oh, but she did. She wanted his steadying arm and his low, quiet voice in her ear. She wanted to lean into his strength. Truth to tell, her senses were full of him. The stronger her limbs felt, the more she wanted to touch the exposed area of his throat where the open shirt collar gaped, draw in the clean piney scent of his skin.

Good Lord almighty! That mad horseback ride had knocked all the sense out of her. She felt all upside down and inside out.

Rydell stood just a step away from her, hands on his hips, watching her with a curious half smile playing about his mouth. Without conscious thought, she took a step forward.

Holding her gaze with his, he removed his hat and dropped it on the plank floor. His hands came up to cup both her elbows. His touch sent a tremor through her. His fingers were warm and steady; the inside of her wrists tingled.

"Jane." His breath was sweet with mint and warm, so warm. "Jane, kiss me."

She raised her face and his arms went around her. His lips found hers, his mouth fine and strong on hers, the sensation so exquisite it hurt. For the second time in her life she felt her soul rise from somewhere deep inside her and call out. *Love me. Take me.*

She was mad! Wanton. If she were at home in Montclair she would be ostracized from polite society for the rest of her life.

But you are not home in Montclair. You are here in Oregon, and a man is kissing you, slow and sweet and deliberate, and you want it to go on and on. You want more of it. More of him.

Her heart pumped hard against her rib cage. Her breasts seemed to swell, and a delicious drowsy heat washed over her.

Rydell lifted his mouth a fraction of an inch from hers. "Tell me to stop," he whispered. "Now, before I— Oh, God, Jane. You are so…much."

He kissed her again, then purposefully set her apart from him. She noticed that his hands shook.

"Are you hungry?" he asked, his voice rough.

"No," she breathed. "I mean yes."

He chuckled. "I mean for the picnic. Should be starting about now, and I thought we should…"

"Oh, yes, we most certainly should. However, I must look in on Mama, and—"

Rydell smoothed down his dark hair and replaced his gray hat. "Odelia and Mose Freeman went to check on her."

"Mose? Why, whatever makes you think that?"

Rydell laughed outright. "Instinct, I guess." He took her arm. "Just thinking about that hundred-dollar prize Mose won in the race today. Sometimes a hundred dollars is enough to give a man ideas."

And when it came to ideas, Rydell admitted, he had a couple of his own that would fry the bloomers off a proper, overprotected female like Miss Jane Davis.

Chapter Ten

Lefty Springer bowed stiffly and with a flourish handed Jane the beribboned straw hat she had lost at the start of the race. She squeezed his hand and gave him a shaky smile. He blushed to the roots of his hair.

She waited until her breathing returned to normal before she approached the cloth-draped table, took the plate a kind-faced older woman handed her, and put a dab of potato salad and a very small morsel of barbecued ham on it. Rydell had disappeared, but Lefty hovered at her elbow.

"I'll spread out my jacket fer you to sit on, Miz Jane. Grass stains ain't gonna do that pretty green dress no good."

"Where is—"

"Dell, he's checkin' whether that uncivilized varmint's still hangin' around. An' I spy Odelia just now comin' down the hill."

She followed Lefty to a flat grassy area and settled herself on his gallantly offered jacket. Only when a sudden silence descended on the other picnickers did she inspect her surroundings more closely. Evangeline Tanner and Letitia Price sat just a few yards away, a number of other young ladies surrounding them. Jane gave them the best smile she could summon, and the two women pointedly looked away.

Her cheeks heated. What were they thinking? That she should have screamed for rescue when that dark man had grabbed her? That she had spent a scandalous long time alone in the schoolhouse with Rydell Wilder?

She studied her plate of food, her neck burning from the imagined stares of the women behind her. Deliberately she forced her hand to pick up the fork. The potato salad tasted like a lump of cotton inside her mouth. She swallowed it down with effort and laid her fork aside just as Odelia huffed her way to her side.

"Miss Leah's readin' that Mistah Tennyson, happy as a cat lappin' up cream. Won't need tendin' till dark." She inspected Jane with a practiced eye. "You be all right here with Mr. Springer, lamb?"

"Yes, Odelia. Of course." After her earlier adventures, eating barbecue with a sweet old one-armed man wasn't likely to raise any eyebrows. All she really wanted to do was sit quietly until the dark swallowed her up and made her invisible.

"I will be quite all right, Odelia. You go on and enjoy yourself."

"I's spect I will, honey. Ol' 'Delia know a good thing when she see it."

Jane watched the dark woman load up two plates of food, top them both with a slab of chocolate layer cake, and stride off in the direction of the big gray-green cypress tree at the far end of the meadow.

A man stepped forward to meet her. A well-built black man wearing a red plaid shirt.

Jane closed her eyes. A feeling of emptiness swept over her, choking her breath into a sob. She felt as if she were floating outside herself, looking down on the people eating their picnic suppers in small groups scattered about the meadow. A tiny pain bit into her chest.

At her side, Lefty coughed politely. "Anythin' wrong, Miz Jane?"

A full minute passed. "Miz Jane?"

"Mr. Springer, it would be an untruth if I said no. I feel I am not part of things here. The townspeople are polite, but...well..." She swallowed over the ache in her throat. "I have not one friend here in Dixon Falls except for you."

"Well, ma'am, as I see it, folks 'round here don't know 'xactly what to make of you."

Jane lifted her head. "Whatever do you mean?"

"Well, jes' look at it. Yer momma disapproved of common folk like us."

"Mama was a Beaudry, from Charleston. It was hard for her to adjust to life out here in the West."

Lefty's eyebrows drew together. "And yer daddy, he kept you home while ever'body else was goin' on hay rides and hellin' around at the socials."

"Yes, he did." Once she had spied a wagonload of chattering young people about her age headed for the river to swim and have a picnic lunch. She'd begged her father to let her join them. Instead, Papa made her practice an extra hour on the piano for even asking.

"The way I see it, your folks kept you to their-selves. And now yore an orphan, kinda like."

"Yes," she said softly. "Yes, you're right. I know hardly a soul outside that picket fence Papa built around our house." She drew in a deep breath. "I feel like an onion in a petunia patch."

She lowered her forehead to rest on her drawn-up knees. Tears burned beneath her closed eyelids. Keeping her head down, she let them spill over.

"You ain't no onion, Miss Jane."

She hadn't the strength to reply. She would rest here, hide her weak-kneed weeping in the folds of her skirt until she could speak.

The quiet soothed her. Voices seemed far, far away. She became aware of crickets chirping, a baby crying. And then she heard a stifled laugh. A woman giggled and someone hushed her.

The noise grew into ripples of laughter and finally a raucous shout. "Where'd ya get them duds, Mary?"

Lefty laid his hand on her arm. "Miz Jane? You might want to see this."

Jane looked up. "Oh dear Lord and little feathers," she murmured.

The Indian woman, Mary Two Hats, circled the supper table, her head high, her back straight. Tied around her chin, bonnet fashion, was the ruffled red muslin apron Jane had sold her. Another apron, a blue one, spanned her waist, and secured from each shoulder was one of Jane's flounced creations, tied on like epaulets. The garments fluttered about her upper arms like gaily colored wings.

"How come Modoc Mary's wearing your aprons?" Lefty whispered.

"She bought them. Five of them."

"Mary's the best midwife in the territory," Lefty intoned. "Lives out of town a ways and supports herself and her daughter tendin' women in their time of trial. By golly, is she ever a sight!"

The laughter bloomed into guffaws as the woman paraded back and forth to shouts of amusement. When she turned her back to load up a plate at the supper table, Jane saw the last of her creations, blue with two red pockets, tied like a breech cloth around Mary Two Hats' hips. The ruffles bounced at her every step.

Jane's face burned. Everyone was laughing at the Indian woman, laughing at Jane's beautiful aprons! They did look funny worn as the woman had arranged them, but they were still perfectly good aprons, well designed and finely stitched!

Behind her a woman sniffed in disapproval. A low comment drew a waterfall of girlish giggles, followed by loud whispering. Then she heard the words "Queen Jane."

That did it. Queen Jane, was it? After eleven years they still called her that cruel nickname? She clenched and unclenched her fingers, slowly rose to her feet and turned to face the women. She knew exactly what she had to do.

She took three purposeful steps toward the golden-haired young woman and her dark-haired companion.

"I beg your pardon, ladies. I should like to make your acquaintance." Her voice trembled. She straightened her spine and gathered up her courage.

"I am *Miss* Jane." She put the slightest emphasis on the Miss. "Jane Charlotte Davis. I believe you are Miss Price?"

She extended her hand to the younger woman, then turned to her companion. "And you must be Mrs. Tanner. It is a pleasure to meet you both."

The two women turned red as radishes. Evangeline Tanner opened her mouth, but closed it when nothing came out.

"I do not mean to be rude," Jane continued. "But why do you laugh at a woman simply because she wears a garment in an unusual way? Just imagine, if we females never experimented with a shawl or a hat, we would still be wearing fig leaves, would we not?"

The two women looked at each other.

Jane drew in a long, calming breath. "I do admire your gown, Miss Price. It is stylish and suits your coloring very well. But surely you have another, or perhaps two or three, and all of them are worn differently, are they not?"

She did not pause for an answer but plunged on, hiding her shaking hands in the folds of her skirt. "It is my calling in life to be a dressmaker. The garments Mary Two Hats is wearing are my own designs, sewn by my own hand. You will not find others like them anywhere."

She smiled as best she could and turned to go.

"Don't want no fancy ruffles," a voice sang out. "We're farm wives," another called. "We scrub overalls and milk cows. We need plain clothes that wear good and don't fade.''

''I like them aprons!'' A man's voice. ''Reminds me of the calico girls down in—''

''Josh, you shut yer trap! This here's polite company.''

Jane cringed. Of course, a farmer's wife wouldn't need a fancy apron. Why hadn't she thought of that? The fanciest thing a farmer's wife did in her whole life was get married.

She gazed around at the groups of picnickers. Ranchers, farmers, lumbermen from the mill, townspeople. Only the town women wore anything fussier than a plain cotton work dress and an all-over gingham apron. The town women, judging by Letitia Price and Evangeline Tanner, didn't wear aprons at all, at least not in public.

That was it! The notion exploded in her brain. This wasn't Montclair, where women served tea and entertained at supper parties. This was the middle of Oregon. Oregon women did not read *Godey's Ladies' Book* or have a trunk full of outdated gowns to refurbish.

Right then and there Jane knew what she must do. She had to study her potential clientele.

And, she acknowledged, she would have to learn how to fit in. Women, whether country or town folk, would never patronize a dressmaker who wasn't one of them.

Lefty was waiting for her when she returned. ''Whew.'' He gave a low whistle. ''You look mighty soft, Miz Jane, but you got a tongue that could cut steel.''

Jane's spirits soared as she took his proffered arm. "Lefty, it is truly amazing what a little conniption fit does to my appetite. I am simply starving. I think I will have some more potato salad and some pie.''

Her entire body felt lighter than air, as if she would float away over the treetops if she weren't holding on to Lefty's arm.

"In fact,'' she announced. "I feel so much better I am going to have two kinds of pie!''

Chapter Eleven

Rydell blocked the schoolhouse door, watching the man retrieve his holstered revolver from the collection the sheriff had piled in one corner. The stranger buckled the leather belt low on his hip and started to shove a cartridge into the chamber.

"I wouldn't do that, if I were you."

"You gonna stop me?" the man growled. "You took the girl before I could get what I aimed for, what more d'ya want?"

Rydell spoke in a low voice. "I want you to ride out. You can take the gun, since it belongs to you, but spill that shell out on the floor. Nobody'll know the difference except you and me."

The man's sun-leathered face darkened into a scowl. "Why should I?"

Rydell stepped into the schoolroom. "Got an old Indian saying in these parts, mister. If you can't swim the river, you got two choices—bluff it and drown or ride your horse across. One way a man ends up dead; the other way he saves face. The live Indian saves face."

"Yeah? Just how do you know so much?" His gaze shifted from his Colt to Rydell's empty holster.

"I figure I'm part Indian." He picked his own revolver from the pile and held it loosely in his hand. "And I figure you want to save your skin." His eyes locked with the stranger's. "If I were you, I'd empty that cartridge on the floor, like I said."

"You gonna shoot me if I don't? How do I know whether your gun is empty or loaded?"

"You don't." A long moment passed in which the man's narrowed eyes moved from the revolver Rydell held in his hand to the open doorway behind him.

"You won't make it," Rydell said quietly.

Suddenly the man's lips pulled back in a grin that did not reach his eyes. "You're right this time." He shook the shell out into his palm and lifted his hand away from the gun. "Might not be next time."

Rydell holstered his sidearm but let his palm rest on the butt. "You watch yourself, won't be a 'next time.' It's up to you." He tipped his head in the direction of the door.

"There'll be a next time, all right. Found me a pretty woman today. Might want to see her again."

Rydell closed his fingers around his revolver handle. "Don't even think about it, mister. Now get going."

The man ambled through the doorway in an exaggerated show of defiance. Rydell watched until the roan gelding disappeared at the bend in the road. Then, with his jaw still set and blood thrumming in his ears, he went to find Jane.

* * *

Lefty drew Jane to a standstill as Rydell loomed out of the dusky shadows. "You get him to go peaceable, Dell?"

"Yeah." He shot a glance at Jane. Her eyes looked red and swollen, and after she caught his gaze, she studied her shoes.

Damn. She would remember only the terror of being hauled onto a horse and manhandled by a stranger, not the part that had mattered, the few precious minutes he'd spent with her in the privacy of the schoolhouse.

He turned his attention back to Lefty. "He didn't much like it, but he rode out."

"Who is he, anyway? I seen him once or twice. Drifts into town every few months, plays a bit of faro. Seems edgy, like he was on the run."

"Maybe. You see that basket of peach tarts on the supper table, Lefty? 'Bout empty, so if you want some, I'll see Miss Jane safely home."

Lefty eyed him with a knowing grin. "Sure thing, Dell. Always been a sucker for peach tarts. Thanks fer remindin' me."

With a chuckle he raised his left forearm and looked at the small white hand resting there. "I gotta step aside, Miz Jane, but you'll be safe with Dell."

She lifted her fingers off the flannel sleeve. Rydell stepped into Lefty's place, but Jane ignored his offered arm. She moved on up the hill toward her home.

"Jane."

She kept walking, her pace deliberate, touching the

tip of the folded black parasol to the ground at every other step.

"Jane, wait." He caught up, stepped by her side for a dozen yards in silence. "You're upset," he said at last.

"What makes you think that, Mr. Wilder?" Her voice sounded odd.

"Your eyes. You've been crying."

"Only a little. It's just that…a great deal has occurred today."

"Jane, I'm sorry. I didn't want it to be like this for you."

She came to a full stop. "Didn't want it? You mean you didn't *want* to kiss me?"

"Kiss you! Hell yes, I wanted— What are you talking about?"

"You did kiss me, whether you planned to or not. It made me quite…unsettled."

Rydell felt the top of his head might blow off. She was talking about what happened in the schoolhouse, when he'd put his arms around her and held her. *Not* about being kidnapped, jounced up and down, and touched by the stranger.

A warm fist unfolded inside his rib cage, squeezing his heart until it skipped beats. She remembered his kiss, not the forced horseback ride! Not the dark man on the roan gelding.

She remembered *him*. Rydell Wilder.

Speechless, he looked up at the dark blue canopy of sky above them, at the silvery stars winking into view. It was going to come true. He'd waited for years, a lifetime of laboring from dawn until dark, hoarding his savings. Dreaming.

At last Jane was going to be his.

He didn't touch her. Did not speak until they reached the prim picket fence in front of her house. She unlatched the gate and stepped through.

"Jane." His throat was so choked he barely got the word out.

"Good night, Mr. Wilder." Her voice floated to him from the front porch, and he heard the *scrick* of the screen door opening, then shutting with a soft whap.

He stood in the dark, staring at the lighted windows, the shadows moving behind the lace curtains. And then he heard the piano, a simple melody, a slow, rippling underpinning of chords. His chest tightened.

He had stood outside her house a hundred, maybe two hundred, times in the past ten years. Her music had never sounded so beautiful.

Soon, Jane. I swear I'll make it good for you.

Jane closed the lid over the piano keys and let her head droop until her chin brushed the high lace collar of her dress. *Just when I was getting used to yesterday, along comes today!*

What on earth was her life coming to? People had laughed at her beautiful aprons. She had had words with the very women she hoped would be her future customers. And to top it all off, twice in one day a man had touched her! Her senses still spun from being held in Rydell Wilder's arms and kissed until her knees felt like warm jelly.

"Jane Charlotte, are you unwell?" A soft hand touched her shoulder.

"Of course not, Mama. Just tired." She twirled the mahogany piano stool to face her mother. "Have you had your supper?"

"Oh my, yes. And Odelia baked the most delicious peach tarts for dessert. Would you like— Why, Jane, you've been crying!"

Jane blinked away the moisture in her eyes. "No, I— Oh, Mama, my brain feels all scrambled up inside. So much is happening I cannot think straight any longer and I have so many things to sort out, and it's all so new and...and frightening."

Her mother smoothed her hand over Jane's hair. "There is no cause to be frightened. You will find your way, I am certain sure. I did, and I was even younger than you are."

"You did? How did you do it?"

"Your father rode up on a fine black mare and snatched my heart before I could draw a single breath. After that, things just fell into place. Then you were born, and I have rejoiced in my good fortune ever since."

"Good fortune, hunnh!" Odelia's low voice held a hint of amusement. "Yo' good fortune was 'ol 'Delia comin' to care for' dat baby!" She turned her soft, dark eyes on Jane. "When you jus' a li'l bitty thing, you grabbed onto mah finger, and dat was it for 'ol 'Delia. I'se trapped right then an' there."

"Yes," her mother replied with a soft laugh. "We were both lucky."

Odelia nodded her head. "Otherwise, woulda

growed up spoiled an' helpless. Now, what all dis talk 'bout bein' scared?"

Jane took her mother's delicate hand in her own. "I do not belong here. I am attempting to sew for women I know nothing about."

"But Jane, you sew beautifully. Your father always says so."

She flinched at the mention of her father. Mama talked about him as if he were still alive, just out in the orchard somewhere, waiting to be called in for supper. Mama simply did not remember.

"I know how to cut on the bias and inset lace and do fancy hand stitching, but I don't know what garments to make. Do women in Dixon Falls wear morning gowns? Or lace pantalettes? What do farm wives wear to bed at night? Do they wear corsets while baking bread and churning butter? There is so much I must find out, I hardly know where to begin!"

Odelia huffed. "De Lord din't do it all in one day, honey. What make you think *you* can?"

"And..." Jane swallowed back the rush of words that threatened to tumble out. Breathing slowly and evenly, she continued. "I have never before received the attentions of a man, and...well, I do not know what to do."

"A man?" Her mother frowned in concern. "Have you been properly introduced? Is he of a good family?"

"Don't need to do nothin', child," Odelia said in a quiet voice. "Jes' wait an' let it come."

"Let what come?" Jane cried. "I don't want anything to come. I want to earn enough money to go back to Montclair. I want to go home!''

Odelia slipped her arm around Jane's shoulders. ''Honey, you is home. Yo' momma here, 'Delia's here. Nuthin' left at Montclair now 'cept a honeysuckle bush that's growed over the roof and a powerful lot of memories.''

''Mama? Don't you want to go home to Marion County?''

Her mother sighed. ''Someday, perhaps. Your father will take us for a visit in the spring. It's so pretty then, with the azaleas in bloom and the slaves singing in the cotton fields.''

A long look passed between Odelia and Jane. With a brief shake of her head, the dark-skinned woman tucked the older woman's arm under her own. ''Dey don' sing no more, Miss Leah. But yo' right, is a mighty purty sight in the spring.''

She led the woman toward the kitchen. ''You 'member dat big persimmon bush by the summer kitchen? Miss Jane, honey, bring yo' momma's woolen shawl. She kinda chilled-like, and I gonna make her some tea. You an' me, we talk later 'bout dis man business.''

The muscles of Jane's stomach began to unclench. She would try to think calmly about her next dressmaking project, make a list of possibilities. And, she decided, she would also make a list of questions about men. One man in particular.

There was no classroom in the world that could equal a quarter of an hour with Odelia.

Chapter Twelve

With renewed determination, Jane unlocked the door to her dress shop and stepped inside. General Lee greeted her with an ecstatic leap into the air and a ride on the flounced hem of her blue percale work skirt. She bunched up the garment and tried to shake off the kitten, but the animal clung, purring, and swung back and forth with claws enmeshed in the fabric.

"Let go, you little ruffian! I have work to do."

The kitten dropped off and scuttled away to her nest in the sewing basket, allowing Jane to withdraw a small sketchbook from her pocket and sharpen a lead pencil with one blade of her cutting shears. "Now," she announced to the furry ball pawing at a round satin pincushion, "I must carry on my investigation."

She marched the few steps down the boardwalk to Mercer's Mercantile and stationed herself just inside the entrance, partially hidden by the candy counter.

"Something I can help you with, Miz Davis?"

Rafe Mercer's skeletal frame skirted the pickle barrel and advanced down the aisle toward her.

"Oh, no. I mean, yes. Some..." her gaze fell on the bulbous glass jars of lemon drops and jelly beans "...horehound drops, I think."

Instantly he reversed direction. "Help yourself. I'm right in the middle of my summer inventory, so if you don't mind I'll keep at it. Just leave the money on the shelf."

Jane plopped her sketchbook on the glass case and popped one flavored drop into her mouth. With her pencil she made a tiny mark on the first sheet of paper. The perfect thing, she thought with a smile of satisfaction. She could linger at her post all morning long, ostensibly sampling Mr. Mercer's candy selection, and no one would be the wiser.

She rolled the horehound lozenge around her mouth and waited.

A man in work-worn overalls bought a pair of denims and two spools of thread. Another man, a lumberman by the look of him, purchased four tins of beans and a quart bottle of whiskey. Jane ate another horehound drop and tallied it on her page.

For the next hour there were no customers at all except for a redheaded boy who plunked down a nickel and pointed to the jelly beans. She shoveled a scoopful into his outstretched hand and watched him dart out the door toward the bank. Another hour crawled by, but not a single female entered the mercantile. Jane dragged an empty fruit crate forward, sat down, and sketched the view out the front window, letting her mind wander as she worked.

Perhaps the women were too busy to patronize the mercantile on a Monday morning? Maybe they were home doing the washing or tending an infant? She stifled a prickle of impatience. If it took all day from now until Friday, she would not give up. She could not afford to fail. She had to know: What were the women *wearing?*

She couldn't just walk up and down the street and stare at them. She would be talked about from now till Christmas! But her cleverly thought-out plan was not working, and Lord knew she couldn't just sit here and munch horehound drops until suppertime!

She had made up her mind last night, after her talk with Odelia.

"About de male of de species," the black woman had begun. "You got to understand him, got to see him clear-eyed like a hawk to know whether he be good or bad. Mos' of them bad, so it pay to look at 'em sharp."

"I don't *want* to look at them," Jane had protested. "Any of them, good or not."

"'Course you do, child. Underneath. You jes' haven't felt the hungries yet."

Jane wrinkled her nose. "The hungries?"

"Oh my, yes. Tha's when yo' insides gets all tumbled-like and yo' heart feel kinda poorly." Her dark eyes rolled. "Come in the night, sometimes. Ache so bad make you almos' crazy."

"But...Odelia, that sounds just awful!"

"Is awful, honey. An' it hurt an' make you cry, but it also make you so happy you think you kin fly right up to heaven."

"Not me." Jane shook her head. "I have had enough hurt since we left Montclair and Papa died to last me a lifetime. I do not want any more."

"Comes a time, though, when you be ready. When you feel dat longing deep inside, and you want to belong to somebody. A *good* somebody. Like two halves of a walnut, cleaved together so they's whole."

"A walnut? Surely you are funning me, Odelia. A *walnut?*"

Odelia had patted her shoulder. "I ain't never lied to you, Miss Jane. Y'all kin laugh if you want, but it's a'comin', sure as baby peas make big peas, and I's gonna enjoy it some when you get bit. Jes' remember what 'ol 'Delia tell you—eyes like a hawk."

Jane told herself Odelia had sipped too much hard cider at the picnic, and had gone to bed to plan what to do next.

Now, behind Mercer's candy counter and twelve horehound drops in debt, she had to admit her plan had failed. She should pay Mr. Mercer and retreat to her store.

At that moment the bell over the door tinkled, and Jane looked up to see two women in hats and gloves. She poised her pencil over the sketch pad.

"...you're just jealous. After all, last year..."

Hurriedly Jane drew the details of the hat, then with quick pencil strokes she sketched the back of the speaker's dress. Three rows of ruffles below the bustle, caught up with a matching bow. The fabric was something filmy—thin muslin, or perhaps lawn—with a tiny flower print.

"...and then he didn't so much as...so I thought..."

Turn around, Jane willed the woman. *Let me see the front.*

"...she just plain stole him...right under my nose, and she..."

"No, she didn't, Letty. She's not that calculating...queen..." The voice dropped to a whisper.

Jane's hand stilled. Merciful heaven, were they talking about *her?* But it made no sense. She had never stolen a thing in her life. She must be mistaken.

The two women debated the purchase of a pair of stockings until Jane thought she would scream. *Turn around. Let me see who you are. What you are wearing.*

And then the figure in the filmy dress turned toward the entrance, and Jane sucked in her breath. Letitia Price. Her fingers gripped the pencil. A tucked bodice, short puffed sleeves with lace ruching. A neckline low enough to be indecent at this hour back in Marion County.

And eyes that looked directly into hers from a face flushed with angry red splotches.

"Why, Jane Davis, I didn't see you hiding there? What on earth are you doing?"

Jane swallowed. "I am not hiding. I am...investigating."

"You mean eavesdropping, don't you?"

"No." She rose and held up her sketchbook. "I was making a drawing of your dress. And yours, too, Mrs. Tanner. I am s-searching for new pattern designs."

Letitia came toward her. "I think not. I think you are spying on—"

"Letty, for heaven's sake, of course Miss Davis isn't spying!"

Jane bit her lip as Evangeline Tanner moved to join Letitia. "No," she managed. *Spying is something Yankees do.* She clamped her jaw tight to keep the words inside.

"No," she repeated after a moment. "I am not spying." She pointed to the sketchbook. "I admired your dress. I wanted to make a drawing of it, so I could devise a pattern."

Evangeline's dark eyebrows went up. "You could do that? Just from a drawing?"

"Y-yes. That is how I make all my patterns, from pictures in a book."

Letitia turned away with a sniff. "Come, Evie. I'm sure I wouldn't want any dress made up just like one I already have."

With a regretful smile at Jane, Evangeline allowed her companion to sweep her past the candy counter and out the door.

"...simply unthinkable...who does she think... Rydell..."

At the mention of Rydell, Jane's head came up. Of course. Letitia and Rydell Wilder. *That* was why the young woman was so angry. She breathed a sigh of relief.

In the next instant she felt something akin to that hurt Odelia had spoken of. *Letitia and Rydell.*

Odelia was right. It did hurt. She could not fathom why it mattered, but it did. And, she acknowledged with a tightening of her lips, it made her good and mad!

She marched toward the door, pivoted and dug five cents out of her pocket for the horehound drops. Then she straightened her hat, yanked on her gloves, and headed down the boardwalk toward the bank.

Rydell crumpled the foolscap sheet into a ball and tossed it into the now-overflowing wastebasket beside his desk. The clock in the bank foyer chimed faintly. Another hour and he'd give it up until evening. He'd racked his brain trying to guess what she would want—a wide front porch or a wraparound veranda? A music salon or a second parlor? How many bedrooms? Upstairs or downstairs?

He smoothed out a fresh sheet and began again.

The door cracked open. "Mr. Wilder, sir?"

"What is it, Josiah?" He kept on working, making sharp, straight lines with the metal ruler, each quarter inch representing a foot.

"There's a man out front, says he wants to see you."

Rydell kept his gaze on the new drawing. "Tell him I'm busy. Whatever it is, you can handle it."

"Yessir. Except he won't deal with me. Says he's got to see you. I'm awful sorry to bother you, Mr. Wilder, but—"

Rydell shoved back his chair and stood up. 'Not your fault, Josiah. Sharpen these pencils for me while I'm gone, would you?"

"Sure, Mr. Wilder. What are you drawing?"

Rydell gave the young man a long look. "I'm trying to put a round-shaped dream in a square-shaped box with four walls and a roof.''

''Oh, I see, sir.''

''You do?'' he said over his shoulder as he strode to the doorway.

The bank clerk gulped so audibly Rydell stopped in his tracks.

''I—I think so, Mr. Wilder.''

''Then you're smarter than I am, Josiah.'' He closed the door on the young man's blank expression and made his way out to the teller's window. On the other side of the iron grill stood the tall stranger from the picnic.

''Your name Wilder?'' the man rasped. ''Rydell Wilder?''

''It is. You wanted to see me, Mr....?''

''Lucas. You own this bank?''

Rydell studied the man. Dark hair to his earlobes, leathery skin. Gray eyes that refused to meet his. He held a slim black leather satchel in one hand but kept the other in his coat pocket.

Yeah, he did look a bit familiar. Maybe Lefty was right, a drifter with a gambling habit. Or an outlaw with a sidearm in his pocket. He was glad he'd told Josiah to wait in his office. A young husband with a wife and a new baby girl ought not to tangle with a bank robber.

He'd seen his share of outlaws when he rode shotgun for Lefty. He'd killed a good number of them, and little by little the word had spread. By the time he took over the freight line, robbers left him alone.

He guessed this one was new to the territory. He'd take it slow and easy.

"Well, Mr. Lucas? What can I do for you?"

"I'm lookin' for a good bank," the man said, his voice gravelly.

"How do you mean 'good'? Chock full of money or easy to rob? This is the only bank in Dixon Falls, so you don't have much choice."

"Neither." The tall man spilled the contents of the satchel onto the oak counter. Five packets of crisp hundred-dollar bills. "I got five thousand dollars here. I want you to keep it safe."

Rydell looked him in the eye. "Not if it's dishonest money. You want to tell me where it came from?"

"Nope."

"In that case, it's no deal. Take your hand out of your pocket, Mr. Lucas, and put these bills back in your bag."

Lucas didn't move a muscle. The clock chimed the half hour, and Rydell waited.

"All right, I'll tell you. It's gaming money. I won it playing faro."

"You're a gambler." It wasn't a question.

The man nodded. "The money's clean. You can trust me on that. Check with the sheriff if you like. I want you to keep it for me. Yours is the only bank within fifty miles, and people speak highly of it."

Rydell just looked at him.

Lucas coughed. "I'd be a dead man in twenty-four hours, carryin' that much cash around."

"I've carried more. What's different about you?"

The man's face tightened into a sun-burnished mask. "I...I got someone trailin' me."

"The law?"

"No, not the law."

"Who, then?"

"Don't know exactly. I ran out on someone once. Figure it might be a Pinkerton man. You gonna take this or not? I ain't got all day."

At that instant the entrance door flew open and a tornado in a blue skirt whirled toward him. Oh God, Jane. Rydell scribbled out a deposit receipt and shoved it across the counter. "Your money's safe, now get out."

The stranger grinned, turned away and tipped his hat as Jane sped forward. She didn't spare him a glance, and he ambled out the door she'd left open. Rydell swept the bills into the cash drawer.

Jane didn't stop at the teller's window, but whooshed through the security gate, her cheeks pink, her blue eyes shooting sparks. She barely avoided colliding with his chest.

"You," she hissed, "are a despicable man!"

Chapter Thirteen

"And what's more," Jane continued, her breath hot and harsh in her throat, "I know all about it, Rydell Wilder, so you can just cease pretending this instant!"

"Know all about what? Jane, what are you talking about?"

"You know very well. No gentleman from Marion County would ever do something so low-down."

"I am not a gentleman. And you know very well I'm not from Marion County."

"Well, wherever you're from, it just isn't done!"

"I was born..." He shut his mouth with a snap. He didn't know where he had been born. All he knew was that he'd been on his own as far back as he could remember. He'd drifted into Dixon Falls when he was just a kid, so he figured he was from somewhere in Oregon. Exactly where had never mattered. He had his mother's photograph and her name, Etta Wilder, and that was all. Until now, that had been enough.

"Jane, come with me." He grasped her elbow and propelled her down the short hallway and into his private office. Josiah gave them a startled look and fled.

"Put the top cash drawer in the vault," Rydell called after him.

He sat her down at the desk and quickly rolled up his drawings. "Now, Jane. Tell me, what is the trouble?"

"You kissed me!" she blurted.

Rydell grinned. "I did. More than once, as I recall. And you kissed me back."

"I did no such thing."

"Is that what all the fuss is about? You weren't mad yesterday, why wait twenty-four hours before deciding you're angry?"

"I am not angry." She said the words very carefully, her chin in the air.

"Or upset?"

"I am not upset."

"Or whatever you are? Seems to me you've got kind of a slow-burning fuse."

He hoped to calm her down, tease the truth out of her. But after a morning of botched house plans and the appearance of that Lucas fellow with a valise full of questionable bills, he was a bit short on understanding. He wanted Jane, and he wanted her now, not six months from now when her dressmaking business went belly-up and the house he'd planned for her was ready. *Now.*

And she was babbling about him kissing her? Hell, yes, he'd kissed her. And it hadn't been nearly enough. His patience was wearing thin.

"Rydell Wilder, you owe me an apology!"

"Like hell I do. You liked it as much as I did. Dammit, Jane, sure I'm sorry if it upset you. It didn't at the time, so now I'm wondering what's come over you?"

"I can sum it up in one simple word," she snapped. "Letitia."

"Letitia? Letitia Price? What's she's got to do with it?"

Jane popped up out of the chair and faced him, a light in her eyes he'd never seen before. "You kissed her, too! Letitia. Last year."

Rydell stared at her. And then he began to smile. His little Southern fireball was jealous. Somehow she must have heard about last year's Fourth of July race, when Letitia Price had offered herself for the horse race, and he had claimed the winner's kiss.

Jane, *his* Jane, the girl he had loved since the first day he laid eyes on her, noticed him on some level she was not even aware of. Otherwise she wouldn't care a dried raisin who he kissed or why.

But she *did* care. She was aware of him the way a woman is aware of a man when she's interested in him, and the knowledge made his head spin.

Made his smile fade.

Made his groin ache.

Oh, God, he wanted her so much he hurt all over.

"Jane, there is nothing between Letitia Price and me. I kissed her once, yes. Maybe twice, I don't remember. But it has nothing to do with you and me."

"I do not believe you." Her voice shook. She looked about her, a dazed expression in her eyes, and uttered in a small voice, "And I do not believe I came here on such an errand. I must have been quite out of my head.''

She raised her chin and straightened her spine. "It means nothing to me whom you kiss."

''I do not believe you,'' Rydell echoed. And then he chuckled and reached for her. Closing his hands about her shoulders, he pulled her close, breathed in the flowery scent of her hair. He wanted to hold her, possess her.

''Get out of here, Jane,'' he breathed. ''If you stay here one more minute, you're going to be compromised.''

The next thing he knew, he was kissing her. He didn't know how it happened, exactly; he'd ordered himself *not* to kiss her. Under the circumstances, alone in his office, it wasn't a smart thing to do.

But what the hell, he was doing it now, he might as well enjoy it. Her mouth was warm and soft, and the arm she lifted to fend him off drifted around his neck. Rydell prolonged the stolen intimacy as long as possible, knowing that the instant he lifted his lips from hers, the explosion would come.

He pressed deeper, torn between wanting to breathe and wanting to possess her. His tongue teased her lower lip, and she made a funny little sound that sent his stomach flip-flopping. No woman he'd ever kissed had made him feel like this, made him forget who and where he was in the glory of what was happening. He felt himself fill with a sweet, hot light that swirled his senses into physical yearning so sharp it hurt.

He had to let her go. Lift his hands away and release her. Otherwise, he would explode.

"Jane," he breathed against her mouth. "I'm sorry. I never meant—"

"Oh, yes you did," she said, her eyes still closed. "Don't lie, Mr. Wilder. You meant every second of it." She tipped her chin up. "Do it again."

"Oh, God, Jane, you can't be serious?"

"No," she said in an unsteady voice. "Of course not. This simply cannot be happening. Any moment I will wake up and find it is just a dream, and then it will be over. So do it now, please."

Rydell shook his head to clear the singing in his brain. This might make some sense if they were both roostered, but he was cold sober on a Monday morning. At least he'd thought he was ten minutes ago.

So what the hell was happening? Jane stood before him, her face lifted, eyes closed, waiting. He'd be a fool not to milk the moment.

A warning bell went off in his head. He'd be an even bigger fool if he did! This wasn't Maggie or Letitia or a dozen women he'd taken to bed over the last nine years trying to forget Jane. This was Jane herself, her skin soft as flower petals, the scent of her body so tantalizing it made his mouth go dry.

He couldn't. He wanted to, but he couldn't.

"Jane, look at me."

She opened her eyes. The hard blue stones that had shot sparks a minute ago had softened into misty azure clouds.

"Yes?" Her voice sounded dreamy and distant, as if she had been a thousand miles away.

His body began to tremble, whether from tension

or desire he couldn't tell. "You are dangerous, do you know that?"

"Yes. Odelia always said so when I was little."

"I mean dangerous in a grown-up way. A danger to...yourself."

"Oh, no. I am exceedingly proper. Mama raised me to be so, and I am."

Rydell stared at the woman he thought he knew. Either she was liquored up and making no sense at all, or she was being perfectly logical and speaking so honestly it scared him.

"A proper young woman," he said in a low, quiet voice, "does not allow men to kiss her in a bank."

"This is not a bank, it's your office. Your *private* office."

"Jane—"

"And you are not 'men.' You are a man, a particular man. I do not object to kissing a particular man. It is educational."

"It is foolhardy."

"I think not," she said with a dreamy smile. "After all, I intend to return to Marion County as soon as my dressmaking establishment brings a suitable profit, and I will want to be ready. I will want to know...things."

Jane drew her hand over General Lee's soft, orange fur and stared absently out the shop window. *I will never get anywhere, much less return to Marion County, unless I sell at least two dozen dresses with hats to match.* But at the moment, she was stuck. Somewhere between a farm wife's loose prairie dress and a town woman's flounces and pleats there must be a garment that would appeal to both. Something practical but pretty. Something that would wear like iron while a woman did up her chores, yet look light and summery in town. Perhaps a skirt that could be adjusted for horseback riding—split down the middle? With buttons, so that…

She lifted the kitten off her lap and reached for her sketchbook. "Like this," she murmured. Her pencil swept back and forth across the page. Yes. And a tight-fitting jacket with a standup collar and mutton sleeves. Western women were adventurous.

She flipped to a clean page. "And this…" She sketched a quick outline. "A trim top, in a nice color, and a sweeping skirt but without a bustle, so it swings free when you walk. Yes!"

In…let me see. Dimity would be too impractical. Seersucker? Or, why not use the blue cambric? She had yards and yards of it left after sewing those aprons. Besides, after she had paid Mose Freeman the dollar she owed him for making her cutting table, and put another dollar into her Travel Fund, she had little left over for new yardgoods. What she did have—a whole fifty cents—she could spend on lace trim.

She moved her pencil with increasing speed. "An inset here and here, and the skirt trimmed with pleats." With deft strokes she filled in details, added buttons and a stylish hat.

Then her hand slowed to a stop. She did want to return to Montclair, did she not? Despite what Odelia said, she could not quite believe the old familiar plantation would not be there waiting for her. The land was still there, wasn't it? Odelia admitted the house was still standing. And Mama would surely be happier back in Marion County.

She forced her thoughts back to the sketchbook. With a seven-gore skirt, lined in the same blue, and red seam stitching to match the cuffs on the jacket... Oh, the outfit would be so stylish, and ever so useful!

And different. She could not wait to see Letitia Price's face when she saw it. She would *have* to have it—the design would be irresistible!

Eventually, she thought with satisfaction, the younger woman would help Jane to pay off her business debt so she could return to Carolina, and Letitia could have Mr. Wilder all to herself.

From somewhere in the back of her mind a small black cloud floated in and settled on her imagined rainbow. *I do hope the gentlemen in Marion County can kiss as nicely as Rydell Wilder.*

She rose abruptly, stepping over the cat snoozing at her feet. "Wake up, General Lee. Rise and shine. There is work to be done!"

Rydell settled his mare into a pace that matched that of his companion. "Lefty, why does a woman—"

"I dunno, Dell. Whatever it is, I dunno. Women is the most confusin' creatures on the face of the earth."

"She's a mystery, all right. One minute she's perfectly rational, and the next thing I know she's all claws and wildcat."

"Whadja do, go an' kiss 'er again?"

Rydell gave the older man a wry grin. "You know I'm not gonna answer that question."

"You tell her 'bout this house yer building?"

"Nope. It's not the right time."

Lefty turned in his saddle and eyed him. "You got Sam Traft and that brother of his workin' from can't-see to can't-see, payin' 'em good wages, too, I hear. 'Fore you get too far into it, you might wanna see if your ideas and Jane's come anywhere near matchin' up. Be a shame to build a mansion if all she wants is a new picket fence for the house she's already got."

"Oh, she wants more than a new fence."

"That right?"

Rydell nodded. "Jane wants a whole new life." *But she wants it 3000 miles away.* "I figure she'll change her mind when her dress shop goes bust. Maybe even before, if I can…" He left the thought unfinished.

The two men rode in silence through a stand of cottonwood trees, then turned onto the rutted wagon road that curved up a gentle hill. At the crest, Rydell pulled up and gazed out over the knee-high rye grass he'd seeded the year before. The late afternoon sunlight turned the seed heads red-gold, and in the breeze, the undulating waves were so beautiful it made his throat hurt.

Lefty drew rein beside him. "Sure has a forty-dollar view of the valley, Dell. Which way you pointin' the house?"

"South. That way the morning sun will hit the kitchen windows and the porch will face the sunset." He watched the two Traft brothers, one tall, one shorter than Lefty, digging trenches for the foundation.

"How many acres you buy, Dell?"

"Two thousand."

Lefty's rust-colored eyebrows shot up. "Don't want any near neighbors, I guess. Or *any* neighbors."

"Nope." He wanted Jane to see the sunlight wash the hills, watch the evening sky turn from vermilion to purple and then to peach with nothing to mar the vista. He wanted to make something beautiful to give her, and this was the best thing he could think of, something that would last all the years of their lives and beyond. Something of himself expressed in beams and windows and roof shingles.

"How you gonna pay fer all this?" Lefty asked.

"Hard work and penny-pinching. Bought the land with my savings—took every last dollar. But the bank's doing well, bringing in a good profit, like I thought it would. I'll be all right as long as people keep buying farms and building barns. As long as the bank's solvent."

"Dell…"

"I know," he said quietly. "I've got to tell her about the house. Trouble is, Lefty, I don't think she's ready to hear it."

The older man snorted. "Trouble is, Dell, if you don't lay yer claim pretty soon, somebody else will. She's climbin' down out of that tower she's been locked up in and sooner than later, people are gonna take notice. While yer waitin' for her to come to you, cuz you wanna be a gentleman and not crowd her none, somebody else might get there ahead of you."

Rydell shook his head. "No, they won't."

"Dell, the whole town's talkin' about her. Half the folks say she's still just as stuck-up as she ever was; t'other half—mostly men—say she's pretty as a peach and ripe fer pluckin'."

"Yeah?"

"Yeah. If I was you, I wouldn't let her outta my sight fer more'n twenty minutes."

"Jane's got some sand, Lefty. And she's no fool, even if she was raised like a hothouse rose. She has to want this as much as I do, otherwise it's no good."

"You're riskin' a lot, Dell."

Rydell grinned at the man who'd been his friend for the last twenty years. "Damn right."

"Too much, mebbe."

"Nope. She'll try her wings, and she'll land in my lap."

Lefty patted his mount's sleek neck. "Women are like horses, Dell. You gotta let 'em smell you all over, get to know you, before you can saddle-break 'em."

Again Rydell just grinned. "You might have a point there, but I don't want Jane 'saddle-broke.' I want her to…want me."

Lefty picked up his reins. "Then you better git busy, son. If you ain't gonna show her the house 'til it's built, an' you ain't declared for her, she ain't catched yet. Me, I'd go strum a guitar under her window."

Rydell chuckled. "Me, I'm going to take her to Olaf Jensen's barn dance Saturday night." Just the thought of holding Jane in his arms, feeling the silky heat of her skin, made his chest tighten. He nosed the black mare toward town and slapped his hat on her rump. ''Come on, you old medicine man, my throat's getting dry.''

Lefty galloped past him on his gray gelding. ''Last one to the Silver Cup buys!''

All the way back to town Rydell wondered whether Lefty was right. What did his friend see that Rydell didn't?

Chapter Fourteen

Jane looked up from the sewing machine when Rydell entered her shop. Despite the skip of her heartbeat at his unexpected appearance, she managed to keep her voice neutral and disinterested. Odelia had advised her to "jes' be honest with the man," but surely that did not mean telling him how flustered she grew in his presence?

"Oh," she said with studied calm. "It's you." She went back to her basting. Perspiration made her hands so slick she could barely hold on to the needle. Mercy, it was scorching hot in here, and she hadn't stopped for lunch or lemonade since breakfast. She felt a bit dizzy.

Rydell scanned the tiny room for something to sit on. "Are you busy?"

"Of course I am busy. There's a big to-do coming up, and I am sewing a party dress just as fast as I can."

"For yourself?"

Jane flashed him a look. "No, not for myself. It's

for a customer. How can I possibly make one penny of profit sewing dresses for myself?''

"Got a buyer?"

She bit her bottom lip. "Not yet, no. But I will have as soon as I finish it and slip it onto my dress form." She waved her hand at the window, where the apron-swathed bust form stood. "As you can see, I am rather occupied, Mr. Wilder. Was there something in particular you wanted?"

"Well, yes." He shifted his weight, leaned his long frame against the wall. "I have a question for you."

She bent her head over the blue cambric skirt pieces in her lap. "I am listening."

"Hot this afternoon, isn't it?"

"Yes."

"You thirsty?" he said without a pause.

"Yes."

"Will you go to Jensen's barn dance with me on Saturday?"

Jane raised her eyes. He had thought to trick her. "No. I have no time for such gatherings, now that I am a businesswoman. I intend to work all day on Saturday, making up another new design."

Rydell again shifted his weight. "The dance is in the evening."

"I will be tired by evening." She continued basting a side seam. "I plan to retire early."

"Olaf Jensen's one fine fiddle player," Rydell offered. "All the folks in the county will turn out for one of his shindigs."

"I am happy to hear that, Mr. Wilder, but I will not be one of them."

"Everybody brings pies and cakes," he went on. "Older kids learn to dance, younger ones bed down in the hayloft."

"Still, I must refuse."

Rydell shot her a glance. "All the ladies wear their prettiest dresses, and—"

"I thank you kindly, but... Dresses?" Jane's darting needle faltered. A whole barn full of ladies in their best outfits? Dresses she could copy? She licked her lips. Ideas she could adapt and embellish.

"Jane? Miss Davis, would you do me the honor of accompanying me?"

She studied the tall man who now eased himself off the wall and came to stand before her. He would surely not mind if she brought her sketchbook, would he?

The blue cambric gown was finished at last. Jane heated the sadiron and pressed the ruffles one last time, then arranged the garment over the dress form. Oh, yes, just lovely! Yards and yards of Valenciennes lace decorated the full skirt and set off the square neckline. The creation looked just like a spot of blue summer sky in the display window.

And just in the nick of time! Here came some of the ladies down the boardwalk. Jane ducked behind the open door to watch.

"Evie, look! Isn't that a handsome gown?"

Some low words Jane could not understand came from the speaker's companion.

Then she heard, "Well, I don't care if it is. A dress

as pretty as that will make me ever so attractive. He will be unable to resist.''

Out of the corner of her eye, Jane spied the Indian woman, Mary Two Hats, start across the street toward her shop, her gaze riveted on the blue cambric dress.

Oh, no. Please don't let her like it. *If she wears it and everyone laughs again, I could not bear it.*

Mary Two Hats pressed her forefinger against the window glass. ''Pretty.''

''I saw it first,'' Letitia Price protested.

The Indian woman ignored her. ''How much?'' she said in a loud voice.

Jane hesitated. ''Four dollars,'' she said at last.

Quick as a cat, Letitia stepped inside, snapped open her reticule, and pressed four greenbacks into Jane's hand. Without a word she indicated she would wait while Jane lifted the garment off the dummy and wrapped it up.

''I,'' Letitia announced to her dark-haired companion, ''intend to be the prettiest girl there.''

''Come now, Letty. Pride goeth before...''

Their words were lost as Letitia grabbed her parcel and the two women continued down the board walkway. Jane sent Mary Two Hats a palms-up gesture of helplessness, and the woman grinned.

''Dress not make woman pretty. Inside make pretty.'' She tapped her chest. ''I pretty inside.''

Jane nodded. How had Odelia put it? *Beauty ain't nuthin' if it only outside-deep.*

She smiled at Mary Two Hats. The Indian woman and Odelia were sisters under the skin.

And then she laughed out loud. All *three* of them,

different as they were on the outside, were sisters under the skin.

The path leading to Olaf Jensen's barn, outlined with colored paper lanterns illuminated by candles secured in wet sand, looked more like the entrance to a castle than a place where farm implements and grain were stored. How beautiful it was. Things were certainly transformed on a soft summer night with the scent of honeysuckle in the air and a canopy of brilliant stars overhead. With a little imagination, this might be the ballroom at Montclair!

Except for the smell of hay, she noted as she stepped through the double-wide doors that stood open. And sweat and...tobacco smoke. Men lined the walls, milled about the long plank table laden with food and a suspicious-looking keg of something at one end. Spirits, no doubt. Nothing genteel like champagne or mint juleps.

Women scurried about, shushing children, greeting friends, laying out pie tins and cake platters, baskets of cookies, trays of fudge and fondant balls. With their full skirts swaying as they moved, they looked like bright-colored butterflies. What did the women drink when *they* were thirsty? She searched in vain for a pitcher of lemonade or cold tea.

At her side, Rydell Wilder touched her elbow. She started, and he chuckled, then said in a low voice, "You're not scared are you, Jane?"

"Certainly not," she said quickly. Clenching her hands together, she moved forward. In her whole life she'd never seen so many people in one place at the same time—not even at the train station in St. Louis. It was overwhelming. Suffocating.

Behind her, Odelia and Mose Freeman murmured together in velvety tones. Jane caught only bits and pieces of their conversation. ''...be all right...Mistah Rydell...'' Odelia and Mose served as her chaperons, she reminded herself. One or the other would keep an eye on her throughout the evening, but she decided she need not tell that to Mr. Wilder.

Yes, she was scared. Her hands felt sticky with perspiration, and her mouth was as dry as a tumbleweed. All these people she didn't know. What would she do if not a one of them spoke to her?

The sound of a fiddle tuning up rose above the din, and couples laughed and shouted as they scrambled to form sets in the center of the plank floor. Why, she'd never seen such behavior at a Marion County dance. Or at a barbecue, or even a horse race! Out here in the West, people were more...direct. There was no gentlemanly decorum, no well-phrased lines of polite small talk or pleasant flattery. It was...she started to say *uncivilized* but changed her mind. Out here people were not versed in poetic niceties; they were straight-to-the-point.

The fiddle launched into a two-step, and a guitar joined in. That must be Olaf Jensen playing the fiddle, his shock of wheat-colored hair bobbing in time to the music. The tune was spirited, full of unexpected figures and embellishments. People began clapping to the beat, and the next thing she knew a barrel-chested man climbed up on a wooden box and began calling out directions to the dancers.

"Swing that pretty gal on your right, then promenade home and step it light…"

Rydell's arm slid around her waist. "Care to
dance?"

Jane watched the couples change partners, form
ladies' circles, break away into twos again—intricate
moves that kept the squares constantly changing patterns. They were the most complicated steps she had
ever seen. In Marion County, a Virginia reel was a
challenge, but even that had a predetermined opening,
a middle, and an end. These sets of whirling men and
women obeyed the whim of the caller with no delay
between his words and their steps. The whole concept
was beyond her comprehension.

"Jane?" Rydell's arm tightened.

"I can't," she whispered. "I've never seen dancing
like this—I don't know how."

"Nobody does, at first. You just grab a partner and
hang on tight."

"Oh, no, I couldn't." Out of the corner of her eye
she saw Odelia and Mose off in one corner, their arms
linked, high-stepping in grand style to the music.
Odelia's gray-collared dress swirled up, revealing the
white petticoat underneath. She smiled at Mose, her
teeth white against her dark skin, and Mose gave her
a look that stopped Jane's breath.

Why, he loves her! Surely a man did not look at a
woman that way unless he… But Odelia had not been
in Dixon Falls more than a week! What on earth could
have happened between the two of them in such a
short time?

Shaken, she looked away. There, in another corner,

an old gray-haired man with work-rounded shoulders waltzed slowly with a plump woman in a pink gingham dress. His wife, she guessed. The fiddle wasn't playing a waltz, but they were waltzing anyway, looking into each other's eyes and smiling, not even listening to the music. Jane saw the woman reach up, tuck his string tie under his vest, and he put his hand over hers and held it to his chest.

Tears burned under her eyelids.

"Mr. Wilder, do go and join the dancing. I prefer to sit and watch. I brought my sketchbook, and—"

"Sketchbook! You plan on sitting on the sidelines all night making drawings?"

"Not *all* night, no."

"It's the first social you've ever attended in Dixon Falls. Don't you want to join in?"

"Not at the moment, thank you."

"Not at the moment," he muttered, frustration evident in his voice. "What does that mean? 'Maybe later,' or 'Not by a long shot'? Jane, I don't exactly know how to say this, but you look beautiful tonight, and, dammit, I want to dance with you."

Her heart skittered to a stop. She wore a full-skirted dress of yellow dimity, made over from one of Mama's old morning gowns, and he thought she was beautiful? Under the lace-encrusted bodice her heart began to hammer.

"It means maybe later." She was stalling, and she knew it. Perhaps he knew it as well. What he didn't know was how she threatened to soar out of herself at this moment, and that this was something she would never, ever tell him.

She was afraid to dance with him. Afraid of the way she felt when his arms were around her.

Without a word, Rydell escorted her to a wide board bridging two bales of hay. He brushed it off with his pocket handkerchief, and she sat down without speaking. He strode off, returning a few moments later with a cup of cider. Jane nodded her thanks, set the cup beside her, and took her sketchbook out of her pocket.

"Hey, Dell," someone called from the floor. "We need a fourth in our set, come on and help us out!"

"Go on," Jane urged. "Please. I will be quite content."

He laid one hand on her shoulder and bent toward her. "Wait for me. There'll be a waltz later."

She watched him move out onto the polished plank floor, his long-legged gait slow and graceful, his dark head erect. Her chest tightened. Then the crowd swallowed him into their midst, and she was alone.

She sipped the cider. She sketched sleeves and bustles, necklines, embroidered waist insets, and sipped some more. She scrutinized the attire of every female she saw and jotted notes next to the drawings. She filled six pages, pausing only when Odelia settled her ample hips beside her, breathing hard.

"Mose gone up to check on yo' momma. Ol' 'Delia need to set a spell."

Jane waited until the older woman had caught her breath. "Odelia?"

"Yas, honey?"

She swallowed. She couldn't ask. She wanted to know, but she couldn't make herself say the words.

"Yo' thinkin' thoughts, Miss Jane? I kin always tell when somethin' leanin' on yo' mind." She pressed Jane's shoulder with her warm, black fingers and waited.

Jane's drawing pencil made tiny squares inside bigger squares all over her page.

"Lemme guess, child. You wanna know 'bout dancin' wid a man, I bet. Dancin' wid Mistah Rydell."

"I don't want to dance with Rydell."

Odelia gave a soft laugh. "'Course you don't. Jus' like you don' wanna ride a horse or have your heart broke. It's more scarifyin' than seein' a haunt in an old graveyard."

"But why is it, Odelia? Dancing with a man is…well, it's just like going fishing or playing whist or anything else—you just do it *with* someone."

Odelia rolled her eyes. "Hunnh, think so? Like fishin'? Honey, lemme set you straight on somethin'. Dancin' wid a man, with a partic'lar man, is like, well, is like makin' love wid him."

"Odelia!"

"Now, honey, ain't so shockin'. How you think you got borned on dis earth? Yo' daddy and yo momma, they meet up in a 'Ginia reel one night, an' pretty soon you come along. Dancin' be God's way of remindin' folks what life all about."

Jane stared at her. "I— I am afraid to dance with Rydell." There, she'd said it. She hadn't meant to confess it, the words just slipped out. But now that they had reached Odelia's ears, an enormous weight lifted off her shoulders.

Odelia rocked back on the bench and smiled.

"Tha's because Mistah Rydell not like them others." She gestured at the sets swirling about the barn floor. "Mistah Rydell, he mean sumpin' to you."

Jane jerked upright, knocking her empty cup off the bench. "Nonsense. He means absolutely nothing to me. Besides, he's a Yankee!"

Odelia bent to retrieve the cup. "That may be, Miss Jane. But if you like him, make no diff'rence whether he a bluebelly or a one-eyed sailor-man."

"Well, I don't like him. I never have, and I never will." The penciled squares grew smaller and smaller.

"Sho', honey. You don't like dat man."

"That is correct."

"An' you prettied yo'self up tonight so's you could set here like a wallflower and show how much you don' like dat man."

Jane pressed her lips together and counted to fifty.

"Odelia, I have never, not since I was three years old, asked a question you could not answer. How is it that you know so much about everything?"

Odelia's black eyes shone. "Cuz I'se a woman, honey. An' pretty soon yo' gonna be one, too."

Chapter Fifteen

Never in his entire life had Rydell wanted a square dance set to end more than he did at this moment. He forced his feet through the steps automatically, smiled at whatever lady he swung and promenaded home, but his mind was elsewhere.

Bedding a woman had always been easy for him. Courting a woman—a lady—was another matter entirely. Jane had let him kiss her in the schoolhouse on Fourth of July, but she preferred to walk home with Lefty Springer. She had agreed to come to the social, but she wouldn't dance with him. With any other female it would be simple. With Jane, it was one step forward and two steps back.

What was he doing wrong?

The minute the set ended and the caller stopped for a cider break, Rydell excused himself and walked outside to clear his head. Through the open doorway he watched the crowd of ranchers, mill hands, townspeople and their women and waited for the fiddle to strike up a waltz. As he waited, he thought out what he had to do.

By the time Olaf Jensen had refreshed himself at the beer keg end of the trestle table and played maybe twenty more reels and square dance tunes, Rydell's nerves were ready to snap. He ached to hold Jane in his arms, inhale the light, sweet scent of her hair.

Jane uncurled her hand from the pencil she clutched and flexed her stiff, cramped fingers. She was beginning to think perhaps Letitia Price would not attend the social. For over an hour she had watched for the young blonde woman, praying she would wear the new dress of soft blue cambric Jane had sewn. Half eager, half fearful, she scanned the crowded barn with a question burning in her brain. What would the women of Dixon Falls think of her creation?

Was it too simple a style? Perhaps she should not have added so much lace around the neck and hemline? She had squandered her last fifty cents on it, purchasing over ten yards at half price because she spotted a sun blemish in the middle of the roll and Mr. Mercer had granted her a generous discount.

So where *was* the young woman who wanted to be the prettiest girl at the dance? *Appear and claim your title,* Jane willed in tense silence. *And model my creation for the women of Dixon Falls.*

After another quarter of an hour, Odelia gave her shoulder a pat and went off to eat cherry pie with Mose Freeman. "Yo' momma fine, but you too wiggly to set by," the black woman said in parting. "I bring you a slice of pie, will you eat it, Miss Jane?"

Jane shook her head. The knots in her stomach left no room for pie.

Again, her gaze swept the gathering. Four tiny girls in starched pinafores snitched cookies from one of the heaping plates, then crawled under the tablecloth and shared them with three little boys in overalls. That nice gray-haired woman, the one who had ladled potato salad onto Jane's plate at the picnic, sent her a friendly smile from behind a white-frosted four-layer cake. Jane waved. Men ambled outside to smoke or talk, then strode back in to replenish their empty glasses at the beer keg.

Girls old enough to dance, dressed in flounced ankle-length skirts, giggled in corners until fathers or grandfathers invited them to two-step around the floor. Jane sniffed. Were there no eligible young men to be found? In Marion County, boys the same age would have had years of lessons at Miss Poppy's dancing school.

Up until the Northern Aggression, she amended. Then all the young men of the county ignored mastering quadrilles and reels in favor of practicing with their sabers and learning to march in formation. At a dance in Marion County, she would be assured of partners. Here in Dixon Falls, she was a wallflower.

She sat up as straight as she could and pressed her lips together. She wasn't going to feel sorry for herself, not tonight. She had work to do. A reputation as a dressmaker to establish.

Across the floor she spotted Rydell among the whirling couples. Without conscious thought she let her gaze follow him while he passed one woman under his arm, then grabbed the next, a tall farm wife with a beaming face, and stepped around the circle with her. He moved with a lazy, deliberate grace, never in a hurry, never wasting a motion, never missing a step. She could tell from the expression on the face of every woman in the set that dancing with him must be pure pleasure.

He handed one partner off, turned toward a new one. Even from this distance, she could see the skin around his eyes crinkle when he smiled. An odd ache bloomed in her belly. Watching Rydell Wilder made her throat catch.

Purposefully she looked away, and when she looked back, the music stopped and the square was breaking up.

She would dance with him, if he asked her, she decided. Even if it wasn't a waltz. Rydell was so sure of himself on the floor she simply couldn't get tangled up. With Rydell, she would be safe.

Besides, all of a sudden she wanted to feel his arms around her.

Why, Jane Charlotte Davis, wherever did that thought come from?

She must be overwarm in the stuffy barn. Or lightheaded from hunger. Odelia was right, she needed to eat something. A slice of apple pie, perhaps, or…

A stir at one end of the long building drew her attention. Mercy, it was Letitia Price, making a grand entrance at last, and looking simply luscious in Jane's lace-trimmed blue cambric gown! She wondered if Letitia had purposely waited until the dancing stopped so she would be the center of attention.

Disapproval warred with admiration in Jane's mind. If this were Marion County, such a tactic might make sense. Mama had instructed her on "picking her moment" for making an entrance. But out here, people just mixed and mingled willy nilly. Besides, Letitia's social skills were neither here nor there at the moment. What was important was The Dress.

She craned her neck to follow the young blonde woman's slow progress across the floor. Laughing and chatting with the knot of admirers that gathered around her, Letitia spun in a slow circle to make her skirt bell out, clapping her hands in delight at the oohs and aaahs her action prompted.

Yes, Miss Price was the prettiest girl at the social. And the dress—Jane's dress—was truly beautiful! Her heart swelling with pride, she searched for Rydell, but he had disappeared.

Jane bit her lip. She wanted him to see her creation, wanted him to know that she would succeed at her business, would pay back his three-hundred-dollar loan if it was the last thing she did on this earth.

Letitia slid her gaze sideways, as if searching for someone, and her bright smile faltered. Then with a toss of her blond ringlets, she linked arms with Evangeline Tanner and moved toward the refreshment table. Fascinated, Jane watched Letitia position herself so she was visible from all directions. The young woman fluttered her eyelashes and drummed her fingers against her cider cup, apparently waiting for something to happen.

Olaf retuned his fiddle and the dancing began again. Reels and two-steps, schottisches and landlers poured from the perspiring musicians. Letitia Price was besieged with partners. Jane watched, trying to memorize the steps.

At last a waltz tune floated on the air, so sweet and haunting it brought tears to her eyes. "Beautiful dreamer, wake unto me..."

Rydell appeared at the doorway, scanning the crowd. In the next instant he was headed toward her.

When he was halfway across the floor, Letitia glided out of nowhere and laid her hand on his arm. He smiled and spoke a few words. Jane heard only a phrase or two. "...later...lovely dress..." and then the young woman's chiming laugh.

Over Letitia's head, Rydell's eyes met hers. Jane rose.

Rydell gently disengaged Letitia's fingers and moved toward Jane.

Letitia's face went white with comprehension. She planted her hands on her hips, staring at Rydell's back "What, you mean this outdated old thing?" Her words cut through the music like a bucket of ice water. "I only wear this when I've nothing better."

A lance ripped through Jane's chest. Hurt settled over her, so raw it made her stomach feel as if it were full of lead balls.

Rydell kept coming. Without uttering a word, he put his arm around her waist, and in silence she raised her left hand to his shoulder.

"She's wrong," Jane said in a choked voice. "She is mean and rude and she is wrong. It *is* a lovely dress. I made it."

Rydell invited her body to move with his, taking

small steps, his fingers caressing her back. "I've never understood that about women," he murmured. "How they can feel so soft and bite like a bear trap."

Jane clamped her jaws together. She would *not* cry. Not here, with everyone watching. She raised her head and looked into his face.

"She fancies you," she said when she could trust herself to speak.

"Some, yeah."

"It was you she spoke of at the mercantile that day. Last year, you and she—"

"Some," he said again.

Another prick of pain, sharper and more deep-seated.

"It is a beautiful dress, Jane."

"I wanted everyone to notice it," she said in a low voice. "I wanted everyone to see what I could produce, so…" she drew in a shuddery breath "…so I could sell another, and then another."

Rydell held her eyes. "You don't have to, Jane," he said quietly. "You know that, don't you?"

"But I *want* to," she whispered. "At first it was the only thing I could think of to do, but now…" She frowned, searching for words. "I am proud of what I can create. It—it makes me happy."

His arm tightened around her. "Yeah, I was afraid of that. I thought you might fail to make a profit, and that would be hard for you to swallow. I figured you'd get over it in time. But a man can't fight that other thing."

"What other thing? Rydell Wilder, whatever are you talking about?"

He took his time before answering.

"That thing in you that makes you different. That thing you're just finding out about yourself."

"What thing?" she murmured. "Tell me."

Again he was silent for a long minute. When he finally spoke, his voice was low and gravelly. "Some women are like a clear pond on a summer day. It's pretty, and a man can satisfy a thirst if he's got one. Other women…"

He hesitated, looked up to the rafters, then down at her. "Jane, I don't exactly know how to say this. Some women are like a stream in the dead of winter. There's a layer of ice on top, so you can't see clear to the bottom, but underneath the current's there, moving, and the man who's got a thirst has some work to do. He's got to wait."

"Wait for what?" Jane said in a small voice.

"Wait for the silt to settle out. Wait for the water hidden under the ice to flow free."

"You're talking scandalous nonsense!"

"I'm talking good old-fashioned horse sense."

Jane tipped her head back to look at him. Under her fingers she felt the muscles of his shoulder move beneath the soft linen shirt. "I do not want to marry."

"I know."

"Papa was the best catch in Marion County, but Mama was miserable anyway. Especially after we moved out west. I used to hear her crying in her room at night after she thought I was asleep. Sometimes I think the reason she doesn't remember much…" she closed her eyes, steadied her voice "…is because she doesn't want to. I do not want to end up like Mama. Ever.''

"Yeah," Rydell said. "I know that, too."

"You understand about Letitia's dress? *My* dress? How important it is to me? Most men are good men, like Papa, aren't they? But their women still go crazy with unhappiness."

"Jane, there's another thing about men and women." He bent his head until his lips brushed her temple. "They can be friends."

"Oh, yes, I know that, I suppose."

"And they can be something else to each other, as well."

A blaze of heat suffused her body. She didn't understand exactly what he was talking about, but something inside her wanted to know. *Tell me. Show me.*

Aghast, she stopped in her tracks. "Mr. Wilder, I feel quite faint all of a sudden. May we sit down?"

Rydell chuckled. "Sure, if you want."

"Yes, I—"

"Or," he interjected, "we could do a little, uh, ice fishing. Someplace where it's not so crowded."

"Ice fishing?"

"Oh, hell, Jane. I'm not very good at this. With some women it's simple, but with you—I'm afraid of saying the wrong thing, doing the wrong thing. Afraid of scaring you."

"Scaring me? That's silly. I haven't been scared of a Yankee since the war! Why should that matter now?"

Rydell groaned. "It just does." He grasped her hand. "Come on, Jane. I've got to get out of here."

Without speaking, Rydell walked her a good twenty paces down the lantern-lit path leading from Olaf Jensen's barn. The air was warm on her skin, and she turned her face up to catch the honeysuckle-scented breeze. The sound of fiddle music gradually faded into the rasp of crickets and the *swish-swish* of their footsteps brushing the tall grass as he turned them off the path.

"There's a willow tree yonder," he said at last. "Up on a little rise. Will you come?"

Jane said nothing. She should not be traipsing about at night with a man; she had not been reared to engage in such compromising behavior. But every fiber of her being whispered *Yes, I will come*. She lifted her hand and touched his arm.

The tree stood by itself on a knoll, its pendulous branches dappled in soft light from the fat orangey-gold summer moon that floated near the horizon. With his free hand, Rydell parted the branches and led her underneath, to the shadowed area near the trunk.

"You have been here before," Jane breathed.

"Many times. Not with a woman, though. By myself."

"Oh. I see."

"I used to come here when I was a kid. I'd put my butt on the ground and my back against the tree and look out over the town, and think about my life. Wonder where the hell I fit in."

"I wonder that, too," Jane murmured. "Not about you," she added quickly. "You have made a place for yourself here."

"Have I?" Rydell said, his voice quiet. He looked

out across the lights of the town spread below them. "I made just one rule about being here, under this tree. You only say what's the truth, to yourself or to anyone else. It's not easy."

"Yes, I think I understand."

"That's why I've never brought anyone here before." He stepped forward, away from her, and put his spine against the dark tree trunk. When he faced her, he reached out his hand. "I'll take you back if you say so, Jane. I just wanted you to know how it's to be if you're up here."

"Very well." Jane heard herself agree and in the next instant she wondered if she would regret it. She didn't mind if Rydell Wilder told her his true thoughts. As a matter of fact she'd grown a little curious about him. Where had he come from? How had he managed to establish the first bank in Dixon Falls?

But when she thought of being equally honest about herself, about her own private feelings—oh, no, she didn't know whether she could do that.

And is part of the reason because you don't know what your real feelings are?

"Certainly not," she said aloud.

Rydell straightened and dropped his arm to his side. "Change your mind?"

"No. Yes. Oh, I don't know," she blurted.

He laughed softly. Then he reached out both hands and drew her forward until her forehead grazed his chin. "Good. I like a woman who thinks on her feet."

He smelled of soap and something like leather, but not as strong. She closed her eyes, listening to their combined breathing. Something was happening to her, something wonderful and frightening all at the same time.

Something that happened only when she was with Rydell.

"Jane," he murmured. His breath near her ear sent a spark dancing down her backbone. "May I kiss you?"

"You never asked before," she said without thinking. "You just did it."

"This is different. This time I'm asking."

She didn't know what to say. Did she want him to kiss her or not?

She did, she decided.

And she didn't.

She did because she always felt so strange and wonderful inside when his lips touched hers. And she didn't because...well, because he was a Yankee. And because soon as ever she could, she was going back to Marion County. And because...

She tipped her head up so his mouth could find hers. He looked straight into her eyes for the longest moment, and she thought she saw a mixture of hunger and amusement in the depths of his gaze.

"Jane?" he breathed, his lips inches from hers.

"Yes?" she whispered. And then "Yes."

His mouth closed over hers, warm and seeking, asking something she could answer only with her lips and tongue. A drowsy, silky feeling spread over her, as if a fiery torch were turning her bones to molasses, scalding her skin with want. Any moment she would break free, like a butterfly, and soar into the heat.

Rydell lifted his mouth and she felt his body tremble. "Jane, do you want this?"

In answer, she drew his head down to hers and felt his arms tighten until the tips of her breasts brushed his shirt. She took a single step forward and fitted her body to his, pressing against his hard male frame. She opened her mouth to him and he groaned.

His hands lifted, slid down her sides from her shoulders to the flare of her hips, then returned to her neck and glided slowly, oh, so slowly across her bosom, down to her waist, and back up, his thumbs moving, caressing.

She would melt if he kept that up! Or die. Dear Lord, what a throbbing ache fluttered inside her. She felt completely possessed, as if she were someone else, not Jane Charlotte at all. It was glorious. *Glorious.*

Her fingers moved to the top button of her dress. She heard his breath suck in and his hand stopped her.

"Don't, Jane. I won't be able to stop."

She opened her eyes. What was he talking about?

He folded her hand into his and held it gently against his chest. "You won't want it this way."

She opened her mouth, but no sound came out. Her pulse pounded in her ears. Perhaps she was dreaming.

"Miss Jane, dat you up 'dere?" a soft male voice drawled.

"Yes, Mose." Rydell answered for her. "She's here with me."

"'Delia done start to fuss some, Mistah Rydell."

Rydell chuckled. "We'll be along, Mose. Tell Odelia not to worry."

He gave Jane a quick, hard kiss. "Just in time," he murmured. "One thing before I let you go, Jane."

Dazed, she lifted her eyes to his.

"I love you. I've loved you ever since the first day I saw you."

"But—"

"I'm just telling you. It's got nothing to do with that three-hundred-dollar loan."

She gazed at him. "What loan?"

Rydell laughed out loud. Then he kissed her, kissed her again and spoke into her hair as he held her.

"You'll remember the minute we start down this hill."

Chapter Sixteen

The minute they set foot in Olaf Jensen's noisy barn, Jane knew something was different. *She* was different. She had kissed a man under the drooping branches of a willow tree, had let him kiss her, touch her, until her body burst into flame. Until this moment, she had not known such feelings existed.

Odelia knew. Mama knew. Even Aunt Carrie must have known about these things. The world, and everything in it, looked different now.

"Dell, honey. I've been searching everywhere for you!" A feminine arm reached out and pulled Rydell off to one side.

And Letitia Price knew! With a flurry of blue ruffles, she plucked him from Jane's side like a ripe apple. "Why, darling, they need us for the Grand Reel! Surely you remember?"

Rydell sent Jane a look that made her breath catch—half amusement, half raw longing. Then Letitia dragged him off to where couples were lining up on the dance floor.

"Miz Jane?" Lefty Springer appeared before her,

offering his good arm. "Keer to step lively with an old man?"

Jane smiled at him. "Mr. Springer, I accept with pleasure."

"Most women don' know how to dance with a man that's got only one arm, but you ain't most women. I figure you'll know how."

"Oh, yes, I can be very creative." She patted his left hand.

"I seed that right off. That blue dress you sewed for Miz Letitia, why it's the purtiest dress I ever laid eyes on."

"Why, thank you, Lefty. I didn't know you were an admirer of ladies' dresses."

"I ain't, usually. Usually I jes' admire the ladies *in* the dresses, but that one's kinda special. I mean the dress," he added. "Not the lady wearin' it. Come on, Miz Jane, they're linin' up!"

They moved into place at the end of the line and waited with the others while the fiddle warmed up, then plunged into a lively reel. The lines of dancers swept forward, bowed to their partners opposite, and stepped back as the head couple met in the center. Rather than watch Rydell and Letitia join hands and swing each other around, Jane focused on Lefty, deciding how best to compensate for his missing arm.

A flash of blue skipped past her, and then her row stepped forward to join their partners and promenade under the bridge Rydell and Letitia formed with their upraised arms.

Keeping her left hand at her waist eliminated the need for Lefty to use his missing arm. Jane's use of this small subterfuge worked perfectly, earning an appreciative grin from her partner. His extended left hand grasped her right, and they swung around each other with as much style as any other couple.

Maybe more, Jane noted. With a completely straight face, Lefty threw an occasional double-kick into the routine steps. His heels made a smart snapping sound on the offbeat when they connected, and more than one youngster lined up at the edge of the plank floor and tried out the tricky maneuver.

"Learned that in the cavalry," the rusty-haired man puffed. "From my horse!"

Jane laughed and let him spin her in a new way—his good arm clasping her around the waist, her arm skirting his belt buckle, her thumb hooked in his wide red suspenders.

"I call this the Civilian's Quick March," he said as they ducked under the upraised arms of Rafe Mercer and his partner, the kind-faced woman in the gingham check dress. His wife, Jane guessed. She never saw Rafe issue one word of instruction, yet the two moved as if connected by a single cord.

In contrast, Lefty talked continually as they worked their way through the steps of the reel, advancing one couple at a time to the head of the line. "Watch that loose board, Miz Jane…see, I throwed in one more turn, you notice?…you're light as thistledown on your feet—don't have no trouble a'tall follerin' a rambunctious old geezer like me!"

Jane's breath was too short to answer him, so she just concentrated on keeping up. She gulped air when she could and marveled at the old man's stamina. And his footwork.

Forward and back, around and around, make a chain, duck under the bridge—Jane barely had time to think.

When it came time for the corner man and woman to meet and circle with each other, she gave Lefty a smile and side-stepped away from him toward the center. The man caught her with two hard hands about her waist, and before she could draw breath, she was imprisoned. The silky black shirt looked vaguely familiar, as did the snakeskin-banded black Stetson with the hard rolled edges.

"Caught 'cha, pretty lady," a rough voice exulted.

Jane sucked air into her lungs. It was the stranger at the picnic, the man whose roving hands had assaulted her before she could get off his horse.

"Didja miss me?" His sour breath reeked of spirits.

She tried to circle out of his grasp and get back to Lefty, but the tall man with the shaggy dark hair held her fast. He spun her two extra turns while she tried to think what to do.

Reverse direction, that was it! She slammed her shoulder against his upper arm and broke free without losing a beat. To make up the time, she skipped back to her partner and safety.

"He hurt you?" Lefty asked as they met, twirled one turn, and peeled off for the promenade. They met at the back of the line, raised a one-armed bridge between them as if by unspoken agreement.

"No, I am fine," Jane answered as the couples started under their arch.

"Look white as cake flour," he observed.

Over the jostling bodies and bent heads filing between them, Jane tried to smile. "I am tougher than I look."

Lefty grinned at her.

Rydell and Letitia were the last ones under the bridge. When they emerged, Lefty and Jane took up positions next to them. Jane could not help but note how gracefully the blue dress rippled with each motion Letitia made. It was the cut of the skirt, she thought with satisfaction. On the bias but full-gathered on the waistband as well. A flash of dress-making inspiration.

By the time the reel ended, Jane had recovered some of her equilibrium. The tall stranger was nowhere in sight, and she breathed a sigh of relief as the fiddle struck up "My Bonnie Lies Over the Ocean."

Lefty offered his arm, and before she knew it they had worked out another method of waltzing—one hand high on his right shoulder, she let him guide her about the floor by pumping their clasped hands up and down. It must surely look ungainly, she acknowledged, but it was fun. And anyway, she noted as she watched the other couples over Lefty's shoulder, none of them looked remotely like a Miss Poppy's Dancing Academy graduate, either.

Lefty began to hum the tune, and after a moment she joined him. "...Bring back, bring back, oh, bring back my bonnie..."

"To me," a cracked voice finished. Jane found herself whirled out of Lefty's grasp and crushed in the arms of the dark stranger. She tried to escape by refusing to move her feet, but he tightened the long arm about her waist and swung her up off the floor.

"Release me this instant!"

He acted as if he hadn't heard her, twirling her around and around, held fast to his chest, until she grew dizzy. She noticed he was moving her toward the barn door, and she stopped breathing. If he forced her outside, away from the crowd...

"I will scream," she warned, keeping her voice as steady as she could.

"No, you won't," he rasped. "You're gonna like it. You're gonna beg for more."

"I—"

All at once something spun the man backwards, and her feet stumbled as they met the floor. Fingers of steel closed over her wrist, pulling her free.

"I told you to keep your hands off her," Rydell said in a low voice.

The tall man straightened, tossing his chin-length black hair out of his face. "It's a free country. I can dance with anyone I want."

"We're not going to do this here, Lucas," Rydell said. "Let's take it outside. No need to spoil a fine evening for everyone." He moved toward the door.

A long arm reached out, caught Rydell's sleeve. "Not so fast. I came to see the lady, not the dark side of a barn."

Rydell shrugged free. "You've seen her. Now we talk."

The man's angular features darkened. "I'm gonna beat the— Just who do you think you are, ordering me around?"

"I am Miss Davis's escort."

"That don't mean you own her! Let *her* decide, why don'tcha?"

Rydell clenched his fists and turned to the trembling woman at his side. He kept his tone neutral. "Jane?"

She shook her head.

"That's it, Lucas. Come on." He strode away, sure Lucas would follow him. Rydell figured he'd be torn between trying to convince Jane otherwise in public or saving face. If he measured his man correctly, Lucas would stick to what made him look good.

Once outside and a good distance from the barn, Rydell turned to face him. "I'm not armed, Lucas. We can talk or we can fight, but it's gonna be quiet. I'm not going to disrupt Olaf Jensen's shindig."

Lucas tramped up to him, thrust his weather-lined face so close Rydell could see the sweat on his upper lip. "Ya know, mister, you need me. We need each other."

Rydell tensed. "That so?"

"Sure. You're keepin' my money safe in your bank."

Rydell said nothing. He half expected the tall man to jump him any second. Instead he jammed one hand in his back trouser pocket and poked a long forefinger into Rydell's chest.

"I'm a smart man, Wilder. I'd be a damn fool to smear yer face in the dirt now."

"True."

"If it weren't for that pretty gal waitin' inside…"

"Still true. She doesn't want you, Lucas. Leave her alone."

"Maybe I will. On one condition." He poked again, and Rydell swatted his hand away and waited. He wanted to tear the man into pieces, but he knew better. A hurt man will try to get even. A proud man will want to preserve his image. Lucas was proud. Cocky, even. It showed in his stance, the arrogant tilt of his chin, the surly bravado in his speech. It reminded him of something he didn't want to be. God help him, if he hadn't pulled himself up by his bootstraps when he was a kid, he might have turned out just like this man.

"What condition?" he prompted.

"I bring some more cash, lots more, and you keep it in your bank for me."

Interesting. At the moment, Lucas seemed more concerned about his money than Jane, and that left Rydell with some control over her safety.

"Agreed."

It crossed his mind that Lucas might be lying. Not much he could do about it outside of asking Lefty and Mose Freeman to help him keep a close eye on Jane. He would talk to Odelia about accompanying her when Jane walked into town. Maybe he should get her a horse. Mounted, she might be safer.

Without speaking, the two men moved toward the barn entrance, each wary of the other.

Which, Rydell reminded himself, was just the way he wanted it. He knew nothing about Lucas, yet something about the way he walked, the timbre and inflection of his gravelly voice, left an uneasy feeling in Rydell's gut.

The man was hiding something.

Chapter Seventeen

The house was dark and quiet when Jane and Odelia climbed the steps onto the front porch. Lefty and Mose Freeman had walked them up the long hill to the picket-fence-enclosed structure. After seeing the two women safe inside the front door, they turned and headed their separate ways—Lefty back to town and his cozy cabin near the livery stable, Mose continuing up the road to the little shack he rented outside of town.

"Us darkies not 'llowed to own property," Odelia announced as Mose trudged off. "Dat why he live out near de woods."

It was something Jane had never thought of before. As a house servant, Odelia had always lived with the family, in a room off the kitchen at Montclair. Here in Dixon Falls she slept in the extra downstairs bedroom. Now she realized that, unlike herself, Odelia owned nothing she could call her own except the clothes on her back and those she'd brought with her.

I've been asleep all these years. So absorbed in her

own troubles she had never thought much about what went on around her.

In the dark, Jane felt her way into the front parlor. "Mama?"

"Ah'm over heah, Jane Charlotte." The quavery voice came from the damask upholstered settee, her mother's favorite resting place.

"Mama, why are you sitting here in the dark? Odelia, light the lamp, will you?"

"Sho' thing, Miss Jane." She scrabbled in the kitchen for a moment, then emerged with a flaming match. In the glow of lamplight, Jane knelt by her mother, scanning her face. "Mama? Are you all right?"

"Of course, dear." She pronounced the words slowly, her voice sounding odd. Distant. "I've been waiting for you. We must begin to pack."

Jane's heart leaped into her throat. "Pack?" Over her mother's head, she met Odelia's dark eyes, wide with concern.

"You promised, Jane. You said we would go back to Marion County. I have been talking it over with your father, and he says it is time to go home."

"Mama…"

"I want to go home, Jane. More than anything in the world. We will leave tomorrow, and soon I will see Carrie, and the air will smell like jasmine again. Oh, I do so miss the scent of jasmine."

Jane forced herself to look into her mother's tear-streaked face. The pale blue eyes looked back at her with a longing that made her chest ache.

"Please, Jane," her mother whispered. "Oh, please. Say we can go."

Odelia turned away abruptly. After a moment she spoke in a choked voice. "Cain't do that. Ain't nuthin' there no more, jus' brambles an' a big ol' empty house...."

Jane wrapped her arms around her mother's thin shoulders. "Mama. Oh, Mama, I'd do anything to make you happy, but..." She could not bear to destroy the hope in her mother's eyes.

"Then we will go? You will take me home?"

Jane bowed her head and laid her cheek on her mother's soft hair. "I will try, Mama. I will try to take you home, just as soon as I am able." She pressed her fingers over her mouth and clenched her teeth together.

Don't you dare cry, Jane Charlotte! She would not let her mother see her cry.

"Come on, Mama, it's time for bed. I'll make you a nice of cup of warm milk to help you sleep." She managed to keep her voice steady until Odelia and her mother went up the stairs. Then, while she poked up the fire and heated the milk in a small blue-speckled saucepan, she could not stop her tears.

"You's gettin' Miss Leah's cup all full o' salt water," Odelia announced when she returned for the milk. Her voice sounded watery. When she entered the kitchen a few moments later, dabbing at her eyes with a corner of her apron, the two women clung together and wept.

"What we gonna do, honey? Yo' momma maybe not in her right mind."

Jane drew a breath past her tightening throat. Her eyes ached from crying over the pain in her mother's life. Marriage was not worth it, she decided. It led to heartache and dreadful, numbing loss.

"I don't know what we're going to do, Odelia. I pray to God I will think of something."

"It's that Lucas fellow again, Mr. Wilder." Josiah peered at the drawings on the broad oak desktop. "Says he wants to see you."

Rydell rose, massaging his stiff neck with one hand. He'd been expecting him for the past three days. Now that he'd finally turned up, he felt an inexplicable sense of relief. Always better to know where a wildcard like Lucas was and what he was up to. Like keeping your eye on a snake.

"Gosh," the young clerk blurted. "My wife would sure fancy a house like that, with a veranda 'n everything. You plannin' on getting—I mean, 'scuse me, sir."

Rydell chuckled. "Walking that new baby of yours all night is turning your brain into cheese, Josiah."

The young man turned the color of beet juice. "Yessir, it—it's plumb wonderful! To be a father, I mean. Of course, first you got to get marr— Oh, beg pardon, Mr. Wilder. You're absolutely right." His Adam's apple bobbed over the high starched shirt collar.

His young clerk swept the door open for him, and Rydell grinned. "I'm right about the cheese, that's for damn sure."

Lucas was waiting for him at the cashier's window,

his tall frame lounging against the oak counter. He nodded once as Rydell approached. "Wilder."

The man wore dark trousers and a fancy embroidered vest. He didn't remove his black Stetson, Rydell noted. "Lucas. What can I do for you?"

"You got a short memory, sonny. Same as before, keep my cash safe." He hefted a black leather satchel onto the counter.

Rydell gritted his teeth. "How much this time?"

"Eighteen, maybe twenty thousand. Didn't bother to count it close."

Rydell studied the man. His eyes were opaque, hard and expressionless. Something about him made Rydell want to spit. "Where'd this come from?"

"None of your business. What do you care? It's honest money."

"Is it?" He leveled his gaze on the satchel. "How come you don't know exactly how much is there?"

Lucas stiffened. "Hell, I can't read nor keep accounts. That's why I'm bringin' it in here. I can't keep track of every poker pot I win in every two-bit town I ride through."

"What towns do you ride through, Lucas? Where are you from?"

The tall man punched a thumb over his shoulder. "Up north."

"Idaho? Montana?"

"Maybe."

Maybe. Getting information out of Lucas was like shoveling quicksand. He'd checked the wanted posters at the sheriff's office; no outlaw matched Lucas's description. So what was it that made his gut tighten every time he laid eyes on the man?

As if reading Rydell's thoughts, Lucas gave him a twisted smile. "Galls ya, don't it? I said I won't bother Miz Jane, but you're wonderin' if my word's good. You're wonderin' about where this money came from." He slapped a bony hand onto the satchel.

"You think too much, Wilder. You got no choice. Take the money and I leave the girl alone."

Maybe he didn't have a choice, at least at the moment. He snapped open the valise, counted the neat packets of hundred dollar bills, and wrote out a deposit receipt for $19,500.

"I'm a pretty good gambler, wouldn'tcha say?"

Rydell drilled him with a look. "Either that or you're a pretty good liar. I don't trust you, Lucas, so watch your step."

"Fair enough," the tall man growled. He reached for the satchel. "Next time, though, I might have a surprise for you."

The encounter left a sour taste in Rydell's mouth. So sour that as soon as Lucas left, he headed across the street to the Silver Cup and ordered a whiskey. Then he rode out to his building site, dismounted and sat for over an hour watching the Traft brothers nail up framing studs.

It would be a fine house, finer than any house in the whole county. But that wasn't what was important, was it?

What's important is that you've scratched yourself up from that skinny, lost kid who didn't know where he fit in, who mucked out stables and ate hardtack to make a life for himself that counted.

Now he was respected. He could afford to build the house that was taking shape before his eyes. He'd kissed Jane with all the unspoken ardor he'd felt all these years, let his lips and tongue tell her what he could not yet put into words, and she hadn't turned away.

But something cold had lodged in his gut and wouldn't move on. He'd gotten what he wanted, what he'd worked so hard for. Now he was beginning to realize how much he had to lose.

The smell of new yardgoods rose to meet Jane as she unlocked the shop door and stepped inside. The kitten sprang to meet her, trailing a tangle of blue thread, and Jane bent to stroke her soft fur. She had spent all morning cutting out pieces for two new dresses, and the floor was littered with scraps of mint-green Swiss muslin and rose sateen. She sidestepped General Lee and reached for the broom.

Not one customer for the past three days. She'd hoped—prayed, even—that following the dance at Olaf Jensen's barn she would be flooded with requests for her dressmaking services. Only Mary Two Hats exhibited any interest in her business. The Indian woman made a daily trip across the street and past Jane's establishment, peered in the display window, and then moved on down the boardwalk.

There was nothing new in the display window yet. Not until tomorrow would Jane have even a basted version of either gown to pin over the dress dummy.

She pushed the colorful scraps into a pile, but before she could gather it up to dump in the stove, the cat leaped into the center of the mound and scattered the bits and pieces.

She grabbed the animal by the scruff of the neck, lifted her out of harm's way, and again wielded her broom. A tall figure drifted by the open front door, but she was too busy to look up.

Rydell Wilder, perhaps. Or that stranger, Mr. Lucas. The first thought filled her belly with hot flutters; the second possibility dumped ice all over the pleasant warmth.

But neither man came in. Good. She had seams to baste and press open, gathered lace ruffles to attach, buttonholes to mark. "Besides," she said out loud to General Lee, "I am not interested in either man. Both of them are Yankees, and just as soon as I can, I am going home to Marion County where my mama longs to be. And," she added under her breath, "the gentleman are not so bold."

The kitten looked up at her, cocked its head, and mewed.

"Well, yes, I did like Mr. Wilder's kisses. Quite more than I should have." She scooped General Lee up into her arms. "As if it's any of *your* business."

The cat began to purr. Jane smiled at her foolishness and paced absently about the floor, stroking the ball of fluff. She had to force her mind off kisses and concentrate on her sewing!

Toward dusk, just as she finished the last buttonhole, she glanced up and caught her breath. Evangeline Tanner stood in the doorway.

"May I come in?"

Jane hastily stuck her threaded needle into a pin-cushion and lifted the bodice front off her lap. "Of course, Mrs. Tanner." She rose from her chair as she spoke and met the young woman halfway across the tiny shop.

"I've been wanting to stop by," the dark-haired woman began. "I wished to tell you—"

General Lee scampered under Mrs. Tanner's corded walking skirt and pounced on her shoe.

"Oh, my, I didn't know you kept a cat."

Jane dropped onto one knee and slapped her palm on the floor. "Come, kitty. Come away from there."

"Oh!" Evangeline jumped.

"I am afraid she is partial to ruffled petticoats," Jane explained. "General Lee, come here at once!" She glimpsed a twitching orange tail and dove forward without thinking. Her fingers grasped the kitten and she dragged it out from under Mrs. Tanner's skirt and hoisted the wriggling animal aloft.

To her intense relief, Evangeline laughed. "General Lee, did you say?" She smiled. "What an unusual name. But of course, you're from the South, are you not?"

Jane rose, her face flaming. "I am so sorry, Mrs. Tanner. Please forgive me. Us."

"Nonsense. No harm has been done, except perhaps to my shoebutton."

Jane bit her lip. "May I offer you some...?" The automatic words flowed from her mouth before she realized she was not at home but at her dressmaking shop. Other than a pint jar of lukewarm water, she had nothing to offer a visitor.

"Thank you, no. I just stopped in to say how much I admired that charming blue dress you made for Letty. I thought it most handsome, and wanted to tell you so."

Jane stared at her. She must surely be dreaming.

"Letty…Letitia is not one to praise the efforts of others, but I think something must be said to acknowledge your skill with a needle. All the women admired it, you know. Not just myself."

"Thank you, Mrs. Tanner. Oh, thank you so very much!"

The dark-haired woman glanced about the shop, her gaze moving from the half-basted mint-green skirt to the rose sateen bodice draped over the sewing cabinet. "What are you making now?"

Making? For a moment Jane could not remember. Then the short length of rose thread caught on her work skirt jolted her memory.

"Morning gowns," she said. "Two of them—one in Swiss muslin, that pale green over there; the other in rose sateen, with an apron front and pleating on the hem."

"I see. You have a good eye, Miss Davis. I would like to see the muslin when it is finished."

"I will put it in the window the instant it is completed."

Evangeline smiled. "Letty will want it, no doubt. But she will delay as long as she possibly can, and—"

"But why?" Jane interjected.

"Why, my dear, it never occurred to me you did not know."

Jane's heart stuttered. "Know what?"

Evangeline gazed directly into Jane's eyes. "Letitia does not wish you well, Miss Davis. She is extremely jealous. You see, last summer, Letty set her cap for Rydell Wilder. This summer he seems to prefer you."

"Oh, but he doesn't!" Jane blurted. "It's just that…" She racked her brain for some sort of explanation. She would much rather have Letitia Price as a customer than Rydell Wilder as a… Well, that was certainly out of the question. She planned to return to Marion County.

And Letitia Price would help her do it!

"Mr. Wilder and I are…business partners." At least that was not much of a lie. Jane detested lying.

"Ah, I see." Mrs. Tanner gave her a quizzical look.

"Rydell Wilder means nothing at all to me," Jane went on. "I don't value him a button."

Jane Charlotte, you are prevaricating! Ignoring all that you do not care to acknowledge.

Evangeline nodded. "I see," she said again.

"For anyone to think anything else would be…would be…unmitigated spooniness."

Mrs. Tanner burst into laughter. "I will keep an eye on your display window," she said with a broad smile. "And you, Miss Davis, keep your eye on your…business partner. Letitia can be unpredictable."

Chapter Eighteen

"Fer pity's sake, Dell, she's slippin' right through yer fingers! Never knowed you to get so tangled up in your brandin' rope. Here, have another shot."

Lefty Springer splashed a whiskey into the empty glass on the table between them and topped up his own. The Silver Cup was deserted except for the bar-keep, a pear-shaped man with a permanent mournful expression on his long face.

"I don't want to tie her up and brand her," Rydell replied. "I want her willing, not stampeded into it."

Lefty snorted. "Dell, you wake her up and 'fore you know it, some other gent—or not-so-gent, like that Lucas fella—he'll steal yer prize right from under yer nose."

Rydell shook his head. "He won't. He might try, but he won't."

"What makes you so all-fired sure?"

Rydell thought a minute, drawing in a lungful of the tangy saloon air. "I'm doing Lucas a favor, like I told you."

Lefty snorted. "Oh, yeah, the money. Ever wonder how come he picked *you* for that little favor?"

"Yep. All the time. Must be because I run the only bank in the county."

"Huh," the older man scoffed. He downed a gulp of his whiskey and coughed. "Mos' likely he picked Dixon Falls cuz Miz Jane's here. I'd watch it, if'n I was you. Hurry things along some. Man, she's turning out dresses fast as hens can lay eggs. What'll you do if she's a success?"

"Won't matter, I've decided. By that time I'm hoping she'll want me more than the three hundred dollars."

"Dell, I hate to bust yer bubble, but it's not you she's in love with, it's that sewin' machine of hers."

Rydell grinned at his friend. "Yeah, maybe. But time—and nature—is on my side."

Lefty choked on his drink. "Nature! You mean what I think you mean, you better press yer advantage some. Walk her home at night. Lollygag in that swing on her front porch."

"Yeah. Partly."

Lefty's rust-colored eyebrows shot up. "Partly! What the devil's wrong with your intelligent parts, Dell? What else you gonna do?"

Rydell finished off his shot, rose, and laid a hand on his friend's shoulder. "Want me to help you limp home, old-timer?"

"Heck, no, I don't need no help. I ain't so old."

Rydell chuckled. "I'm working on a plan," he said casually.

"Plan?" Lefty's blue eyes snapped. "A plan about Miz Jane?"

"Could be. I was maybe going to tell you about it on the way."

The older man shot out of his chair. "Come to think on it, Dell, my leg is a mite sore tonight."

Rydell laughed and slapped four coins onto the bar. "Thanks, Bill. See you in church Sunday." He turned back to Lefty, who was hobbling dramatically toward the door.

"Blue blazes, cowboy, you don't need me," he joked. "You're walkin' better than you ever did!"

Lefty slapped his battered brown felt hat against Rydell's chest, and the two men left arm in arm.

Bill the bartender caught himself smiling, shrugged, and went back to polishing the counter.

Jane sewed the last tiny button on the pale green spotted muslin gown and bit off the thread with her teeth. She could hardly wait to drape it over the jersey-covered dress form and then stand back and admire her handiwork. Why, the dress looked so cool and green it reminded her of a mint julep! With her dark hair and high coloring, Evangeline Tanner would look handsome in it.

She fluffed out the gathered skirt and set about sweeping up the bits of lace and thread that littered the floor. When someone purchased her creation it would add another four dollars to the savings jar she kept hidden behind the flour bin in the pantry.

If someone purchased it. She prayed Mrs. Tanner would see it before Mary Two Hats. Instinct told her

Evangeline would prove a more steady customer for Jane's services. Yesterday at the mercantile, Rafe Mercer had told her that Mrs. Tanner's husband owned the sawmill. "Tanner's Mill employs thirteen men, and all of them buy their supplies at the mercantile," the store owner had confided. Then he added in a significant undertone, "Walk right past your dressmaking establishment ev'ry day, Miz Jane. And eight of the men got wives who gussy themselves up now and again. To say nothing of Mrs. Tanner herself, who's a fine-looking woman."

And dresses accordingly, Jane surmised. She appreciated Mr. Mercer's unspoken encouragement, and right then and there she decided to turn out some garments the mill workers would see when they passed by her shop, garments they could buy for their wives.

She made her purchase—twelve yards of fine white cambric, pearl buttons and two spools of white thread—and flew back to her shop with her spirits chirked up, as Odelia would say. Now she wondered if she would have the courage to display lacy chemises and ruffled petticoats and nightrobes in her front window.

Her broom slowed and then stopped as she made a quick calculation in her head. "Mercy," she murmured. "Even if I save every penny I make, at four dollars each I will have to sew seventy-five whole dresses to earn the three hundred dollars I owe Rydell Wilder."

Absently she swept and reswept the same spot. But of course she could *not* save all her profits! She had to buy fabric and trimmings for the next garments, and the next and the next....

And then there would be the train fare back to Marion County.

"It will never end," she said aloud. The hard work didn't bother her; it was the futility of trying to get ahead. Did other business people—Rafe Mercer, for instance, even the mill workers—carry the same burden?

Papa always said it was degrading to work with one's hands. She always thought he disapproved because your hands got dirty, but perhaps he meant the day-to-day struggle for survival people of the working class endured—dragging yourself out of a warm bed each morning and doing your job no matter whether snow blew down your collar or the sun seared your skin. No matter if you felt ill or your head ached or someone suggested a picnic lunch under a shady tree.

She thought about Rafe Mercer, opening his store every morning, sweeping the boardwalk twice a day. And Mose Freeman, the blacksmith; and Maggie, who waited tables at the Excelsior dining room. She even thought of Rydell Wilder, who owned the Dixon Falls bank. How hard he must have worked, for years and years, to get where he was today.

Could she do that? Sew seventy-five dresses whether she felt like it or not?

All of a sudden she saw things in a completely new light. It took tremendous drive and courage to work every day of your life. She thought of the young men she'd known back at Montclair, so gallant and gay. So fortunate.

And into her mind flashed something she'd read once, about an officer among the Federals. *He laughed his fill at our ragged, dirty soldiers, but he stopped laughing when he saw them under fire.*

She caught the broom to her chest. There were soldiers everywhere, she realized. In the South. Out here in the West. Quiet, uncomplaining men and women who simply did what they had to do. She guessed she was now one of them.

"Miz Jane?"

Jane jumped as Mose Freeman's broad-shouldered frame loomed in the open doorway. "Oh, Mr. Freeman. I am so sorry I did not hear you. I am deep in a slough of despond, I'm afraid."

"Didn't mean to startle you, Miz Jane. Come to buy a present."

"Come in, Mose. What sort of present?"

"Well, it's kind of a...female present. For Odelia, ma'am. I figure she'd fancy a new petticoat, the kind that makes a swishin' sound when you move."

Jane suppressed a smile. Bless the man. He would spend his hard-earned pennies on a gift for someone else? Instead of overalls for himself or a fancy saddle for his horse, Mose wanted to buy something for Odelia? Her throat tightened.

"It's taffeta you want," she said. "Red taffeta."

Mose grinned. "Yes'm. Taff'ta. Kin you make one up in the right size?"

"I'll make you a fine petticoat, Mose. You just leave it to me." She brushed aside his effusive thanks, and when he tramped on down the boardwalk, Jane found herself humming as she scooped the sweepings into a tin dustpan.

Some men, like Mose, were soldiers *and* princes, she decided. His hands might get dirty, but his spirit was fit to walk with kings.

"Well, now, did you ever?" she said aloud. "The minute I started figuring how many yards of taffeta I will need, my 'despond' just evaporated as if by magic." Maybe Mose was not only a soldier and a prince, but a conjure man as well!

By late afternoon Jane's eyes stung and her back ached from bending over her makeshift cutting table. She laid the pattern pieces for four chemises over the back of the single chair, then began to hang the lengths of yardage for five petticoats—one of scarlet taffeta—and three long cambric nightgowns over a smooth wooden dowel she'd nailed into one corner to serve as a closet pole. If she worked quickly, she could mark the darts and baste them before suppertime.

With her back to the doorway, she draped the gored pieces of red taffeta over the rod. When she turned back, she jumped and emitted a little squeak of surprise.

"Oh, Mr. Wilder! Where did you come from?" She pulled the straight-back chair in front of her, to serve as a barrier between them.

Rydell's dark eyebrows lifted. "Something wrong with my being here?" He looked pointedly at the piece of furniture.

"Oh, no, of course not." She gripped the hard maple.

He advanced a step. She stepped back, dragging the chair with her.

"I've got a buggy outside. There's something I want to show you."

"What is it?"

Rydell grinned. "Come with me and see for yourself."

"I cannot. I am terribly busy, and it's almost suppertime."

"You can," he contradicted. "I had Maggie pack us some sandwiches and a jar of cold tea."

"No," she said. "I cannot. Will not." She straightened her spine and clasped her unsteady hands at her waist. "When I am close to you, I...I quite forget that I am a lady."

Rydell strode around the chair, stepped over the orange kitten stretched out on the floor, and cornered Jane before she could escape. "I won't touch you, Jane. I give you my word."

She stared up into the penetrating gray eyes. There was no way to explain. How could she confess it wasn't *him* she did not trust, but herself?

"You have my word," he repeated, his voice quiet. "Come."

Even if she could think of what to say, she could not make a sound. Her throat felt as if it were clogged with straight pins; if she uttered a single word, whether Yes or No, it would hurt.

"Jane?"

When he said her name and looked at her like that,

his eyes steady, his mouth curved in a half smile, she felt her resistance melt away like so much strawberry jam. *What was the matter with her when he was near?*

Nothing was the matter, she told herself. And to prove it, she would go and look at whatever it was he wanted to show her, and that would be that. Besides, he promised he would not touch her. She knew that much about Rydell Wilder. Yankee or not, he was a man who kept his word.

In silence she bent to lift General Lee away from Rydell's boots, settled the animal into her sewing basket, and lifted her shawl and black mesh reticule from the sewing cabinet where she had laid them.

Rydell pulled the door shut. Jane turned the metal key in the lock and tucked it into her skirt pocket. Then he handed her into the black buggy, patted the harnessed gray mare and stepped around to the other side. Only when he lifted the reins and Jane felt the buggy jerk forward did the tightness in her throat ease.

The balmy air felt like silk on her face and smelled of dust and the bushy pink rose Mr. Mercer grew in a barrel outside his store. She lifted her head and inhaled. A mockingbird called. The buggy wheels crunched over the ground and all at once Jane felt deliciously alive.

"What kind of sandwiches?" she blurted.

Rydell laughed all the way to the edge of town.

The partially framed house came into view as the buggy reached the crest of a gentle, grass-carpeted hill half an hour from town. Rydell watched Jane's face as he guided the mare down the gradually sloping road and pulled up near a lush sugar maple. More than anything else, she looked puzzled.

"Plenty of wind protection from those fir trees to the north, and a year-round spring," he said. "Good area for a garden, too."

Her eyes glowed at the word "garden." Still she said nothing. Rydell began to sweat.

What if she didn't like it? What if she didn't care a fig how he'd positioned the house to be shaded in summer, sun-bathed in winter? How he'd dug a cistern halfway between the spring and the kitchen door so it would be only twenty-five steps to water? What if she preferred living in town, with close neighbors and fences?

You've never even asked her how she likes Dixon Falls. He just assumed that since he loved her, she would like what he liked.

What *he* liked was the peaceful feeling he got out in the open countryside. The view of the hills from any room in his new house. What Jane liked was a mystery. At times, like right now, everything about Jane was a mystery.

He didn't even know how she felt—really felt—about him. He was pretty certain she hadn't done much in the way of physical interaction with a male. She hadn't had much opportunity when her father was alive, and the townfolk still called her Queen Jane behind her back. Except for that forward stranger, Lucas, no man dared to approach her but himself.

He looped the reins into a loose knot and shot a glance at her as he climbed down from the buggy.

She gazed at the half-framed house, the soft, green hills and the grove of maple trees on the next hill, her blue eyes wide, her fine dark brows lifted in a question.

He reached to help her out of the buggy, and she grasped his hand. "Whose land is this?" she breathed.

"Mine. Do you like it?"

"Y-yes."

Rydell's heart did a somersault inside his chest.

"And no. It seems awfully…" She searched for a word.

"Remote?" he supplied.

Jane shook her head as she stepped onto the ground. "Big. It seems very large, for a…well, for a man who lives in a single room at the Excelsior Hotel."

He released her hand. Every fiber of his being wanted to sweep her into his arms and hold her close, but he had given his word. "My needs are very simple, Jane."

She looked at him, tilting her head so the late afternoon sunlight shone through her dark hair; it brought out auburn highlights he'd never seen before. A curious expression spread over her face, her mouth forming a soft pink O. Rydell gritted his teeth and stuffed both hands in his trouser pockets.

"Tell me," she began in a low voice. "If it is not too personal, that is. How did you manage to acquire all this?" She swept one hand toward the house. "How did you start out?"

Something occurred to him then. While he had

been all too aware of Jane for years, watching her grow up, chafing at her virtual imprisonment in her father's house, gauging the state of her emotions by the music she played on the piano in the evenings, Jane had not been equally aware of him. In fact, she knew very little about him.

Rydell swallowed. He was just an ordinary man, not a gentleman such as she'd been groomed for. Still, he couldn't lie to her.

"I started small. Came to town broke and hungry and Aaron Legerman let me sleep in an empty horse stall at his livery stable."

"Where was your family?"

"Don't have one." He took a deep breath. "My mother died young. I—" he hesitated "—never knew who my father was."

She nodded, but did not look away. "How ever did you survive?" She took a step toward the shade under the spreading maple.

"Worked. Shoveled manure. Brushed down horses. Ate a lot of beans and tried to get some schooling."

"I know," she said in a soft voice. "I used to see you walk past the house in the morning. Your trousers were always too short."

"I grew up pretty fast, I guess."

"And you did, didn't you? Get schooling, I mean?"

"I did. Not as much as I'd like, but enough."

"After that first day, when they teased me so awfully, Papa and Mama tutored me at home. I always wished...but it doesn't matter now. Tell me then, how did you advance yourself? I don't mean to pry, but I need to know—I mean I would like to hear how one succeeds at earning a livelihood."

He shot her a quick look. Her wide blue eyes looked into his with utter honesty. "Lefty Springer hired me to ride shotgun on his express wagon. I saved every penny I could and when Lefty wanted to retire, I bought him out."

Jane studied him with such intensity it made him squirm. "What about the bank? And all this land?"

"I figured the town needed a bank, what with the sawmill and all. I used the freight business as collateral and started one up. For a while I worked the freight line and the bank at the same time. Later, I bought the land. For the house, well, I'm using the last of my savings."

"And that is exactly what I intend to do," Jane announced. "Work very, very hard and earn money. But I must confess it seems extraordinarily slow and difficult at times."

Rydell grinned. "How about 'back-breaking' and 'soul-bending'? Every working man—or woman— feels that way most every day of the year. Goes with the territory." He retrieved the wicker lunch basket and a blanket from the buggy and spread it in the shade.

"It isn't the effort I mind so much," Jane said when she had settled herself on the soft wool. "It's the slowness. I'm afraid Mama's going to get sick before I can—"

Rydell turned to face her. "You don't have to go back, Jane." His eyes held hers for a long moment. "You could stay out here in Oregon."

"Oh, but I cannot. I promised Mama, you see. I promised I would take her home to Marion County. She does love it so. She has been dreadfully unhappy ever since we came out west."

"What about you?"

She stiffened. Working her fingers back and forth on the blanket weave, she blinked away tears. Rydell's gut tightened. Jane—his Jane—was suffering and he could do nothing.

Nothing except offer her rescue.

"Your mother has lived her life. It's your turn now."

Her chin snapped up. "My mother's life is certainly not over! Why, she reads Mr. Tennyson every evening, and her appetite is much perked up since Odelia came."

Rydell groaned. It was the wrong thing to say. To a woman looking for something to hook her life onto, an aging mother could serve as a perfect excuse to avoid living her own life.

"Jane," he began again. "Jane, listen. Think for a minute. You can give your mother the care and attention she deserves. But you don't owe her your life."

"Oh, but I do so want to make her smile again. I want Mama to be happy, like...like she was years ago, at Montclair." Her voice broke.

To keep himself from touching her, Rydell shifted the picnic basket between them. "Goddammit, Jane, I'm trying to ask you—"

"I know," she interrupted. "And I wish you wouldn't. It's burden enough that if I cannot repay the three hundred dollars I pledged myself to—"

"Forget the loan," he blurted. "I told you that night behind Jensen's barn that I love you. By God, I want to marry you! Not because of some damned bargain we made, but because I've wanted you for so many years it's like you're part of me."

"But...but I don't think I love you." Jane's eyes grew shiny. "Up until a few days ago, I wasn't sure I even *liked* you."

"Yes, you do. You just don't know it yet." He rummaged in the basket. "Here, have a sandwich. You can't consider a proposal on an empty belly."

Jane laid her hand on his forearm. "Mr. Wilder..."

"Rydell," he snapped. "Look at me, Jane. I may not know who my daddy is, but I sure as blazes know who *I* am, and what I want. And you know these things, too." He unwrapped the napkin-swathed sandwich and held it out. *Damnation, his hand was shaking!*

"Marry me. I can care for you and keep your mother safe and as content as she's ever gonna be out here. That house I'm building is for us. It's big enough for your momma and for Odelia, too. I can give you a good life."

Without a word, she took the sandwich, bit off a mouthful, and chewed for such a long time Rydell thought he would explode. He upended the jar of cold tea and gulped down a mouthful.

No use. The fire in his gut was flaring out of control. He didn't know what it was—frustration? Anger? Desire? He just knew that it was burning him up inside, and he was trapped just like a fox cornered by baying hounds.

He'd spent his whole life wanting her. He couldn't give up. He couldn't let her go.

And blazing balls of lightning, it was beginning to look like no matter what he did, he couldn't have her, either!

Chapter Nineteen

Jane stared at him. Had she heard correctly? He wanted her to marry him? *Break her promise to Mama?*

Now, wasn't that just like a Yankee? Go marching willy-nilly after whatever they wanted, running roughshod over people, over plantations that had been built up from nothing but raw earth and had flourished for a hundred years? It made her so mad she could spit nails!

And, she had to admit, she was mad because it scared her right down to her shoe tops. Rydell Wilder, and everything he stood for, scared the wits out of her. All this talk about Mama and houses and... marriage. To say nothing of the dangerous, shimmery way she felt when he kissed her.

Heat rose in her midsection at the memory of his mouth on hers, the silky, floating sensation of well-being she had never before experienced. Oh, mercy yes, she liked the feeling all right. Liked it almost as much as the heady combination of elation and pride that filled her when she watched her beautiful blue dress and the mint-green Swiss muslin take shape.

Well, Jane Charlotte, now you find yourself in a muddle!

Beside her, Rydell cleared his throat. "I'm offering you a good solution."

"Ye-es," Jane said, drawing out the word. Thoughtfully she nibbled her sandwich down to the crust. "It is indeed admirable how you rose to success. I see that I have much to learn. Much to do."

She did wish her mentor in the business trade wasn't a Yankee. It was humiliating, really, to be tutored by the enemy. Not only did he hold her loan, but he stood to gain when...if...

Pooh! She wouldn't let him win, not for all the tea in China. And she wouldn't marry him, no matter what. She refused to be settled into the rough, uncivilized life of a married woman out here in the West. A woman could not vote, had no say about who served as sheriff or what laws were adopted, could not even own property in her own name. Why, she was no more free than Odelia was back home at Montclair, before the war. It was a sobering thought.

Rydell handed her the jar of cool tea. Lost in her own thoughts, Jane sipped and swallowed until he drew the container out of her hand and replaced it with another sandwich.

"To think," she said, gesturing at the half-built house, "you did all this by yourself. I can hardly imagine what it must have taken to accomplish so much."

"What it took was hard work," he replied, his voice low. "And something I wanted a whole lot."

"Mr. Wilder...Rydell," she corrected. "I do regard you with admiration. There is something I want a whole lot, as well."

She thought he sat up a little straighter. His hands, which had been digging in the wicker basket, stilled and lay idle, one on his thigh, the other on the blanket near her skirt.

"In fact," she continued, "I want it more than anything!"

She watched his fingers dig into the fabric of his trousers. After a moment, his hand relaxed and he turned his head toward her. The slate-colored eyes sought hers and his lips formed a lopsided smile. His tone, when he spoke, was tinged with exasperation.

"When I kiss you," he began, his voice rough, "it might appear we have something to say to each other."

Jane's breath stopped. Would he...? No, he'd given his word. A man like Rydell would never break his word.

"But," he continued, "when we exchange syllables and sentences, it's like one of us is on the moon."

A sharp needle of guilt pricked her conscience. "Well, I suppose that is true." She had to admit she made no great effort to divine his meaning at times. Words could be so...exact. Binding. Words spoken out loud forced one to think, and there were times— right now, for instance—when she didn't *want* to think. At least not about anything other than earning enough money to purchase food for Mama and Odelia, and making Mama as happy as she could.

"The truth is, Jane, I can't figure you out."

She opened her mouth to reply, but he cut her off. "I can't get close enough to you to figure you out!"

"Why you most certainly do! No other man..." Mercy! She felt the flush start at her chest and surge up to her neck into her hot cheeks.

"...has been as close to me as you. Has held me, and t-touched me, and...well, kissed me. Most thoroughly!"

Rydell laughed softly. "Good God, Jane, stop talking."

She stared at him, perplexed.

He stood up abruptly and faced away from her, jamming both hands into his back pockets. "You say one more word along those lines, and I'm liable to...do all those things, and more, right here and now."

"No, you won't," Jane said, her tone matter-of-fact.

"I won't," he echoed. Anger sharpened his diction.

She tipped her head up. "You said you wouldn't touch me. And if there is one thing I am sure of in this topsy-turvy world, it is that you will not break your word."

He pivoted and gazed down on her. "You know, a sane man would plop you in that buggy and hightail it back to town as fast as old Sugarfoot there can trot." He withdrew his hands from his pockets and folded both arms across his chest.

"A crazy man," he continued, "would say to himself, Hallelujah, she trusts you. Guess that's some progress!''

"I do trust you," Jane said. "And I—well, I do like you. Up to a point, that is."

Rydell groaned. "Come on, Jane. Get in the buggy." He bent to grasp the handles of the picnic basket. "I'm going to get a double whiskey and try to figure out whether today was a Victory or a Defeat."

A dash of cold water trickled into her heated veins. *For you, it was a Victory,* she acknowledged. Rydell had kept his word; he had not laid one finger on her. *For me, it was a Defeat.* A small, insistent part of her innermost-self wished he had.

Rydell drove her home, returned the buggy to the livery stable, then set out on foot for the willow tree on the hill behind Olaf Jensen's barn. When he reached it, he slipped through the pendulous gray-green branches and put his back against the trunk.

Damn, he'd forgotten the whiskey. Two shots of the Silver Cup's private stock bottled in a clean pint jar had seen him through many trials in the past; today he'd have to think things through on his own. He plucked a spear of bunchgrass, rolled it between his lips, and studied the town below him.

Golden light dappled the building fronts along the main street. Dust swirls stirred lazily when a horse passed, puffed against wagon wheels and ladies' black high-top shoes, licked at their skirt hems. The just-scrubbed front window of the Excelsior Hotel winked in the fading sunlight. Maggie would be in the dining room, bustling from the kitchen to the tables. For an instant he thought about supper.

Not hungry, he decided. Or maybe he just didn't want to move. He just wanted to watch the sun go down and not think any more about Jane. *If you can't fix it, better learn to live with it.*

Wispy strips of cloud blushed peach and then flamed into burgundy and purple as the fiery globe sank toward the distant smoke-colored mountains. He chewed the grass blade slowly.

What the heck was he doing wrong? Was he supposed to learn something from all this? Whatever it was, it was more slippery than a fish.

He thought over what he'd revealed to Jane about his earlier life. She seemed impressed, not by him personally, but by the idea that hard work could gain what you wanted.

Well, maybe. For the first time in his life, Rydell questioned the belief that had guided his life up until now. Maybe there was more to it than hard work and a dream. Winning a woman wasn't as straightforward as delivering a payroll shipment or establishing a bank. Even building a house, holding a respectable position in society—none of it mattered in the end. Regardless of how hard he'd worked all these years, *she* had to want it. She had to want *him*.

He guessed maybe she didn't. At least not enough to give up her bone-deep prejudice against the North. Not enough to give up her preference for a ''gentleman,'' or the social position her ma and pa thought was so important.

Hell's bells, she thought he wasn't good enough.

Rydell straightened. Well, by Jupiter, she was wrong. Once he'd seen something in Jane, or thought he had, that first day when she'd come to school and the other students had taunted her. *Queen Jane... stuck up...and plain.*

She hadn't cried or hung on the teacher's skirts. She had stood up to them with a kind of courage and honesty reflected in her eyes. She probably would have fought back if he hadn't stepped in and done it for her.

Now...

Now he didn't know. He watched the clouds turn from vermilion to lavender and then to gray. He hated it when the rich colors of the sky finally faded away; it was like working up a hunger and then going to bed with an empty belly.

Like wanting Jane and watching her slip out of his grasp.

He bit down on the grass blade as something in the town spread below him caught his eye. A man, tall in the saddle, with lanky dark hair and a dark hat with a sharp curl in the brim.

Lucas. He narrowed his eyes and studied the man's slow progress along the now-shadowed street. Just before Lucas reached the bank building, he drew rein. Bending low, he peered in the window of Jane's dressmaking shop, then righted himself and moved on toward the bank.

Rydell got to his feet. If Lucas had intended to make a deposit, he'd have come earlier in the day, before the bank closed. Unless he wanted to...

Rydell sucked in his breath. But why would a man steal from the same bank that held his own money?

For a full minute he tried to control his breathing and sort out the possibilities. Maybe he should borrow a horse from Olaf Jensen and go for the sheriff.

Lucas reached the edge of town and doubled back. The tall man walked his mount at an unhurried pace, pausing every few steps as if looking for someone. Despite the balmy summer air, the man looked like he was cold. Lonely, maybe.

An irrational surge of fellow-feeling welled up in Rydell's chest. Poor bastard. Except for some good luck and a few breaks, that might be himself down there, riding alone into a town that didn't want him. The thought made his jaw tighten.

When Lucas dismounted in front of the Excelsior Hotel, Rydell shook off the nagging sense of foreboding he felt. He decided he'd take his supper tonight with Lefty Springer.

He shouldered his way through the drooping willow fronds and headed down the faint trail to Lefty's tidy cabin in back of the stable. Later, he'd mosey on out to Jane's house, just to check on things.

It was full dark when Rydell set off from Lefty's small cabin and headed up the hill toward the house at the crest. He kept a sharp eye peeled for Lucas's roan gelding, noting that it was no longer tethered to the Excelsior Hotel hitching post. Had the man ridden into town just for a drink or some supper? Or was it a poker game that drew him?

He didn't care, as long as he wasn't anywhere near

Jane. Rydell lengthened his stride. For some reason
he didn't completely trust Lucas. The man had all the
markings of an hombre who was hiding something.

Halfway up the hill the big two-story house came
into view. Jupiter, the place was lit up like a circus!
As he walked, a light winked on upstairs, and just as
quickly was extinguished. Someone going to bed.
Jane? He knew she slept on the second floor; he'd sat
across the road enough times, listening to the piano
until she blew out the lamp and his gaze followed the
wavering light of a candle carried up the stairs.

Tonight no music drifted on the warm, still air.
Shadows moved behind the white lace curtains, and
then he heard the front screen door slap. Someone—
Jane, he guessed from the slim shape silhouetted
against the lighted window—stepped out onto the
porch and settled into the porch swing. At the same
instant, something moved beside the house.

Rydell quickened his pace. The rump of a horse
disappeared around the corner. In the dark, he
couldn't tell the color, something dark. Maybe a roan,
maybe not.

"Who's there?" Jane's voice carried over the rasp
of crickets.

Rydell waited to see if the horseman would answer,
straining his ears for the sound of hooves. Silence.
Either the rider had noiselessly slipped off behind the
house, or he was still there, waiting. He peered into
the dark.

"It's me," he called at last. "Rydell. Didn't want
to scare you. I was just passing by, thought I'd walk
off my supper before turning in."

"I'm making fudge," she said. "The kitchen is like an oven, so I came out here where it's cooler to stir it."

Fudge? Educated, refined Jane Davis would stand over a hot stove making fudge?

"Mind if I stop by after I finish my walk?" He didn't wait for her to answer, but strode past the porch and circled the house to make sure no one was there. Too dark to see tracks, he acknowledged. He sure would like to know which direction they led.

The back of his neck prickled. He decided he would sit with Jane until she went inside.

Odelia bustled through the screen door. "Miss Jane, you want Ah should crack dem walnuts for de—?"

One look at Jane and Rydell side-by-side in the swing, and the sturdy woman pivoted back toward the house. "'Scuse me, honey. Ah din't know you was entertainin' a caller. Evenin', Mr. Rydell."

Rydell suppressed a chuckle. "Good evening, Odelia."

The screen door swished shut behind her. "Y'all jes' go right on with yo'…" The rich, deep voice faded.

"Stirring," Jane supplied. She cradled a blue speckled enamel saucepan on her lap, making figure eights in the dark chocolate with a wooden spoon. For a moment there was no sound but the thud of the utensil against the bottom of the pan.

Rydell watched her fingers grip the handle. "I made fudge once."

Jane laughed. "You! Are you fooling me?"

"Nope. 'Bout ten years ago. Boiled it till it looked sticky enough and dumped it out in an old tin cake pan."

Jane's stirring hand slowed. "And then what?"

"It cooled so hard I had to bust it up with a hammer to get it out. Tasted good, though. Too hard to chew, so I just rolled it around in my mouth. One piece would last for an hour."

Jane laughed again, and Rydell began to relax. Whoever had been hanging around earlier was gone, the night air was soft and scented with the rose rambling along the picket fence, and Jane was smiling at him. He lifted the pan of fudge out of her hands and took over the stirring.

"When it's not shiny anymore, it's ready," she said.

Rydell peered at the mixture. "Too dark to tell."

"Let me taste it, then." She dipped her forefinger into the pan and licked it clean. His groin tightened watching her. "Stirred enough?"

Without speaking, she again coated her finger and offered it to him. He closed his lips over the tip.

"Oh!" She sucked in a gasp of air and snatched her hand away.

"Sweet," he murmured.

She grasped the pan with both hands. "It must be ready. I'll just step into the kitchen and—"

The screen door whapped open and a dark hand held out a tin pie pan. "Ah done buttered it already, jes' need the choc'late poured in."

Rydell grabbed the tin pan. Odelia shot him a wide grin and retreated into the house.

He upended the fudge container, scraped out the contents with the wooden spoon and spread the candy evenly around the edges of the tin. His mouth still dry from the exquisite feel of Jane's fingertip against his tongue, he didn't speak until he thought he could trust his voice.

"Want to lick the spoon?" he said at last.

"What? Oh, the spoon. Mercy me, I haven't done that since I was a child."

He held the utensil up between them. With a girlish laugh, she closed her hand over his wrist, pulling the spoon to her lips. "Oh, it is good."

Rydell gave her the spoon, then set the pan of warm candy on the wide porch railing to harden. From inside the house Odelia's rich voice accompanied the sound of dishes sloshing in the kitchen sink.

"…way down in Egypt's lan'…tell ol' Pharoah…let mah people go…"

The rattling continued, and the singing went on as well, punctuated by the muffled clank of iron cookware. He stretched his legs out in front of him and nudged the swing into silent motion.

"My mother used to sing," he heard himself say. "'Pop Goes the Weasel' and 'Shenendoah.' Yankee tunes," he added.

"Mama sang, too. Hymns, mostly. And sometimes 'Lorena' or 'Bonnie Blue Flag.' Confed—Southern songs." As an afterthought she said quietly, "She doesn't sing much anymore."

He could hear her steady breathing, along with a soft, liquid sound. Her tongue, stroking the spoon.

Think about something else! He lifted off his hat

and fanned himself with the brim. Inside, Odelia thumped something onto the stove and lifted her voice in another song.

"Oh, Shenendoah…Ah love yo' daughter…."

Rydell closed his eyes. Hunger such as he had never known gnawed at his insides. He wanted a home. A wife. Children.

Oh, Lord, he wanted to belong to someone!

To Jane.

He reached for her. She met him halfway, tipped her face up to his and let him find her mouth. She tasted of chocolate. He pulled her against him, stroked the back of her neck where her collar dipped. He couldn't get enough of her. When she made a small moan in her throat, Rydell's entire body seemed to burst into flame.

Jane. Oh, God, Jane.

Something whooshed through the doorway. "Miss Jane, come quick! Yo' momma's gone."

Chapter Twenty

Jane jerked out of Rydell's arms. "Gone? Gone where?"

"Dunno, child," the older woman panted. "She readin' in the parlor las' Ah looked. Now she not dere no mo'."

"Perhaps she went up to bed?" Jane offered in a small voice.

Rydell was on his feet before she finished the sentence.

Odelia wrung her hands. "I look ever'where upstairs. Ain't no place."

"Check the root cellar," Rydell ordered. "Jane, go inside and look in every room, every closet. The pantry, too, and then the attic. I'll search the garden and the orchard."

Odelia tramped down the porch steps and headed around toward the back of the house. White-faced, Jane turned to Rydell. "She had on her lilac wrapper. And bed slippers, blue ones."

He grasped her shoulders. "We'll find her. She can't have gone far."

She spun away and disappeared inside the screen door. He heard her choked voice call out. "Mama? Mama, where are you?"

Rydell started for the peach orchard. Once he left the porch, darkness enveloped him, so thick he couldn't see his hand before his face. He paused to let his eyes adjust, wished he had a horse.

He took a stumbling step forward. He remembered that Jane's father had planted his peach trees in neat rows; if he could locate just one, he could estimate where the next one would be, and then could continue until he reached the back edge of the property. With every step he took, he prayed that Leah Davis was safe.

Rydell waited to move forward until he could make out the shape of a small tree in front of him. A peach tree, he guessed from the pungent scent. Good. From here he could search every square foot of orchard if he had to. If Jane's mother was out here, he'd find her.

"Mrs. Davis? Can you hear me?"

He kept walking, branches slapping against his face, until he stumbled into another tree. Again he cupped his hands around his mouth. "Mrs. Davis?" Maybe she'd come to visit her husband's grave site. He wished to hell he knew where it was.

It took the better part of an hour to comb the entire orchard, and still he found no trace of her. Sweat soaked his shirt collar, plastered the linen fabric to his back. Where the devil could she—

A faint cry, high and thin like a child's, stopped him in his tracks. He cocked his head, listening.

Behind him. Good Lord, he must have walked right by her in the dark. He pivoted, straining his eyes into the blackness. "Mrs. Davis? Leah Davis, where are you?"

He waited a moment, then moved toward a rustling sound.

She sat under a tree, almost hidden beneath the thick branches, her back straight as a ramrod, her hands folded in her lap. The lilac wrapper covered her bent knees. Rydell knelt in front of her and she raised her head.

"Ah'm waiting for the train," she said in a small, clear voice. "Ah would not want to miss the train."

Rydell took her small hands in his. "What train is that, Mrs. Davis?"

"Why, the passenger coach home to Marion County. Are you the station master?"

Rydell swallowed over a lump the size of a lump of coal. "No, ma'am, I'm not. Your daughter, Jane, sent me to find you and escort you back to the house."

"Oh, but you see, suh, Jane Charlotte is going with me. She'd best hurry."

He closed his eyes as pain sliced into his heart. "Allow me to help you up, ma'am."

She smiled up at him. "Oh, no thank you. The train, you know. Jane promised."

What could he say to her? With all his strength he wished he could save this frail, beaten woman from the agony she endured. And Jane...God almighty, how she must suffer, watching her mother drift away like this. No wonder she was distracted when he showed her the house he was building.

He leaned over and gathered Leah Davis into his arms. "I'm taking you back to the house." He slipped one arm under her knees and stood up. "Watch your head, ma'am."

Rydell trudged over the uneven ground as fast as he judged safe, the small burden trembling in his arms. "Don't be afraid, ma'am. You're safe now."

Far ahead through the trees he saw a flickering light. Someone moved toward them with a lantern.

"Mistah Rydell?" Odelia's scratchy voice floated to him from far away. "Y'all out dere?"

"Rydell?" It was Jane's voice. A bubble of joy floated into his chest at the sound of her voice calling his given name.

"Mama?"

Rydell stepped toward the wavering glow ahead of him. "She's safe," he shouted. He strode on, using his shoulder to shield Mrs. Davis from drooping branches. The light bobbed toward him, and he quickened his pace. "Just a few more yards, now, ma'am."

She patted his arm. "Yoah very kind, suh, to see me home."

Out of the dark loomed a large figure, a lantern held high over her head. "Dat you, Miss Leah?"

In the next instant Jane was beside him. "Mama? Oh, Mama, we were so worried! Are you all right?"

"She's fine," Rydell said. "Just a bit…confused."

She fell into step at his side, holding on to her mother's arm as he moved out of the orchard and through the kitchen garden toward the back door.

Odelia scrambled ahead, shining the lantern on the back porch steps.

"Right through dat door an' up de stairs. Her room's de fust one you comes to."

Unwilling to relinquish her grip on her mother, Jane squeezed through the doorway alongside Rydell. "Right up here," she directed. She slipped ahead of him on the staircase.

Odelia panted up behind them, still holding up the lantern. "Ah'll make some hot cocoa fo' Miss Leah and tuck her into bed."

At the indicated doorway, Rydell halted. Odelia fluttered around to one side.

"You gotta let go of her sleeve, honey. Else we all gwine stuck in de door."

Jane obeyed. "A-all right."

"Miss Jane, go on down t'the pantry an' see if Mose brought 'nuf milk for to make fo' cups o' co-coa."

The black woman watched Jane head back down the stairs. "An' heat up some water to wash her pore feet!" she called after her.

"Gots to give dat chile sumpin' to do," she said under her breath. She pointed the way to the quilt-covered double bed. "Otherwise, she go crazy her-self."

In the kitchen, Jane paced back and forth while a teakettle of water slowly came to a simmer. The re-mainder of the milk Mose had left warmed in an en-amelware saucepan. What could be taking so long upstairs? Surely Mr. Wilder…Rydell, she cor-rected…was not needed to help Mama into her night clothes? That would be most improper. She must offer him something when he came down, some hot cocoa, or perhaps a bit of the fudge she'd made earlier. It must be cool by now, and ready to cut into pieces.

Oh, she couldn't keep her thoughts in coherent order to save her life!

When Odelia ushered Rydell into the kitchen, she heaved a sigh of relief.

"You go on up, honey. Say good-night to yo' momma. She plumb tuckered, and her feet, my oh my, they's black as mine!"

Jane bolted through the doorway. Rydell heard her light footsteps running up the stairs.

Odelia stirred the pan of milk. "Ah don' know what we gwine do 'bout Miss Leah. Look to me like she done lost her mind."

Rydell could think of nothing to say. He understood with perfect clarity what Jane was facing, could only imagine the anguish and the sense of helplessness he would feel in the same situation. For the first time in his life he was glad his mother had not lived. Nothing could frighten her or hurt her, ever again. She was safe.

There were things worse than death, he thought suddenly. Watching someone you love lose touch with reality was one of them.

When Jane returned, he rose from the chair Odelia had pressed him into and moved toward her. "Come out on the porch," he said in a low voice.

She followed him without speaking, and when the screen door flapped shut behind them, she turned to face him. "I—I want to thank you for what you did."

"Is she all right?"

Jane sucked in a breath. "Physically she is un-harmed. Her spirit, however…"

Rydell nodded. "She said she was waiting for the train."

"To Marion County," Jane supplied. "I know. I made her a promise."

Rydell's heart wrenched at the weariness in her voice. She kept talking, her tone thoughtful.

"There's something I want to tell you." She swal-lowed, pivoted away, and then turned back to him. "I have never had a friend in Dixon Falls. Perhaps that was mostly my fault, as I made little effort to extend myself socially. But I want you to know this, Mr.…Rydell."

He let out a long, slow breath, afraid to speak, afraid to move a muscle. His heart hammering, he waited for her next words.

"I acknowledge that I have not been kind in the past, partly because of your Northern background. And for that I wish to apologize. But I want you to know that, after tonight, I would be proud to call you a friend."

If she had offered him the crown of a kingdom, he could not be more moved. Slowly he took her small, soft hands in his and lifted them to his lips.

"My dear Jane," he whispered over her knuckles. "Queen Jane." He turned her hands over and pressed his mouth against her palm.

"Always."

He lingered over her other palm, then raised his head and looked into her eyes.

"I will always be the queen's man, Jane. Always."

Chapter Twenty-One

Jane slapped her cutting shears down onto the plank table with a resounding thunk. She hadn't the foggiest idea how to proceed. "Stitch up a shirt for Mose," Odelia had begged. "One that's coolin', not like that ol' flannel he wear all de time. Sumpin' dat breathes when he work over dem hot coals."

Something that breathes? Yesterday morning she had purchased four yards of tan linen, sponged it off to size it, and spread it out to dry overnight. Now she pursed her lips as she stared down at the pattern pieces, taken from one of Mose's "shirts fo' de rag-bag," Odelia said.

How could a shirt, plastered to a working man's perspiring body on a hot day, possibly be "cooling"? Linen was better than wool, certainly; that was one step in the right direction. He could roll up the sleeves. Unbutton the collar. He could even flap his arms to make a breeze of sorts—anything to let some air...

Of course! She snatched up the scissors. Why had no one thought of it before? True, the idea was a bit odd, but it was such a simple solution! Afire with her idea, she cut out the pieces, marked the gathers, and laid all but one over the sewing machine. The back section she would cut double, one layer of linen, and one of…what?

She rummaged through her remnant basket. Something light, something— yes! She snatched up a length of hat veiling. The very thing!

Sidestepping the kitten, its fluffy orange body arched on the floor in a patch of sunshine from the open door, she snipped out a large piece of the sheer material and mated it with the matching one in linen. Like an interlining, only better. *Cooler!* She couldn't wait to tell Odelia about her innovation.

Now what? She still had the red taffeta petticoat for Odelia to hem, a half-dozen white batiste corset covers to baste and stitch up, and, let's see, the rose sateen morning gown. Perhaps she should finish that first.

She turned a thoughtful gaze on the now-bare dress form in her display window. Yesterday morning Evangeline Tanner had stopped in to admire the green dotted muslin dress and ended up purchasing it, along with some pale green netting for a matching hat. Her heart swelling with pride, Jane had stammered her thanks for the four dollars and fifty cents Evangeline pressed into her hand. Last night she added three of those dollars to the savings jar under her mattress.

How many new dresses might the mill owner's wife buy in a season? Jane resolved to have some tempting new confection in her window every time Mrs. Tanner passed by the shop.

She lifted the cover off the sewing machine and found the basted-together top and the skirt pieces, the lining neatly hand-stitched in place. Just as she reached for a wound bobbin of rose cotton thread, Evangeline Tanner herself stepped through the doorway.

"Oh, Jane, you will never guess what!"

Jane looked up in alarm. "The green muslin did not fit?"

The woman smiled. "No, it's not that. It fits most beautifully."

"I regret that the rose sateen is not yet finished. My mother is…unwell." She lifted two of the skirt pieces and pinned them together. "I have been sewing only at night, and am just stitching it together this minute."

Evangeline laid her hand on Jane's arm. "Then stop. I have a much larger order for you."

Jane gaped at her. "Order? Whatever do you mean?"

"Just listen." The woman's dark eyes shone with pleasure. "I have a…friend who wishes you to sew an entire wedding trousseau—everything, nightgowns, petticoats, morning wrappers and, best of all, the wedding gown!"

"Wedding gown? But I have never sewn a—"

"Oh, say yes, Jane. My friend is most anxious to engage your talents."

"Why does she not come herself? Does she not wish to select the fabric and discuss the style?"

Evangeline dimpled. "My friend has seen your work and admires it and prefers that you make the decisions. After all, your gowns are very lovely. Very unusual.''

"But I must know her measurements," Jane protested. "Otherwise, things may not fit correctly."

Evangeline pointed to the dress form in the window. "That size. Make everything to fit that form and it will be just perfect. And oh, Jane, I have not yet told you the best part!"

"Best part?" Her head spun so she could barely articulate the words. "There is more?"

"Much more. My friend will pay handsomely if you will undertake this—three hundred and fifty dollars. In cash! Providing that the wedding gown is finished by September first." She sent Jane a beaming smile. "Oh, I almost forgot—and a hat to complement the dress."

"Hat," Jane echoed.

"The ceremony will be outside, so a broad-brimmed straw would be appropriate, don't you think?"

"Broad brim," Jane repeated. "Wedding gown. Three hundred and fifty…"

She could pay her debt to Rydell Wilder and have money left over for train fare! She could—she *would*—take Mama home to Marion County as she had promised.

"Mrs. Tanner…"

"Evangeline. Do call me Evangeline. I feel we are to be friends."

Jane swallowed over the tightness in her throat. "Evangeline, then. Tell Letit— Tell your friend I will be pleased to do this. Tell her that I…understand the reasons for not coming to me personally.'' She spoke over a tremor in her voice. ''Tell her that I intend to sew the most beautiful wedding gown this county has ever seen.''

The mill owner's wife smiled, a delighted gleam in her eye. ''Oh, I do so love a secret, don't you?''

''I—I suppose so.'' She wouldn't spoil Evangeline's fun by confessing she had already guessed who her ''friend'' was.

But she also began to wonder who Letitia Price was planning to marry.

Rydell clapped his arm across Lefty Springer's shoulders and propelled him across the schoolyard. ''Come on, old man. I hear a big, juicy steak calling me.''

''Now don't you rush me none, Dell. I'm an old man, like you say. I'm entitled to move no faster'n I need to. Need to slow down and savor things along the way, like that rose bush Rafe Mercer keeps waterin'.''

''Right now I need to savor a steak. Maggie promised me a plate-sized hunk of beef.''

''Now, lookee there, Dell.'' He pointed to the worn plank teeter-totter balanced on a sawhorse in the center of the yard, a child on each end. ''Why, that gets my heart all swole up!''

Rydell recognized the red-headed boy with the freckles. Tommy, the boy with the nickel and the orange kitten he'd taken to Jane. The little girl at the opposite end, perched on a folded blanket, had bright blue eyes and wheat-colored corkscrew curls. Tommy, Rydell noted, couldn't take his eyes off her.

Her starched white pinafore fluttered as the board tipped up and down, hoisting first one, then the other child high into the hot summer sunshine.

Lefty chuckled. "Looks kinda like true love, don't it?"

"Kinda like courting Jane," Rydell murmured. "Whenever one of them makes a move, it pushes the other out of reach."

"They're sure 'nuff balanced opposite each other. Saw a circus once, had a flyin' trapeze act. The girl turns a somersault in midair and her partner reaches out and catches her. Perfect timing."

He sent Rydell a significant look. "Ya ask me, you an' Jane doin' the same thing, only her timing's off. She swings up high, but you ain't there to catch her. She's here, see." He demonstrated with his left hand. "And you're over here. You come toward each other, but jumpin' jigsaws, Dell, you don't—"

Rydell glared at his friend. "Lefty," he said in a quiet voice. "Shut the hell up."

"Dell, I'm not gonna. You want me to hush up 'bout you an' Miss Jane, you hurry up and marry that girl."

"Don't think I'm not trying!"

"Oh, I see you tryin' all right. *Tryin'* ain't good enough in a romantical sit-y-ation. Gotta *catch* her."

Rydell gave the older man's shoulder a friendly punch. "Why don't you mind your own business?"

"Cuz I'm old—you said so yourself. When ya get

old is when you get to mind ev'rybody *else's* business!''

Rydell laughed in spite of himself. ''Here's a proposition, Lefty. If you shut up, I'll buy your dinner.''

''Deal. Thought you'd never ask.''

Rydell punched him again.

''Well, I swan, Miss Jane.'' Odelia held up the completed linen shirt Jane had made for Mose Freeman, shaking her head as she turned it over and over in her dark hands. ''Nevah saw nuthin' like dat it in all my born days. You sure it's decent?''

Jane laughed with delight. ''Of course it's decent. Only the wearer will know there's a flap here…'' She lifted the wide back panel, revealing the sheer netting under-piece. ''…and these vents here, in the gussets under the arms.''

''Uh-huh.'' Odelia looked doubtful.

''Whenever Mose moves,'' Jane assured her, ''the air will flow in and cool him off. Don't you see?''

''Uh-huh,'' the older woman said without enthusiasm. ''If'n he even consent to wear it. Mose mighty set in his ways, like mos' men.''

Jane thought over the remark. Her only knowledge of a man's daily habits was based on observation of her father. True, Garrett Davis liked his shirt collars starched stiff and his eggs boiled soft, and she had never seen him in anything other than a wool suit coat and trousers, even picking peaches in the orchard. Would Papa have laughed at this unusual shirt she had dreamed up? Would he have worn it?

More to the point, would Mose? ''There is only

one way to find out," she announced. She lifted the garment from Odelia's hands and folded it the way shown in the mercantile catalogs—collar and front exposed, sleeves hidden but for the cuffs.

Odelia patted her hand. "Is a fine shirt, honey. He goin' specially like dem buttons."

Jane couldn't help smiling. The buttons were handsome. She'd snipped them off one of Papa's shirts, still hanging in the upstairs hall closet next to her mother's old afternoon dresses. The mottled brown tortoiseshell looked even better against the tan linen. She scanned the black woman's still pensive face. "Don't worry, Odelia. If Mose doesn't like it, I'll make him another one."

"Y'all don' mind, Miss Jane, ol' 'Delia go down an' give Mose his shirt right now. Ain't too soon to start coolin' his skin. Dat man work so hard in dis heat he likely fry up 'fore summer's over."

"Yes, go on, Odelia. I will stay with Mama. It's too hot to go back to the shop until evening."

"Yo' workin' too hard, too, honey. Lookin' peaked mos' ev'ry mornin' an' half-dead by nightfall."

"I am perfectly fine," Jane assured her. "I—I have not been sleeping well ever since—" She broke off as her throat tightened.

"Since dat night. 'Delia know it, and 'Delia know why. Nuthin' you can do fo' yo' momma, child, 'cept give her love. Dat's 'bout all you kin ever do fo' a needy folk." She squeezed Jane in a hug so tight she thought her stays would snap. Mercy, she must loosen her corset in this heat!

Odelia clumped off the porch steps and headed

down the hill toward town, her gray skirt billowing in the hot wind. Just before Jane turned away she glimpsed a flash of red underneath the ballooning garment.

The taffeta petticoat! A funny little hiccup prodded her heart.

Odelia dealt with life as it presented itself. She did what she could in whatever situation she found herself. She worked hard and she loved without reservation. Odelia "made do" with whatever came along.

Well, Jane Charlotte, you shall do the same. To start with, take yourself upstairs and unlace this whalebone prison encasing your rib cage!

"And another thing," she murmured aloud. "I have worn yet another hole in the thumb of my last pair of gloves, but with all the sewing needed for the wedding trousseau of Evangeline's 'friend', I haven't the time to mend them. I think I will simply stop wearing gloves when I go out!"

Evangeline went bare-handed, she had noticed. If the mill owner's wife could, *she* could as well. After all, this wasn't Marion County. This was Douglas County, Oregon. Women out here wore holes in aprons, not gloves. Women out here worked with their hands. Even Evangeline Tanner and Letitia Price must cook and boil laundry and scrub floors at some time or other.

She sank onto a damask-covered chair and studied her hands. A permanent depression marked her forefinger where the cutting shears pressed. She kept her nails cut short now, to avoid snagging the threads of delicate fabric. Her left wrist ached from guiding acres of material under the sewing machine presser foot.

Were these still a lady's hands? She labored day after day, week after week; did that mean she was no longer a lady?

In one way, it did not matter any longer. She had to work. She needed the money. Come September, a mere five weeks away, she would be paid for Letitia Price's completed wedding trousseau, and she and Mama and Odelia would take the train east.

Until then, she would emulate Odelia. She would "make do." And, she resolved, she would do what she could about Mama—love without reservation, as Odelia did. She rose and moved to the foot of the stairs.

"Mama? Mama, I'm going to make you a nice cool glass of lemonade and come sit by your side while you drink it."

Later, when she was alone, she would think about the pile of sewing that awaited her at the dressmaking shop. About Letitia's wedding gown. About Rydell.

Her breath caught. *But I will try ever so hard not to think of the two of them together.*

Chapter Twenty-Two

By mid-August, the summer heat and the hot, dry wind began to take its toll on Jane. She worked in the early morning and went back to the stifling shop each evening to replenish General Lee's water dish and do her pressing. Even though she no longer laced up her corset so tight she could barely move, heating the sadiron or the fluting iron she used to smooth out ruffles and standing over the padded plank she used for an ironing board made her feel faint and short of breath. When it grew too dark in her little shop to thread a needle, she set the kerosene lamp on a nail keg and sewed until midnight with the kitten stretched on the floor beside her. Some nights it was so hot she dragged the single chair into the open doorway to catch even the whisper of a breeze.

In the morning, she avoided looking at her face in the glass over the bureau. Her cheeks were pale, the dark circles deepening under her eyes. September loomed just two weeks away, and Jane drove herself to finish the garments she and Evangeline had chosen—a pretty striped seersucker suit, calico and lawn

Mother Hubbard wrappers, night robes, slips and un-der-petticoats, chemises, embroidered collars, a dozen sheer linen handkerchiefs trimmed in lace, even a lawn dressing sacque and a fine muslin bridal set edged in lace.

And the wedding gown. Jane suggested ivory bro-caded silk with a full train, puffed in the back, with a pointed waist trimmed in lace. Evangeline approved with enthusiasm and insisted on a full-length sheer veil, to be secured at the crown with flowers.

The mill owner's wife stopped in every few days and stayed to chat. At each visit, she lingered a little longer, so that Jane now knew how hard her husband, Mr. Tanner, worked running the mill and how des-perately Evangeline wanted a baby. Once, thumbing through the pattern catalog, the young woman had paused at a page of infant sacques, and Jane had glimpsed tears in her dark eyes.

Rafe Mercer brought her an apple every evening before he locked up the mercantile for the night, and one sweltering morning Maggie stepped in from the Excelsior Hotel dining room with a pitcher of cold tea.

Jane fitted all the garments on the dress dummy in the window, but as she completed each one she laid it away, wrapped in tissue paper, on the top shelf of her wardrobe at home. Already the stack reached three-quarters of the way to the top cedar panel, and she wasn't near finished.

Every week, Mary Two Hats padded quietly through the open door, batting one long-fingered hand at the lazy flies around her face. "You busy-busy, but why lady in window still not dressed?"

"I use her only for fitting," Jane explained. "I am sewing clothes for a lady's bridal trousseau, and the items should not be seen before the wedding."

"With my people, it is different. Every one look on dresses—only bride is hidden." She grinned at Jane. "Who you marry?"

Jane's sewing needle stabbed into her thumb. "Me! Oh, it is not I who will marry. It is to be another lady."

The Indian woman shook her head. "Big waste."

To turn the conversation, Jane gave her a length of blue calico she admired. Still, she smiled every time she recalled Mary Two Hats's words.

That same evening, Jane returned to the shop, turned her chair to catch the fading twilight, and began stitching a delicate lace border around the sleeves of a cambric chemise. Her neck felt hot and sticky in the ruffled white waist, buttoned to her throat. She was so warm the sleeves stuck to her arms and shoulders, and her back prickled, as if someone were watching her.

The sensation grew stronger with every passing minute until she could stand it no longer. She let the fabric fall to her lap. Then she stood up and peered out the doorway.

Both sides of the street looked deserted. Directly across from her shop, the Excelsior Hotel sat bathed in shadows; she guessed it was too hot inside to light the lamps. She drew in a deep breath of the warm, dust-scented air and gazed at the windows on the hotel's top floor.

Was someone watching her? She knew Rydell lived at the Excelsior. Mercy, could he be spying on her?

Her gaze moved to the rooftop and the words died in her throat. Beyond the tall wooden building the sky glowed an ominous red-orange.

Without thinking, she began to run. Suddenly the street was alive with horsemen, wagons, men shouting. The church bell began to clang. In the middle of the street someone grabbed her by the shoulders. "Jane! What are you doing out here?"

She clung to Rydell's arm. "The sky," she gasped. "Look at the sky!"

"It's a range fire," He had to shout over the noise. "To the north. Probably started by lightning, but the wind's blowing it this way."

"This way! You mean toward town?"

"We think we can stop it before it reaches the Jensen place."

Jane froze in horror. "Stop it? How?"

"Quilts. Gunnysacks. Shovels. We'll try to beat it out, clear a firebreak, anything. If we don't it'll take the town."

He yanked her out of the path of a hurtling wagon. "Keep moving, Jane. Otherwise you'll get run down."

"Wh-where are you going?"

"To the mercantile. Rafe got in a shipment of blankets. We'll start with them. Mose Freeman's bringing a pile of jute sacks."

"I can help, too," she screamed over the din.

"No. Go home, Jane. Stay out of the way, where it's safe."

"But my shop? If the town burns…"

He jerked to a stop and gave her a long look. His gray eyes seemed to penetrate her very soul. "Aren't you scared?"

"Of course I'm scared! I'm frightened to death. But it's my town, too!"

An odd look crossed his face. He pulled her into his arms, hugged her so hard her ribs hurt. Irrationally she pictured her corset stays bending to fit his body.

"All right," he said. "But stay close behind me and do exactly what I tell you."

Jane nodded. When he released her, she grasped the back of his shirt and held on tight as he strode toward Mercer's Mercantile.

Bearing an array of shovels and blankets, an army of townspeople marched out past Olaf Jensen's peaceful farm where the fire licked and curled along the ground toward his big red-stained barn. They would make their stand in front of Olaf's winter rye field. The men spread out, tied bandannas over their faces, and began beating at the flames.

The women worked alongside them, dishtowels tied over their heads to protect their hair from sparks, kerchiefs over their mouths and noses. The air was thick with brown smoke. The smell was awful, sharp and sour. Jane thought she would be sick from the searing heat and the stench.

Rydell pulled her to a halt and tied a white handkerchief over the lower half of her face. It smelled clean, like pine soap, but as soon as she drew near the fire line, the smell of burning grass and sagebrush overwhelmed her. She unfolded the blanket he shoved into her hands and began to flail away at the creeping line of fire.

A woman beside her—Maggie from the Excelsior Hotel dining room—whacked away with a multicolored quilt, coughing and choking as the smoke billowed up. A man heaved a shovel full of dirt at her feet, and the smoke thinned.

Jane slapped her blanket against the hot ground until she thought her spine would crack in half. Straightening for a moment, she gasped for breath.

Rydell's voice cut into her tired brain. "What's wrong?"

"I can't get my breath."

"Your corset's probably too tight. You shouldn't be out here, Jane."

"Yes, I should." She turned toward him. "Cut the lacing," she said.

He shot her a surprised look, then reached for his pocketknife. "In front?"

She nodded and began to unbutton her blouse. *Jane Charlotte, are you out of your mind? What on earth would Mama say?*

Mama would not begin to understand. But Jane had a dressmaking business to save. She was part of a town that needed help.

Rydell flicked open the blade. "Sure you don't want to quit and go home where it's safe?"

"Cut them!" she ordered. She drew in a shaky

breath and spread the two halves of the blouse just enough to give him access to the lacings.

"Don't move," he warned. He steadied her with one hand on her shoulder and slit the embroidered muslin corset cover from her neck to her waist. "You women wear too damn many clothes," he muttered.

Carefully he ran the blade down the front of the rigid boned undergarment. The lacings popped apart, and Jane dragged in a gulp of smoky air. Rydell turned away and snapped the knife closed while she hurriedly rebuttoned her blouse. Without a word, he picked up his shovel and resumed scraping a widening patch of bare earth.

Jane stepped forward, swatting the blanket onto the flames at her feet.

It went on for hours. Olaf Jensen's gray-bunned wife brought a wood kindling box filled to the top with sandwiches. Lefty Springer passed up and down the line, a bucket of water and a dipper in his good hand.

They didn't talk, just beat at the flames while smoke blew into their faces and stung their eyes.

"I'd give my eyeteeth for some rain," someone yelled.

Mary Two Hats started to sing, then dropped her smoke-blackened blanket and began to stamp in a circle. "Dance for rain," she called. Just as quickly she snatched up the blanket and resumed her attack on the smouldering grass. She indicated the line of twisting figures, bending and straightening, flapping blankets or banging shovels against the ground. Some of the men stomped at crimson embers with their booted feet.

"White men dance pretty good!" she shouted.

The wind picked up, blowing smoke in their faces. Jane choked in the hot, thick air, her throat raw, her nostrils burning. Lefty moved toward her with the water bucket, but she kept on swinging the square of singed wool. Sparks spat at her feet, swirled under her petticoat.

"Keep moving," Rydell yelled. He leaned against his shovel and gulped water from the dipper Lefty offered. Jane waited while Maggie drank, then took the dipper and sucked in the cooling water as fast as she could. It dribbled off her chin and down the front of her blouse. She swiped one hand at it, leaving a grimy streak across her chest, then noticed smoke curling behind her. Her blanket had caught fire!

Rydell yanked it out of her grasp and stamped out the flames with his boots. When he held it up, a hole the size of a washtub was burned out of the middle. Jane groaned. It was completely useless.

The line of flame danced forward, toward her. She stamped her shoes down hard, then kicked dirt onto the popping sparks. They swirled like fireflies in the suffocating air. She needed something to smother the flames. Anything would do.

She cast a look around her. Maggie flapped her smoking quilt. Rydell bent over his shovel, scooping earth onto the fire.

Jane turned away. Reaching up under her dirt-stained sateen skirt she untied her petticoat and let it shimmy down over her hips. She stepped out of it, gathered it up and swung it against the advancing flames. She worked until she was winded, her throat parched from breathing hot, acrid air, her legs trembling with exhaustion.

Little by little, the flames were beaten back, flying sparks extinguished with shovels full of dirt. Then the men set to work scraping a firebreak between the smouldering prairie grass and Olaf Jensen's rye field.

At first it was only a boot-wide band of bare earth. One tired crew of shovel-wielding men was replaced by another, and while the first crew threw themselves down to catch their breath, the clearing went on. The barrier grew to a yard, then two yards, and still the men worked.

Mose Freeman began digging a trench while the other men argued about starting a backfire.

"The wind's wrong," someone said. "It'll carry that backfire right down our main street!"

"Tanner's right," Rydell shouted. He grabbed a shovel and joined Mose. "Come on, let's dig!"

A dozen men sprang to join them. Maggie and Mary Two Hats found a second water bucket, filled it at Jensen's well, and carried it among the men. Jane went to help Lefty.

"You shore do look a sight, Miz Jane!"

Automatically she touched her hair, then glanced at her front. She'd mis-buttoned her blouse; the two sections of white muslin were awry. Sparks had burned tiny black holes in her sateen skirt, and her petticoat—good heavens! Singed around the hem, the blackened length of once-white cambric stank of smoke and soot.

Mama must not see her in this state! It would frighten away what remained of her wits. She tried not to think about it, concentrated instead on offering the dipper to the men digging the trench.

"Water, Mose?"

The big man straightened. "That mighty kind of you, Miz Jane." He swallowed a mouthful of water, then dumped the rest of the dipper contents over his head.

"Oh, Mose, your new shirt!" Jane stared at the soot-blackened linen garment.

"Don' you worry none, Miz Jane. Ain't nuthin' a bit of lye soap cain't clean up. This the best shirt I ever have! Lets mah back breathe. Not gonna give it up fo' a little dirt!"

"I'll make you another one, Mose. I'll make you a dozen more, if you really and truly like it."

Mose's sweat-streaked face split into a grin. "I do like it, Miz Jane. Best fire-stompin', hole-diggin' shirt I ever did see!"

Suddenly Jane's tiredness lifted, as if the air she drew in filled her body with bubbles of a sweet, strengthening elixir.

Mose sobered as he handed back the dipper. "But, Miz Jane, you'd oughtta clean up best as you can 'fore you let Odelia and yore momma clap eyes on you. Top part look pale as a ghost; the rest, my goodness, look jus' like a log been rolled down a hill." He took up his shovel and turned away.

"Down a long, muddy hill," she heard him murmur.

Well, Jane Charlotte, you've done it now. You

know you don't dare go home looking so awful.
Mama would...well, Mama might not make much
sense of it, but Odelia would wear her out with words
if she saw her in such a state.

The wind ruffled her skirt, puffed up a new flurry
of sparks, and her heart twisted. Oh, no, not again.
Her petticoat was beyond use, and anyway she had
not one smidgeon of strength remaining to lift her
arms. *Dear God, please let the firebreak hold.*

The next thing she knew, Lefty was pounding her
on the back. "We done it, Miz Jane! We done
stopped that fire and saved our town!" He planted a
whiskery kiss on her cheek. "I allus knew you was a
special lady, but you shore can surprise a man!"

If I weren't so tired, Jane thought, *I could think of
something to say.*

Instead, she began to cry.

Chapter Twenty-Three

Rydell was beside her in an instant. "Jane, what's wrong?"

"N-nothing. Just relieved it's over, I guess. And tired. My back feels like somebody picked me up and broke me over his knee like a piece of kindling." She blew her nose on the handkerchief he offered.

He studied her face, then let his gaze travel over the rest of her. "You know, I don't think you should go home looking like that."

"Like what?" She brushed the hair out of her eyes, leaving a dark smudge on her forehead. She was so exhausted she didn't care one whit what she looked like—all she wanted was to crawl into bed and rest her aching body.

Rydell grasped her elbow and pulled her to a halt. "For starters, your corset's undone. Your skirt's burned clear through in four places, your face is soot-streaked, and your hair's coming down."

Her hand flew to the once-neat bun at the back of her neck. Strands of hair straggled free of the confining net. "Oh, my, I expect I am a bit mussed."

Rydell chuckled.

"Odelia will have a conniption fit! And Mama…it will upset her no end to see me like this."

"Then don't."

"Don't what?"

"Let her see you like this." Gently he turned her toward town. "Come up to my hotel room and clean up first."

Jane gasped. "Oh, I could not possibly do such a thing. It would be terribly improper." She shot a quick look at him. "We…we have no chaperon!"

The sound of his low laughter sent a dart of fury into her brain. "How *can* you laugh? It is a perfectly reasonable concern."

He gripped her shoulders. "It might be a perfectly reasonable concern for a young woman in North Carolina, but you're not in North Carolina!"

"South Carolina," she corrected.

"It doesn't matter. You're here, in Oregon. You've just spent half the night flapping out flames with your petticoat, you're dirty and tired and, dammit, you know I won't lay a hand on you."

"I am *not* tired." It was a lie, but she couldn't dispute the rest of it. Oh, why did this man have to make such good sense all the time? She pursed her lips in exasperation. "I do hate it when you're right."

He squeezed her shoulders. "I know you do. Doesn't mean I'm going to stop."

"What if someone sees us?"

Rydell groaned. "The whole town watched me cut your corset laces. Why worry now?"

"They did not! They were so busy fighting the fire nobody even looked up."

"And right now they're all out at Olaf Jensen's place, celebrating. They won't be back for hours."

"I can't, Rydell. Odelia will worry if I don't return."

He smiled at her. "I sent Mose to tell her you're with me. The hotel clerk goes to bed early, and the hotel staff owes me a favor. In ten minutes you can settle into a tub of hot water with bubbles up to your chin."

Jane shut her eyes. The thought of soaking away the grime and perspiration, of feeling clean again, was overpowering. "What about my clothes? My skirt is ruined, my waist is filthy and the sleeve is torn." She kept her eyes closed. She couldn't bear to look at her damaged garments.

"We'll stop by your shop to pick up what you need. That green outfit in the window looks about your size."

Her lids snapped open. "Oh, I couldn't. That dress is for…" She caught herself just in time. "…a lady's wedding trousseau."

His dark eyebrows lifted, but he said nothing. Inwardly, Jane sighed with relief. The identity of her client was supposed to be a secret. Even though she had guessed who the bride was, she could not reveal it. Thank the Lord, he had not asked. She found it impossible to lie to Rydell.

They stopped at her shop for clean clothes, then crossed the street to the hotel in silence. Climbing the carpeted stairs to his room, Jane had just one thought—would he want to bathe as well? Would there be two bathtubs, or would he…?

Suddenly she felt hot all over. She must think of something else—let's see, she could think about…what dress pattern would she cut out next?

What would Rydell look like without his shirt and vest? Without his trousers?

Her breath hissed in. She had never, ever wondered such a thing about a man. She resolved she would not spend one more such thought on him. Not in a thousand lifetimes would she ever let herself think of Rydell Wilder in that way again!

But another thought flashed into her mind, stopping her cold in her tracks on the second-to-the-last step.

Was he thinking the same thing about her?

Rydell saw her hesitate at the door to his hotel room. He understood her reluctance. He could hardly believe proper Miss Jane Davis, steeped in Southern gentility and social decorum from the day of her birth, was here with him.

As a matter of fact, the whole thing seemed unreal. All through the long night, side-by-side with her in the hot, smoky air fighting the fire, he found himself wondering who she really was underneath all that lace and ruffles. Certainly not the old Jane, the Jane he'd known these past ten years. The Jane who never ventured out of her house on the hill without her father by her side.

Part of him still didn't believe he had cut her free from her corset lacings! *Snick, slash* and she had thanked him and smiled up at him with an innocence that aroused all his protective instincts.

And some other instincts as well. Instincts he was having a hard time corraling as she stepped over the threshold and entered his private domain.

Immediately she moved around the blue-quilted double bed and went to the window. "Why, mercy me, you can see right into my shop!" She pulled aside the starched muslin curtain. "And all the way to the end of the street."

"If it wasn't so dark," Rydell said without thinking, "you could see all the way up the hill, to your front porch."

She tipped her head, pressing her forehead against the glass. "How long have you lived here at the Excelsior Hotel?"

"You mean how long have I been watching your house?"

She turned to face him. "Exactly."

"Ever since you moved to town." He took a single step toward her. "But tonight I see something I've never seen before. Your face is dirty, your clothes are torn, but you have never looked more beautiful."

Her eyes widened and, to his bewilderment, filled with tears. "I—I think I am so tired my mind is playing tricks. I thought you said—"

"Jane."

"I should not be here, Rydell. I know I should not. If someone should find us, I will be ruined for sure." She turned away and massaged her temples. "But somehow I don't care."

He stifled the surge of happiness that threatened to sweep over him. "That's exhaustion talking."

"Well, yes. Partly. The rest of it is…"

He stepped closer. Two short taps sounded on the door behind him, and he spoke without turning. "Who is it?"

"Is the bathtub you order, *señor*. And Rosita with the hot water."

"Bring it on in, Juan." He held Jane's gaze as the door swung open. "Rosita, leave the buckets. I'll fill the tub myself."

"Bueno, señor." He heard the tub scrape over the carpet, the thunk of the water buckets. Finally the door clicked shut.

Jane did not move. "I…that is…" She swallowed. Rydell moved slowly forward until he stood an arm's length away from her.

"Here's what's going to happen. I'm going to fill that bathtub and you're going to strip off those clothes. I'll turn my back, and when you've finished you can get dressed while I dunk myself."

"In the same water?" Jane said in a hushed voice.

"The same. Water's scarce out here."

She eyed the tub over his shoulder. "Very well. You won't tell anyone, will you?"

He choked back a snort of laughter. She was here, in his room, a thing he'd dreamed of since he was sixteen. He wanted her, wanted to take her and hold her safe in his arms forever.

But he wasn't about to destroy his chances of permanence by one rash move. If he could manage it, he would not touch her, would not even look at her until she was fully dressed.

He turned away, upended both buckets of steaming water into the copper tub, then straddled a straight chair and pulled it to face the doorway. "Toss your clothes in a pile. Soap and a towel are on the floor beside the tub."

There was a long, long silence, and then her shoes thumped onto the floor. A swishing sound followed, and from the corner of his eye he glimpsed the singed skirt settling onto the floor, followed by her dirt-smudged waist. Next came a flash of white undergarments. The corset came last.

"You want me to repair the laces on that?"

She took a long time to answer. "No. You'd just have to cut them again the next time I—"

"You plan on fighting another fire soon?" he said with a chuckle.

"Oh, I do hope not! But without those wicked stays it will be so much more comfortable to bend over and press seams or iron ruffles!"

A splash told him she had stepped into the tub. He shut his eyes, concentrated on keeping his thoughts in line. No use. In his mind's eye he saw her naked form, her dark hair flowing loose down her back, her wet skin glistening.

"When..." He had to clear his throat. "When you're...we're...dressed, I can sneak you down the back stairs."

She said nothing. He could hear her even breathing, accompanied by tiny splashing sounds. He'd bet she was washing her hair to get out the smoke smell. The

thought of the long, damp strands brushing her backbone made his mouth go dry. *Keep talking, you fool!*

He gulped in some air. "The back stairs lead into
the alley. Once you get there, it's just a few steps to
your dress shop."

The splashing ceased. Rydell tried not to think
what she might be doing next. Wiping the soap suds
off her bare shoulders? Running the washcloth up between...

He rocked back on the chair legs and expelled an
uneven breath through his mouth. *Just five more
minutes. Keep it under control for five more minutes.*

"Or," he said when he could trust his voice, "I
could walk you home. Sun ought to be up in another
few hours, so we'd better make our move before
dawn. Folks'll be drifting back into town pretty
soon."

Silence.

"Which would you prefer, Jane?"

No response.

"Jane?"

He waited a full three minutes, then twisted in the
chair. "Jane?"

Her head lolled against the edge of the tub, eyes
closed. Both her arms were draped along the sides, a
bar of soap in one hand, a yellow washcloth in the
other.

Hot damn chile peppers, she was sound asleep! He
almost laughed out loud. The bathwater lapped over
the swell of her breasts, just barely covered her nip-
ples. God in heaven.

"Jane? Jane, wake up."

Her chest rose and fell. Her mouth fell open.

How could he…? Oh, hell, he'd have to. He prayed she wouldn't wake up.

Very slowly he rose and circled the tub. No doubt about it, she was out colder than a doorknob. A straggling wisp of dark hair lifted off her forehead every time she exhaled.

He lifted the washcloth from her hand, retrieved the cake of soap from the other. She didn't so much as twitch. *Okay, here goes.*

He positioned himself behind her, slid his hands under her armpits, and lifted. Water sluiced off her naked back. Her head tipped forward, her arms dangled limp at her sides.

"Up you go," he muttered. He dipped his shoulder and caught one arm beneath her knees. Soaking wet she weighed no more than a hundred pounds.

She moaned and nestled her head against his neck. He felt the dampness of her hair soak through his shirt and moisten his skin. He wanted to lay her down and hold her in his arms, kiss her until she awakened.

He pivoted, snagged the yellow towel and spread it out on the bed with his free hand. Gently he lowered her warm, wet body onto the soft cotton and began to pat her skin dry. She was so beautiful it made his gut ache.

"Mama?" Her sleepy voice brought him bolt upright.

"It's Rydell," he murmured. He waited a moment, then continued drying her ivory skin.

"Feels nice," she muttered.

Rydell froze. *What the devil?* Was she awake or not? Should he stop?

As if in answer she turned on her side and curled herself into a ball. "Rub back."

He drew in a deep breath, then settled his hand on her neckbone.

"Yes," she breathed. "More."

"Jane?"

"Don' argue. Back hurts."

Jumping catfish. He smoothed his hands up and down her back until his groin was hot and swollen. Gingerly he covered her with the thick blue quilt and stepped away from the bed, unbuttoning his shirt and trousers with unsteady fingers. Bath time.

He sloshed into the tub and sat down, resting his forehead against his bent knees. The lukewarm water eased the tension in his muscles, and he managed to soap himself and rinse off before his brain re-engaged. He wanted her so much his limbs trembled.

But he would not take her this way. There was no honor in it. No committed bond. He would wait.

She must come to him, he acknowledged. No matter how much he wanted it, she had to want it, too. She had to want him, just as he wanted her.

He dried off quickly, paced around the room until his skin cooled and his mind cleared. Then he pulled on a clean set of underwear and paced some more. Finally he drew on a pair of trousers. Only then did he trust himself to lie down on the bed beside her.

"What time is it?" she said in a faraway voice.

"Around four."

"Here." She rolled toward him, spread the quilt over his rigid body. "'S cold."

"Jane?"

Her eyelids remained closed. "Yes?"

"Honey, do you know where you are?"

"I'm in your hotel room, Rydell." She spoke slowly, her voice quiet. "On your bed. Poor Mama would be scandalized!"

Rydell stared at the ceiling. "And you're not?" He held his breath.

"I thought I would be, but I'm not." She hesitated. "I like you, Rydell. More than I thought I'd ever like anyone."

Speechless, he pulled her slowly into his arms and felt his heart float up out of his chest.

"'S funny, isn't it?" she went on, her eyes still shut. "Odelia was right."

"Right about what?" He could scarcely breathe. Three words at a time were about all he could handle right now.

"Odelia says if you listen to a man—even a Yankee—long enough, he'll say something worthwhile."

"Jane…"

"Don't kiss me," she murmured. "I feel so funny when you kiss me, I don't trust myself."

"Jane, marry me."

After a long silence, she said, "I'll think about it, Rydell. Truly I will. But I have a trousseau to finish by September, and Mama wants—"

He stopped her words with his mouth. "I don't want to hear about your mama right now," he said against her lips. "I want to hear you say you'll marry me."

"I..." She reached for him, drew him closer, her mouth warm and sweet on his skin.

"I don't want to think about Mama right now, either."

He rolled her close to him and held her, dumb with joy, until the sky in the east turned peach-colored.

Chapter Twenty-Four

Jane opened her eyes to hot sunshine pouring in the window. Merciful heavens, it was broad daylight! Past noon, judging from the angle of the light. She had overslept.

She jerked upright and felt every muscle in her back and shoulders scream in protest. Slapping at a grass fire for hours on end was much worse than ironing a dozen dresses or picking a bushel of ripe peaches. She ached all over.

Her gaze skimmed the empty room. The copper bathtub was gone, as were the two metal water buckets and the yellow towel. Her ruined skirt and waist had disappeared as well, but two white muslin garments—her shimmy and a pair of lace-trimmed pantalettes—hung over a makeshift twine clothesline strung from the window latch to the brass drawer handle on the chiffonier. Dumbstruck, she watched her underclothes sway in the warm breeze wafting in through the open window. Someone—Rydell?—had washed them out and hung them up to dry.

She sat up straighter, turning her attention to the

rest of the room. The furnishings were sparse, just the
bed, and on the opposite wall a chest of drawers and
a small, plain desk of dark wood, topped by three neat
stacks of papers, each weighted with a green river
rock of unusual shape. A framed photograph rested
on top of the chest, a handsome, unsmiling woman
with tired eyes. Next to it lay a black leather-covered
Bible and a set of silver cufflinks.

On one side of the bed sat a wingback chair, upholstered in rich brown damask. Drawn up to the
other side was another chair, with the clean work skirt
and long-sleeved blue gingham waist she'd retrieved
from her shop last night folded into a neat pile on the
seat. A note perched on top.

Back stairs at the end of the hall. R.

Of course. She had to get dressed and walk back
across the street to her shop before anyone saw her.
She couldn't delay one single second.

She jammed one foot into her dry underdrawers
and stopped short. She couldn't believe she was doing
this—getting dressed in a man's hotel room. It was
so unusual she wondered if she could be dreaming.

But she felt perfectly normal. Light as air, in fact,
were it not for her sore muscles. Why was she not
horrified at having spent the night here with Rydell?
Had her wits fled along with her common sense? Except for the problem of slipping down the back stairs
without being seen, her spirits were…well, quite se-
rene.

Jane Charlotte, what is *the matter with you?*

Nothing! Nothing was the matter with her. This
morning she simply recognized herself. Last night she

had taken her place alongside the townspeople against a common enemy. Today she was a person who belonged.

Under her folded navy skirt she found a comb, a man's boar-bristle hairbrush, and her black crocheted mesh hair snood. Beneath that lay her shoes, polished to a shine. He'd thought of everything.

She lifted the brush, drew it through her dark hair. Not only did she view herself differently, but she recognized something else: Rydell Wilder was the only man she had ever known whom she genuinely liked. *Maybe more than liked.*

Her hand stilled. Just imagine, a Yankee! Papa would never understand.

But maybe Papa had been somewhat shortsighted. Rydell had proved himself a man of honor. Yankee or not, he was a real gentleman. She glanced at the woman in the photograph. His parents, whoever they were, must have been fine people, even if they were Northerners. Otherwise, they could not have produced the man Rydell Wilder was. Good breeding was good breeding, and it always showed. Even Papa would agree with that.

She wound her hair into a thick roll at her neck and secured it with the black hair net. The smell of smoke still hung in the air, but everything looked unusually bright and clear this morning, as if a veil had lifted from her eyes.

"Now," she said as she buttoned up the front of her waist, "all I must think about is finding the stairs." She drew her skirt over her head, laced up her shoes, and smoothed the quilt over the bed. Then she tiptoed to the doorway. Putting her ear to the wood, she listened for a full minute before she eased it open and peered outside.

The long hallway was empty. From the floor below she heard the booming voice of the desk clerk, the clink of glassware from the bar.

Now.

She stepped outside, pulled the door shut behind her, and flew down the hallway to her left, away from the sounds. The carpet ended when she reached the back staircase. Gingerly she set her right shoe on the tread, and the bare wood creaked. Clinging to the banister, she descended one cautious footstep at a time. She counted sixteen steps.

At the landing, the door opened into an alley overgrown with wild oxalis and bindweed. A narrow path led through the tangle to the main street. She looked in both directions, took a deep breath and stepped forward.

Five steps from her goal a voice stopped her in her tracks.

"Why, Jane Davis, whatever are you doing skulking about in that alley?"

Lord help her, it was Letitia Price. The young woman stood before her in a pale blue lawn dress, a matching parasol shading her face. Jane's blood turned to ice water.

"Good morning, Letitia. I was just…" A cold fog drifted over her brain. In desperation she searched for some plausible thing to say. "…cooling off here in the shade." She gestured across the street. "It gets terribly hot in my dress shop."

''Well, I should think so!'' Letitia responded. Then her eyes hardened. ''That gown in the window, the green seersucker with the pleats, is it finished?''

Jane blinked. ''Why, yes, but—''

''Is it for sale?''

''No. I mean Yes. I sewed it for…for a client. I thought surely you knew?''

Letitia sent her an odd look. ''Sometimes you make no sense at all, Jane. Just look at you—it's a scorching day, and you haven't a sun-shade of any kind, not even a hat!''

A hat? What had a hat to do with anything? Was it her imagination, or had Letitia purposely changed the subject?

''If you will excuse me, Letitia, I must return to work on your…'' She could have bitten off her tongue. ''…must get back to work.

Letitia nodded, her blond curls bobbing under the blue parasol. ''Of course. Wait! Could you make a hat to match that pleated gown? Trimmed in green ribbon?''

Why, Jane wondered, were they playing this game? Letitia surely knew the green dress was part of the trousseau she had agreed to sew. She just didn't know that Jane had guessed who the garments were for.

Oh, what did it matter? She would finish the buttonholes and start the skirt edging on the wedding gown by the end of the week, and on the first day of September it would be over and done with. She would take the three hundred fifty dollars she'd earned, pack up Mama and Odelia, and go home to Marion County.

All at once she found her throat so tight she

couldn't speak. She nodded to Letitia and stepped off the boardwalk onto the rutted street, her vision blurred with unexpected tears. Didn't she *want* to go home?

Of course she did! What a nonsensical thought. *It's just that, well, you don't really want to leave Rydell, do you?*

"Oh, yes I do!" she blurted. And the sooner the better. She was getting far too involved with him. She was even beginning to think about that house he was building out on Sugar Loaf Hill, about sitting on the wide veranda with him in the evening, about...

And, Lord-a-mercy, she had just spent the entire night in his hotel room! A slow flush of heat moved from her toes up to her chin.

She removed the key from its hiding place above the door frame and stuffed it into the lock. General Lee opened one eye as Jane swept in and repositioned herself in the sewing basket. On top of her cutting table sat a mug of coffee and a napkin-draped plate of cinnamon toast. Breakfast! No matter that it was past lunchtime, Rydell had known she would be hungry.

In fact, she was ravenous. She bit into the toast and gulped a mouthful of lukewarm coffee. As she chewed, her gaze traveled across the street and up to the second floor of the Excelsior Hotel. There, the window on the right, the one with the white curtain. It gave her the most curious feeling to know Rydell could see into her shop, could watch her as she cut and stitched and basted and pressed. She felt looked after. Protected.

After two more gulps of coffee and another slice

of toast, she brushed off her hands and sat herself down with the wedding gown bodice. The design was simple—not the style Letitia usually wore, but the richly patterned moire silk made up for it. It would be a lovely wedding dress, fit for a queen. When the time came, it would be difficult to part with it.

For a fleeting moment she pictured herself in the gown, pink rosebuds in the crown securing the long veil, and a bouquet of roses, white ones, in her hand, moving toward a tall man who waited, his gray eyes calling to her. She felt happy, so happy....

She stared at the silky fabric in her lap, and her heart slammed to a stop. She wanted it to be *her*. Not Letitia, but *her*.

With fingers that shook, she picked up the bodice and a piece of tailor's chalk and marked the first buttonhole.

Impossible.

Not impossible.

She was imagining things.

Good things. Wonderful things.

She wanted to be with Rydell.

Rydell spent the entire morning struggling to keep Jane out of his thoughts long enough to concentrate on the bank's accounts ledger. Once each hour Josiah quietly opened the door and looked in, but Rydell waved the clerk away without looking up.

"Never took you this long before, Mr. Wilder. Anything wrong?"

"No, nothing, Josiah." Nothing that pulling Jane

into his arms and taking her to bed wouldn't cure. "I'll be finished shortly."

"I saw that Mr. Lucas fellow sneaking around outside. Bet he's gonna pay you another one of his visits."

Rydell's hands curled into fists at the mention of the man's name. Something about Lucas made his skin crawl. He slapped the ledger book closed and stood up.

Lucas stood at the teller's cage, his slate-colored eyes glittering through the bars. "Afternoon, Wilder."

Rydell didn't bother to return the greeting. "Making another deposit?"

"Not this time." The thin lips twitched. "I came to make a deal."

Rydell's senses kicked up a notch. "Oh? What kind of deal?"

Lucas hunched his tall frame forward. His breath smelled of whiskey. "So far I've deposited…what would you say, about twenty-five thousand dollars?"

"Twenty-three thousand, four hundred and eighty. I just finished checking the books."

"Yeah, well it don't matter exactly what I walked in with. What matters is what I'm gonna walk out with."

Rydell stared at the lined, sun-leathered face. A knowing smile played around the man's mouth, and his gut tightened. Lucas's eyes were cunning, like those of a predatory fox.

Rydell cleared his throat. "At most banks, you walk out with what you brought in."

"Yeah. Well this here bank's a little different, ain't it?"

"Is it?"

"I been studyin' this some. You own this bank, ain't that right?"

"That's right."

"So, lemme spell it out. You're gonna put my twenty-five thousand in my valise, and then you're gonna add all the rest of the money you got in your safe." His lips stretched over yellowing teeth. "Should be forty, maybe fifty thousand."

Rydell shook his head. "No deal."

"Wouldn't be too sure of that. Like I say, I been studyin'. There's somethin' you want in this town, Wilder. You want it real bad. And I can make it possible." His grin widened. "Or not possible."

"Skip it, Lucas."

"Even if it concerns Miz Jane?"

Rydell felt the hair on his forearms rise. "Leave her out of it."

Lucas gave a guttural laugh. "I'm not interested in the young lady for myself. It's just that I know somethin' she might like to know."

"I doubt that." A dark, choking miasma threatened to cut off his air.

Lucas went on as if he had not spoken. "Here's the deal, Rydell. You open up your safe and turn your back, and I keep my mouth shut."

"Get out, Lucas. You want your own money, you can take it, but that's all. I'm not going to rob my own bank, and neither are you."

"Yes y'are, sonny. You gonna do exactly like I tell

you. I'll even give you twenty-four hours to get the cash together. Tomorrow mornin'—''

"Tomorrow's Sunday. Bank's closed.''

"Not to me, it ain't. Tomorrow mornin' I'm gonna drop in and you're gonna help me walk outta here with a bag full of greenbacks.''

Rydell looked at the tall man in disbelief. "What the hell makes you think so?''

Lucas sent him a calculating look and dropped his voice to a whisper. "The name Etta Wilder mean anything to you?''

A cold hand reached into his gut and turned his belly upside down. "My mother's name. Why?''

The man leaned toward Rydell. "I knew her. Etta. Knew her real good, back in Missouri.''

"You're a lying son of a—''

"You got a chance for a good life out here. Big house. Nice respectable wife. I seen right off how you wanted Miz Jane.''

"I told you to keep her name out of this.''

"Can't do that, boy. Comes a time in a man's life when he's got to play his cards.''

"Spill it, Lucas. Then get out.''

Lucas waited a long time before he spoke. "Y'see, I know somethin'. Somethin' that'll scare Miz Jane offa you quicker'n a dragonfly off a cow pie. But you just say the word and she'll never have to know.''

"Get out,'' Rydell repeated. He wished he'd put his revolver in the cash drawer.

"Oh, no. First, you lissen up. I been waitin' a long time to tell you this.''

An iron fist gripped Rydell's heart. "Tell me what?"

"This. Your momma never got married. You were born a bastard. And that'll matter a lot to Miz Jane."

With difficulty, Rydell kept his voice even. "Lucas, you're nothing but scum."

"Scum? That's rich, you callin' me scum. You don't know one damn thing about me."

"I know all I need to know. You're a liar and a thief."

"Here's somethin' you don't know, sonny boy. Somethin' you won't want Miz Jane to know, neither. My name."

Rydell's chest felt like a horse had kicked him. "Your name is Lucas."

"That's my given name." His thin lips pulled back into a grin that did not reach his eyes.

Rydell held the man's cold-eyed gaze. "So?"

"My last name is Rydell. Lucas Rydell." He expelled a raspy breath. "I'm your father."

For a full minute Rydell thought he would vomit. *This man was his father?* His stomach heaved.

"Never married Etta cuz I was workin' a chain gang in Dakota. I used to rob banks. Now if I tell that to Miz Jane, you ain't ever gonna see her again. I hand-picked this bank because you own it, boy. I figure you'll do your daddy a favor and in return I won't tell your pretty lady that you're the bastard son of an outlaw. So, like I say, come Sunday mornin'…"

He left the sentence unfinished, but the meaning was clear. If Rydell wanted Jane, he'd have to help Lucas—his father—rob the bank.

Chapter Twenty-Five

On Saturday morning, Jane allowed Odelia to feed her hotcakes and bacon until she thought she would pop, then endured the black woman's fussing over her sunburned face with a witch-hazel compress. Finally, when she couldn't stand being away from her shop one more minute, she climbed the stairs to kiss Mama good morning, clapped on a wide-brimmed straw hat, and headed for the front door.

On the front porch she was met by Odelia, a knowing smile on her round, dark face and another compress in her hand.

"You gwine tell dat man how you feel 'bout him, honey?" She patted the aromatic witch hazel over Jane's cheeks. "Don' let a single day pass by without tellin' him."

"Oh, I couldn't just tell him, Odelia. You don't understand."

The older woman sniffed. "Ol' 'Delia understand dese things sure 'nuf. First time you grab on to my finger wid yo li'l hand, I'se trapped forever, so don' tell me I don' know 'bout lovin'."

"This is different," Jane protested.

"No it ain't, child. Lovin' is lovin'."

Jane gave the woman a quick hug and stepped off the porch. There was no arguing with Odelia; the woman had raised Jane from birth and was used to being obeyed.

Hot morning sunshine poured into the dress shop. Jane fed General Lee, poured fresh water into her dish, and settled down to finish the buttonholes on the patterned silk wedding gown. Not ten minutes into the task, a breathless Evangeline Tanner stepped through the doorway, wearing a walking suit of crisp yellow percale.

"Jane, I've come to— Oh, how lovely! How perfectly lovely!" She gazed in admiration at the gown spread over Jane's lap. "Goodness, that dress makes me want to get married all over again. Do try it on!"

Jane looked up sharply. "Oh, I couldn't do that! But it is strange that you should suggest it. The closer I get to finishing this gown, the more I think of it as my own. Now isn't that silly of me?"

An odd look crossed Evangeline's face. "Yes," she said quickly. "Very silly. But that isn't why I stopped in."

She snapped open her reticule and pressed a thick white envelope into Jane's hand. "Here. It's your payment for the trousseau."

"But it's not yet completed! I still have all the buttons to attach and then tack the skirt fastenings on the green seersucker and find some trim for the hat."

"Nevertheless, you are to be paid today. Tomorrow is Sunday and the bank is closed."

Jane peeked inside the envelope and counted four green bills, three one-hundreds and one fifty. "Oh. Oh, my."

Evangeline laid her hand on Jane's arm. "You've earned it, Jane. Now I must fly, as Mr. Tanner expects me at the mill."

"Please thank Let—thank your client for me. Oh, I almost forgot—will she not require a fitting?"

Evangeline dimpled. "Certainly not. Good day, Jane."

Paid in advance with no fitting? Letitia seemed to have a great deal of confidence in her dressmaking capabilities. But then, Evangeline had warned her that Letitia could be unpredictable.

She ran her forefinger over the puffy envelope. My goodness, three hundred and fifty whole dollars. She'd just snip this last thread and step right down to the bank.

The redheaded bank clerk nodded at her when she entered. "Mr. Wilder's in the back office, Miss."

"Thank you, Josiah." She stepped down the short hallway and rapped lightly on the door.

No response. She knocked again, then hesitantly turned the knob.

Rydell sat at the big oak desk, one hand covering his eyes. "Go away, Josiah."

Jane stepped forward. "It's not Josiah. It's me."

"Jane," he said without moving. He said nothing further, and all at once she felt a flicker of unease.

"Is anything the matter?"

He made no answer.

"Rydell, what's wrong? Are you ill?"

Very deliberately he lowered his hand and looked at her. The expression in his eyes made her heart stop.

"No, I'm not ill. I wish to hell I were."

"What is it? Can you tell me?"

"No." She recoiled at the harsh edge in his voice. Slipping the envelope from her skirt pocket, she laid it before him. "I came to pay off my loan. Here is the balance, all three hundred dollars. I cannot thank you enough for—"

"You're free now. You won't have to marry me."

"Oh, but I—"

"Go home, Jane. Go back to North Carolina."

"South Carolina," she corrected automatically. Something was wrong. He seemed so cold, so removed. So different from the man who had held her in his arms, pressed his mouth to hers and made her body come alive.

His lips twisted. "South Carolina, then."

Another long pause, then, "I'm sorry, Jane."

She tried desperately to keep her voice from betraying the pain that gnawed at her. "Yes. Well, I have some sewing to finish up. I...I suppose I should be getting back to my shop." She waited, but he made no move to stop her.

Rydell forced himself to look past her. He couldn't respond, couldn't even think clearly. He'd lost her, lost the one thing he wanted more than anything else in life. He couldn't stand to see the question in her eyes. The hurt.

He couldn't even explain. He was trapped in a box canyon with a hungry wolf. There was only one thing he could do—protect Jane. Keep her from getting tarred by the same brush Lucas threatened him with. Keep her from finding out that he was born a bastard and his father robbed banks.

He couldn't marry Jane. When the news got out about who his father was, her name would be dishonored right along with his. No matter how tempted he was to bury the whole thing, to let Lucas blackmail him and walk away with the bank's money, he knew he could not do it. But without Rydell's cooperation, Lucas would tell the whole town about his sleazy heritage, and Jane would never look at him again.

He closed his eyes to shut out her white, stricken face. "Go home, Jane. Forget everything I ever said to you."

There was no sound in the hot, still room. Outside a horse and wagon rattled past the window. A baby cried. A child shouted something. Suddenly he thought of that boy and girl he'd seen balanced on the seesaw, one riding up as the other descended. They would never get close enough to touch each other.

Oh, God, Jane.

He heard the soft rustle of her skirt as she moved past him and through the doorway.

Her chest constricted, Jane stumbled down the board sidewalk as if in a trance. What had happened? Overnight, Rydell had turned into a stranger. The man she had come to feel strongly about no longer wanted her. She stopped at the door to her shop but could not make her legs carry her inside.

Could Rydell have been promised to someone else?

Letitia Price? Jane was sure the wedding trousseau was intended for the pretty blonde, but in all the flurry of cutting and stitching she had never given serious thought to who the groom would be. Surely it was not…

She let her feet carry her across the street and down the alley next to the Excelsior Hotel to the trim little cabin where she knew Lefty Springer lived. The door swung open at her knock.

"Miz Jane! What're you doin' here?"

She opened her mouth to speak, but the words stuck in her aching throat. She reached out for his good arm and closed her fingers over the soft material of his blue plaid shirt.

"Glory be, yer eyes are brim full of tears. What's wrong, honey?"

"Oh, Lefty, I…" She choked down a sob. "I don't know what's wrong. It's Rydell. He's…" She swiped her fingers across her wet cheek. "Something's happened, but I don't know what it is."

Lefty stepped off his stoop, drawing Jane toward the wooden bench under a maple with crimson-tinged leaves. "Now, you jes' tell me what's been goin' on."

She poured it all out, and when she finished her recital, the man's thick russet eyebrows drew together. "You're right, it don't make sense. I knowed about the bank loan all right. And then he asked Miz Tanner to hire you for some kind of lady sewing, said he'd pay for—"

Jane jerked. "*He* did? Rydell paid for the trousseau? But why?"

"So's you'd have a choice, honey. So you could *choose* to marry him, 'stead of feelin' forced into it cuz you owed him money and made a bargain on it. So you could take yer momma and go back to Carolina if that's what you really wanted. Dell wanted to give you a choice."

"I...I thought Mrs. Tanner was acting on behalf of Letitia Price."

"Nope. Dell's not interested in Miss Letitia. Never has been. Fer as long as I've known him, Rydell's been in love with you."

"You mean that trousseau, that beautiful wedding gown, was..." she wiped the back of her hand across another wash of tears "...was meant for me?"

Her heart soared and then dropped to the bottom of her stomach. "Then why did he send me away?"

"Dunno, Miz Jane. Jus' plain dunno."

She wept against his solid shoulder until her head ached, then dragged herself back down the alley and across the street to her shop. She turned her chair so her back was to the door. At least the townfolk wouldn't see her tear-ravaged face.

For an hour she tried to sit calmly and sew on buttons, but even Maggie's silent visit with a pot of coffee from the hotel dining room failed to ease the anguish inside her. It wasn't enough that she had fallen in love with a Yankee, had scandalized her family and put herself forever on the wrong side of proper behavior for a Southern lady. She jabbed her needle through the pale silk. On top of that, Rydell had spurned her!

Dear Lord in heaven, how could he, after...after...

A shadow fell over her shoulder. Jane bowed her head and shut her eyes. *Please, whoever you are, just go away.*

A familiar voice spoke at her elbow. "Work hard today." Mary Two Hats's soft hand brushed her shoulder, then lifted away.

"I—" Jane swallowed. "I have to finish…" She could get no further, could not face explaining about the wedding trousseau.

"I help," the Indian woman announced. She laid a single, iridescent feather in Jane's lap. "From pheasant. For hat in window."

Jane looked up into the woman's lined face.

"Look pretty with green feather. Match your dress."

"*My* dress? Why do you think it is for me?"

Mary Two Hats's black eyes shone. "Not think. Know for sure. Dress calls to you. And this…" She touched one finger to the silk bodice draped across Jane's lap. "This marriage dress. Many happy years to come. Many children."

Pain shot into Jane's heart. "Oh, no, I don't think so. Not since…" She closed her lips over the words. "Forgive me, Mrs. Two Hats, but I am sure not."

The older woman held Jane's gaze for a long moment and then smiled. "You are young. Many children. You put feather on hat, then you see. Many children."

Jane turned away from the dark, penetrating eyes. She couldn't bear to think of it. Life with Rydell, marriage, children—she would never have any of it. A month ago this was the last thing that would have entered her mind; now it was the only thing she thought about. That and the hopeless, crushed feeling inside her.

She tipped her head to face the tall woman, but the Indian woman had glided away on her moccasins as quietly as she had come. The lovely green feather lay waiting in Jane's lap.

Late that evening she locked up the shop and dragged her numb body up the hill to the house where Mama and Odelia waited. *Her* house. Papa was gone. Mama was gone, too, in a way. She rarely rose from her bed and her mind was confused.

Jane had eaten nothing all day, but the thought of food made her queasy. Feeling as if she were only half-alive, she entered the house, climbed the stairs to kiss Mama and hold her soft, smooth hand in hers, then let Odelia bathe her face and lay a cool cloth across her swollen eyelids.

"You plumb wore out, child. Ol' 'Delia know how yore heart been hurt, and ain't no cure for dat."

Jane struggled to put her feelings into words. "I don't know how it happened. One minute I am standing on solid ground, talking to him, realizing that I— that I love—" Her voice choked off. "And the next minute a chasm opens before me and swallows me up."

"There's two ways to argue with a man," Odelia pronounced. "Neither one of 'em work. You down in a hole, now, so the first thing you gwine do is to stop diggin'."

"Oh, Odelia, I don't know what to do. I thought

I'd want to go back to Marion County, but Mama…''
She caught back a sob.

"You's right, honey. She got no stren'th to stand,
much less travel. 'Cides, Miss Leah, she think she's
back on de ol' plantation now.''

Jane nodded her head. "I don't belong back there
anyway. I've changed, Odelia. Papa would disapprove so, and Mama—oh, how horrified she would
be! But I don't feel like *me* any longer. I feel like
someone different. Someone who—oh, don't let
Mama hear me!—someone who belongs here, in
Dixon Falls. I've given up my dream of going home.
Or maybe I outgrew it, I don't know. And now I have
nothing. Nothing!''

Odelia lifted the cloth from her eyes, swung it in
the air to cool it, and replaced it on Jane's forehead.
"Jes' you rest now, honey. Mose is comin' to lift
your momma so's I can change the sheets. You jes'
lie here quiet-like, an' pretty soon I make you some
tea.''

Jane caught at the black woman's hand. "Odelia,
what am I going to do? There's this awful pain inside
me. I don't want to go back to Marion County, but I
don't think I can stand seeing Rydell every day,
knowing he doesn't want me. And what's more, I
can't…'' She pressed her knuckles hard against her
mouth. "I can't seem to stop crying.''

By dawn, Jane had come to a decision. She would
go down to her shop this morning, even if it was
Sunday. Keeping her hands busy would help her to
not think. Besides, General Lee would need food and

water, and if all else failed, she could hold the kitten on her lap and pet her while she tried to sort out her jumbled thoughts.

In a state of suspended animation, she donned a navy sateen skirt and a white lace-encrusted waist, avoided Odelia's offer of a poached egg, and set off down the hill. As she neared Mercer's Mercantile, she resolved to keep her eyes on the walkway. She would not, absolutely *not,* look up at the second floor of the Excelsior Hotel. Just ten more steps and she would be safe in her shop.

She drew abreast of the barrel in which Rafe Mercer's prize rose grew and made a mistake. She paused to sniff one lush pink bloom. Out of the corner of her eye she caught a glimpse of Rydell's hotel room window. The curtain was drawn shut.

She wouldn't think about that room, or about him, or what he might be doing on this Sunday morning. Sleeping? Writing at his desk? Or was he in the dining room with Lefty Springer, eating breakfast? Maybe he was out on Sugar Loaf Hill nailing boards on that beautiful new house he was building.

A chill sliced between her shoulder blades. Children, Mary Two Hats had said. Marriage. A life with Rydell Wilder.

She couldn't think about it. The longing was too deep, the hurt too raw.

General Lee lapped at her water bowl but ignored the handkerchief-wrapped morsel of cold chicken Jane pulled from her pocket. Instead, the animal curled up in Jane's wicker sewing basket and began to purr.

Jane sucked in a big breath of dusty air and willed herself not to cry. Suddenly she wished she had one of Rafe Mercer's vanilla-scented roses, or an orange—anything at all that was beautiful and comforting.

She wasn't going back to South Carolina. She wasn't going to marry Rydell. She seated herself at the cutting table and peered into her pattern box. She would make another dress.

She didn't have the courage this morning to press the ivory silk wedding gown. Instead, she lifted the straw hat away from the pleated green afternoon dress in the window and pinned the pheasant feather Mary Two Hats had brought to the green taffeta ribbon around the crown. In spite of her drooping spirits, she smiled. The hat was perfectly beautiful with the addition of the feather. She was beginning to believe, truly believe, in her own talent.

A man's footsteps sounded on the boardwalk outside, and for an instant her heart stopped beating. Rydell. She'd know that measured step anywhere. Was he coming to see her?

He moved past her open doorway, and just when she thought he wasn't going to even glance at her, he looked up and their gazes locked. His face looked tight and set, and the expression in his eyes—mercy! In his eyes she read the same despair she was struggling with. Despair…and resignation.

She frowned as he looked away and passed by the window. *Resignation? From Rydell Wilder?* A man who had advanced himself by sheer grit and intelligence from an underfed stable hand to the owner of the first bank in the county? It didn't make sense.

She unbuttoned her cuffs and began to roll up her sleeves. While the sadiron heated on the squat oil stove in the corner, she stared absently into the street. A young boy with hair the color of ripe plums scampered past, hand in hand with a pretty blonde child in a blue pinafore. "Race you," the girl cried, darting ahead. Jane smiled. Would they grow up and fall in love one day? Have children?

She bit back the thought just as another man appeared, striding down the middle of the street, one hand yanking on the bit of a roan gelding. That awful man, Lucas. The one who had accosted her at the Fourth of July horse race. Jane shuddered. The man Rydell had warned her to stay away from.

What was he doing in town?

Her gaze fixed on two large black leather valises tied in back of the expensive tooled saddle. She knew they were empty; they bounced and bobbed at the horse's every step.

And he was heading... She stepped out the door, shading her eyes from the sun. ...straight for the bank.

A nerve jumped at the back of her neck. The bank? *On a Sunday?*

Without a second thought she quietly pulled the shop door closed and headed down the sidewalk in the same direction.

Chapter Twenty-Six

Jane stepped past the roan gelding tethered to the hitching rail in front of the bank, noting that the two black valises had disappeared. Odd, doing bank business on a Sunday.

She stood quietly outside the closed door, straining to hear. A low burr of voices rumbled inside, but the words were indistinguishable. With deliberate care, she laid her hand on the brass knob, twisting it silently until the catch released.

Holding her breath, she cracked the door open just enough to allow entrance, took a single step forward, and slipped into the shadows. Shielded behind the oak panel, she could not see into the room, but she could hear. Voices that were indistinct before were clearly audible now.

"We got a deal?" Lucas's voice.

"No deal, Lucas." Rydell's tone had a steely edge to it.

"Lissen, son. You stand to lose more'n money."

"I am aware of that. It's still no deal. You want to withdraw your own funds, that's up to you."

"Never thought I'd sire such a stubborn kid," Lucas muttered. "I'll tell her, by God. You know how you can stop me—that part's up to you."

"I won't stop you. I won't let you rob my bank, no matter what you threaten. I won't be bought."

"You tellin' me you're willin' to lose her? What kinda man are you, anyway?"

"One that, thank God, wasn't raised by a tin-pot outlaw. If it wasn't for the people in this town—an understanding stable owner and a one-armed man who took me under his wing—I might've turned out just like you."

"You gonna think of that every time you look into a shaving mirror, Rydell. You got your mother's mouth, but you got my eyes, my hair, my build. You're gonna see me lookin' back at you for the rest of your sorry life."

Silence, and then Rydell spoke. "I guess I'll have to pay that price. At least I'll be able to look myself in the face."

"Yore a damn fool, son. Yer high-minded honor's gonna cost you yer woman. Ain't nuthin' worth more than a good woman like Miz Jane. Yer ma was a good woman, leastways till she met up with me."

"Ride on out of here, Lucas. I'm only going to warn you this once."

"It's Jane or me. Choose."

A long silence settled over the room. Jane bit her lip to keep from crying out.

''I already have,'' Rydell said in a quiet voice. ''Now get out. Take your money and get out of my sight.''

''Load it up. But before I ride outta here, I'm gonna have a little chat with one partic'lar pretty lady. And then you ain't never gonna see me again.''

Jane was far down the board sidewalk when she heard the door of the bank slam. She glanced back to see Lucas stomp to the hitching rail and yank the reins free. He carried only one of the valises, which he slung up behind the saddle and secured with a length of rope. With a vicious twist of his arm he jerked the roan's bit.

The horse squealed and tried to back away, but the tall, dark-haired man pulled on the animal's bridle until it stood still. He tried to mount, but the gelding sidestepped, and his boot slipped out of the stirrup. His cursing followed Jane into her shop.

She locked the door behind her, then stood, trembling from head to toe, wondering what to do. A cold, sick feeling washed over her.

Lucas was Rydell's father? How could that odious, hateful man be Rydell's father?

And he wanted money to keep it a secret? It was beyond believable. She knew Rydell Wilder well enough to know that of all men, he would be the last to submit to such coercion. Rydell had worked all his life to get where he was. He would not, could not throw it away. Not even for her.

Right then and there her heart split in two. She

understood all too well the price he was willing to
pay to keep his honor—and hers—from the sullying
touch of a lowlife like Lucas. She was proud of him
for refusing.

A shadow fell across the window. Lucas had ridden
the roan onto the walkway outside her dressmaking
shop, and now he leaned out of the saddle and
pounded his fist on the closed door.

Jane stood perfectly still, her heart jumping in terror.

"Open up! I got somethin' to tell ya!"

She summoned every scrap of courage she had and
opened the door. "I already know," she said. "Go
away."

The man frowned. "You know 'bout Rydell? That
I'm his—"

"Yes!" Jane screamed the word. "I know! Now
go. Leave us in peace."

"Damn fool woman," she heard him mutter.
"Both of you, damn pigheaded fools." He reined his
mount into the street.

The sound of hoofbeats faded into quiet, and Jane
stood alone in her shop, mentally gathering together
the fragments of the life she had begun to build. She
thought about her dream of returning to Marion
County, to the life she had remembered when she was
young. That dream was gone.

She thought about the dress shop, how it brought
her not only money but a feeling of accomplishment,
of pride. She thought about the changes in herself
these past months. She knew things now that she

didn't know before. About Papa, how set in his ways and unyielding he had been. About Mama, her mind confused by all that had happened, her yearning for a world that no longer existed.

About herself, Jane Charlotte Davis, who thought once that it was more important to be a Lady than a Woman. Who now weighed her life in the balance and found it wanting.

She would go on. Must go on. Mama needed care and medicine. The house needed a new roof. ''And I need…I need…'' Her throat closed over the words.

She thought then about Rydell, that awful moment when he acknowledged what Lucas was to him. And then she knew what she had to do.

The soft wind bore the distant sound of the school bell up the hill to the willow tree where Rydell stood looking out over the town.

Children gripped their tin lunch pails and broke into a run, the older boys dodging around the younger ones with shorter legs. The bell clanged again and suddenly it was quiet.

Rafe Mercer emerged from the mercantile and swept the board walkway with a raggedy straw broom, taking time to admire the pink rose blossoms tumbling out of the flour barrel he'd planted. He paused with his hand on the metal watering can.

A horse-drawn hay wagon rumbled down the single dusty street. Long-legged ranchers in plaid shirts and faded denims rolled cigarettes and ambled toward the Excelsior Hotel dining room, tipping their sweat-banded hats to the two women who stood on the hotel steps, heads together, watching something across the street.

Even Lefty Springer poked his head out his cabin door, cut through the alley next to the hotel, and squinted into the sun. "God almighty, what a sight!" he bellowed.

The figure appeared at the far end of town, near the bank, moving in slow, measured steps toward the mercantile. Past the mercantile. The breeze rippled the long, pale skirt. A white parasol hid her face.

The school bell sounded again. She stepped into the sun and light blazed through the shimmery folds of her gown.

The hay wagon slowed. Five ranchers froze at the hotel entrance and stared across the street. The two ladies pointed. Rafe Mercer missed the rosebush and watered his boots.

Lefty Springer stretched as tall as he could and snatched off his hat. "Well, I'll be damned!"

She kept moving, past the hotel, the barber shop, the livery. At the Jensen place, she turned and started up the hill toward him.

Rydell straightened.

The ivory dress had tiny buttons down the front, and the skirt swayed with each step she took. She caught it up in one hand, lifting the hem off the bunchgrass as she walked. With the sun behind her, her figure was luminous, as if outlined in fire.

Rydell waited, unwilling to believe what his eyes told him. He thought of his father. Of his mother. He thought of all the reasons this could not be happening, how she knew everything now, and it could not ever work out.

And still she came, moving toward him at a steady, unhurried pace.

He stepped away from the willow trunk and went to meet her.

Epilogue

They were married that very morning, in the small white church across the knoll from the schoolhouse. Lefty Springer walked Jane down the aisle, her fingers resting lightly on his good arm, the swish of her long ivory silk gown the only sound in the hushed enclosure. Her dark hair was crowned with a filmy white veil secured with pink roses.

Odelia sniffled into her handkerchief. Mose Freeman sat beside her, patting her hand, and the widow Leah Davis, elegantly dressed in mauve satin, beamed from the first pew. Letitia Price, in a sober dark blue dress, tried to catch the eye of the new, young Methodist preacher.

At the altar, Lefty gave Jane over to Rydell, and the instant their hands joined, the sun emerged from behind a cloud and poured soft, golden light through the single church window. Through the open church door, Rydell listened to the song of a meadowlark, punctuated by the *bump-bump* of the schoolyard teeter-totter.

In the middle of the ceremony, Evangeline Tanner gasped as a new life fluttered within her.

And at the back of the church, Mary Two Hats counted on her fingers. She would have a busy year.

* * * * *

Journey to the breathtaking
British Isles with these
riveting tales from
Harlequin Historicals

On Sale July 2002

AN HONORABLE THIEF
by Anne Gracie

*A dashing gentleman falls in love with
a brash and beautiful lady thief!*

A WILD JUSTICE
by Gail Ranstrom

*Will a bluestocking heroine surrender
her heart to the husband who
duped her into marriage?*

On Sale August 2002

BORDER BRIDE
by Deborah Hale

*A former crusader lays claim to an
already betrothed beauty who harbors
a shocking secret!*

A PERILOUS ATTRACTION
by Patricia Frances Rowell

*A newlywed couple encounters passion—
and peril—as they race against time to
unmask a serial killer....*

HHH Harlequin Historicals®
Historical Romantic Adventure!

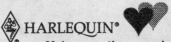

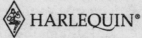

You are cordially invited to join the festivities as
national bestselling authors

Cathy Maxwell
Ruth Langan
Carolyn Davidson

bring you

Wild West
Brides

You won't want to miss this captivating collection with
three feisty heroines who conquer the West and the
heart-stoppingly handsome men who love them.

Available June 2002!

Do Westerns drive you wild?
Then partake of the passion and adventure
that unfold in these brand-new stories from
Harlequin Historicals

On sale July 2002

THE TEXAN by Carolyn Davidson
(Texas, 1880s)
*A U.S. Marshal and an innocent spinster
embark on the rocky road to wedded bliss!*

THE BRIDE'S REVENGE by Anne Avery
(Colorado, 1898)
*An overbearing husband gets more than he bargained
for when his feisty bride demands her independence!*

On sale August 2002

BADLANDS LAW by Ruth Langan
(Dakota Territory, 1885)
*Will an honor-bound sheriff be able to choose
between his job and his devotion for a woman
accused of murder?*

MARRIED BY MIDNIGHT by Judith Stacy
(Los Angeles, 1896)
*In order to win a wager, a roguish businessman
weds a love-smitten family friend!*